PIERCED

SYDNEY LANDON

LEE PIERCED

Cover Design and Interior Format

ALSO BY SYDNEY LANDON

THE PIERCED SERIES

Pierced

Fractured

Mended

Rose

Aidan

Lee

Anthony (Spring 2018)

CHAPTER ONE

———

LEE

A S I LOOK AT THE busy street below from my office window at Falco Corp., I can't help but marvel at the changes in my life. No longer am I a starving kid on the streets with my sole focus on feeding my brother and me. It's been so fucking long since I had to worry about where our next meal was coming from that it seems surreal to me now. Sometimes I find it hard to believe I survived that. My kitchen in the penthouse is always fully stocked, and I eat in restaurants where prices aren't listed on the menu. I'm no longer a gutter rat to be kicked aside like yesterday's trash. I'm a sought-after member of Asheville, North Carolina, society and invited to parties given by the mayor, governor, and the upper crust of society.

If I've learned one thing, it's that money and power will turn many an eye blind and even more ears deaf. Rumors circulate about my past and the fact I've long operated in the gray areas of the law abound, but the good people in this city don't give a fuck. What they do care about is that I donate to whatever charity their guilty conscience prods them to support.

I'm not vain. It's simply a fact that I'm attractive to the opposite sex. I also have a huge cock, and I know how to use it. I could gun someone down in the street on live television and still be welcomed into women's homes *and* beds. Many years ago, this shit surprised me. When you grow up as the son of a crack whore with little more than the clothes on your back most days, being accepted by your peers is the last thing you expect. I was always an outcast, which was fine by me. It's what kept Pete and me alive. Survival isn't taught in public schools, but it damn well should be. Especially the schools I attended.

Even as a kid, I instinctively knew I needed to be the alpha. Even animals are born with this same ingrained knowledge. You assert your dominance early on and reinforce it as needed. It wasn't that I enjoyed fighting as some did. Hell, I never considered myself a violent man by nature. But if it came down to the him-or-me scenario, it was him every time. I've killed to protect myself and those I love, and wouldn't hesitate to do it again. Does it haunt me? Fuck no. I've never physically hurt an innocent person.

That's one of the many things Victor Falco taught me: you don't kill or torment for sport. But on the flip side, you also don't allow others to perceive you as weak. When you make a threat, you back it up. Your word and your reputation are the most important things you'll ever have. Your name, not so much. You can change that at the drop of a hat. But the core of who you are as a man cannot be altered. Evil will remain evil no matter how you try to dress it up. And good will remains true, regardless of the number of times you stumble. On the rare occasion, a person doesn't fit into either category, and that's what I consider myself. I've walked in the darkness, but I haven't completely succumbed to the shadows.

My story might have been different without my brother and Victor, but I don't think so. I've never found any pleasure in violence. It's about necessity. Have I found a certain satisfaction in vengeance? Fuck yeah. Anyone who says they haven't is lying. But at the end of the day, it's all about doing the unpleasant things that need to be done. Another lesson from Victor.

Damn, I still miss the man I considered a father. The day he caught me stealing scraps from his restaurant kitchen was a turning point for me. It was then that my path altered. I learned how successful you could be when the lines between right and wrong were blurred.

Victor's businesses were legitimate. The restaurant, the dry cleaners, the storage buildings, and a host of other entities I can barely remember now. I sold them all off long ago. But where Victor really made his fortune was laundering money for Draco Moretti. Like Pete and me, they grew up together and had been brothers until the day they'd been gunned down by a fucking street thug high on crack cocaine.

The bond you develop when you have nothing but each other to depend on for survival does something that few can comprehend. Victor saw himself in my eyes the night we met, and for that, I'll be eternally grateful. It's not that I wouldn't have made it on my own, because failure has never been an option for me. Being cold and hungry will drive you to accomplish feats you never thought possible. And for all his country club, homeowner's association ways now, Pete will tell you the same thing. My brother can and will kill a man in the blink of an eye if necessary. No matter how you dress us up, we'll never be what society perceives as normal. We've seen and done too much. Regardless of the reasons, our actions and the people we've associated with along the way have left irreversible stains on our souls.

A knock on the door behind me pulls me from my thoughts. *Kara.* What an amazing difference a few months has made in my niece. It wasn't long ago that I was verbally kicking her ass and attempting to pull her from the pity party she was intent on languishing in. Pete's daughter looks so much like my own daughter, Lia, that I get a lump in my throat every time I see her. The girl owned me before I discovered my long-lost child and that hasn't changed. Family is everything to me, and there's nothing I wouldn't do for those I love. Kara survived breast cancer and a serious bout of depression. She also fell in love with Aidan Spencer, my son-in-law's best friend and right-hand man at Quinn Software. They've had their ups and downs, but even now, as she frowns at me in irritation, there's no missing the glow underneath the pissed-off exterior. Of course, I know what she's angry about, and momentarily, I feel like a naughty schoolboy before I remember that I own the company. "Uncle, are you serious?" she begins. "How many does that make? I thought we agreed that Jen was the best assistant since Liza left."

I pick up a pile of papers from the corner of the desk and wave it in the air. "She stapled these reports in the right-hand corner. Who does that shit? Everything is ass backward with her. I swear to God, she refuses to make coffee in the morning, yet brings me a damn triple shot espresso at four in the afternoon. Thanks to her, I haven't slept in a month." Kara gives an exasperated sigh before sinking into a chair in front of my desk. I perch on the corner, knowing she's getting settled in to lecture me. Hell, I don't even know who wears the pants around here anymore. It sure as fuck doesn't seem to be me. *Ever since she left . . . Or maybe even then it wasn't me.*

"What are we going to do now? Most of the temp agencies have stopped returning my calls." Rolling her eyes, she adds, "Don't look at me like that. I'm not going to be your assistant again. You're a horrible boss."

Not in the least offended—because it's damn well true here of late—I shrug. "Just until we find someone else, sweetheart. I promise I'll do better with the next one." *That was a fucking Oscar-worthy performance. I should take a bow.*

"Have you even attempted to talk to Liza lately?" She

moves right in for the kill. *She's so like me. I'm so proud. Except for right now.*

I turn away, pretending to be fascinated by the pen on my desk. "She quit. What is there left to say? I don't go around begging former employees to come back. She's moved on," I add quietly, feeling it like a punch to the gut. The woman I love—who should be mine—now belongs to someone named Harry, for fuck's sake.

Misunderstanding my words, Kara wrinkles her nose in the same way she has since she was a kid. "How do you know she's got another job? Has someone called for a reference?"

I'm confused for a moment by her question before I realize she's taken my comment the wrong way. Although I am aware she's working somewhere else as well, I don't want Kara to know I'm having one of my guys follow my former assistant, so I reluctantly tell a lie to cover my tracks. There's no way I can sell that for anything more than what it is—love. *If only things were different.* "Yeah, months ago. So there's really nothing to discuss here. She couldn't handle the pressure and quit her job. End of story." *Shit, I sound like a complete asshole.* By the expression on my niece's face, she agrees with my thoughts.

She finally stops glaring at me long enough to look down and study her nails. "You know, Uncle Lee," she begins as if making idle chitchat. "I remember that talk you had with me not that long ago. I believe the moral of your words was that I shouldn't be a coward." I tense, knowing what's coming. "So you can imagine how ironic I find this whole situation. We both know you're in love with Liza, yet you just let her walk away and did nothing to stop her."

Running a hand through my hair, I take a moment to rein in my temper. The urge to lash out is strong, but the woman in front of me doesn't deserve it. And in a strange way, I'm proud she has the balls to call me out. Denial

of everything she's said is on the tip of my tongue, but I
don't want to continue lying to Kara. She's also correct. I
said similar shit to her and expected her to get it together
afterward. That's where our situations differ, though. I
can't do anything to change things. Being born a different
man isn't an option. Because for all her assurances to
the contrary, Liza has no idea what I'm capable of or the
things I've done in my life. In her head, I'm the guy from
Fifty Shades of Grey. Maybe I like to throw out a few
spankings because of my fucked-up childhood. Books
and movies like that have women clamoring to find a
damaged guy to save. But my past sins run far deeper
than a rich guy wanting to experience some kink. Don't
get me wrong, a good spanking absolutely has a place in
my life, but so does killing, if it's justified and necessary.
For all her bravado, Liza doesn't have a fucking clue. She's
goodness and light, and I'm forever in the darkness. Not
claiming her and bringing her into my world is one of
the few selfless acts I've ever committed. The fact I'm in
love with her makes it doubly unbelievable that I stepped
aside and let her go. Realizing that Kara is still patiently
awaiting a reply, I say truthfully, "There was nothing I
could do. Liza wanted to be more than an employee of
Falco, and I couldn't give her that."

Ever persistent, Kara asks, "But why not? You don't
have a girlfriend. I mean, I know you must . . . have
women sometimes, but—well, that's a guy thing."

This conversation is spinning out of control. My niece
is obviously alluding to me screwing other women. Even
now as I try to think of a way to end this awkward talk,
her face is flushed and she's stumbling over her words.
It's time to put us both out of our misery. "Kara," I
say sternly, and am relieved when the room goes silent.
Hell, I feared she would ask me next if I used protection.
"Trust me when I say there are some things I'd rather not
discuss. I care a great deal for Liza, which is exactly why

I didn't attempt to change her mind." When Kara opens her mouth, I shake my head, signaling that the matter is closed. She knows me well enough after all these years to see that she'll get no further—at least today.

Getting to her feet, she lets out a long-suffering sigh. "Why are all the men in my life so damn stubborn?" She steps forward to kiss my cheek. "I'll take care of things until I can beg someone else to do it," she grumbles.

"Thank you, sweetheart." We both knew she'd give in all along, but I'm not about to point that out. She has the Jacks' temper and will possibly throw something at me. She walks out of my office and closes the door behind her.

I return to my chair behind my desk and open my email. As usual, there's a daily report from Jenkins. I open the attachment and begin scrolling down it, seeing nothing new. I'm almost at the bottom when my hand freezes. The name seems to leap from the page. *Wrenn.* I haven't spoken that name in twenty years. The last I heard, he was living in Chicago. Even though he's a man I count as an enemy, I haven't bothered to watch him through the years. There are plenty of threats a lot closer with more to be pissed off about. I merely took one of his many companies out of his greedy hands. I did that for Victor and Draco. It hadn't been personal, just another day in the life. Even though it was barely a blip on my radar, I never forget a name from my past. Especially if I wronged them.

According to the report, Liza has been at Hunter's for almost two hours, so it certainly wasn't a case of making a wrong turn. Picking up my cell phone, I place a call to the man who shadows the woman I love. As always, he answers simply, "Boss?"

"What the fuck is she doing at Hunter Wrenn's?" I hiss, unable to hide my frustration. I don't need this shit. My life has had enough drama in the past year to make me feel twenty years older than my current age of forty-five.

Jenkins, well accustomed to my abrupt personality, answers without pause. "Don't know, boss. Wrenn's house is only about ten minutes from her apartment, but she wound around the city, through the country, then onto the expressway. She took a few exits, got back on, then finally made her way there. The whole thing was strange. I just figured she got lost."

I don't bother to point out that I know Liza has a GPS in her car. There's no way she *accidentally* took a route that far out of the way. I could see her making one wrong turn. Hell, I'd even give her two, but the scenario he just described says something else. She knows me well enough to suspect I keep an eye on her. But why would she not want me to know she was at Wrenn's? I never discussed the man with her, so regardless of what took her to his house, she should have had no reason to hide it from me. "I want to know immediately if she goes back there. I'd also like for you to do some digging into her background and his. Find the connection." I've never been a man to believe in coincidences, and I damn sure don't plan to start now. I'm missing something, and I won't stop until I find out what it is. My previous security head, Sears, ran a background report on Liza as he did all employees before her. Of course, I realized Sears himself was a fucking bumbling idiot who missed key information on Lia. He was fired immediately, which I thought solved the problem. But now I wonder if the dumbass had screwed up much more. "Something is off here, and I want to know what it is as soon as possible."

"You got it, boss." I toss my phone onto the desk as a prickle of unease makes its way down my spine.

What are you doing with him, Liza? Hunter Wrenn isn't a good guy, by any means. His father had been a crook, and from what I'd been told back then, the son had been proud to continue the family tradition. Surely to God she isn't dating him. She's supposed to be seeing some safe and boring guy named Harry. I'm not happy about it, but at least he appears to be a solid and unexciting choice. *Much better than the likes of me.* But Wrenn? Fuck no. I'll be damned if I let her be with a man like that. Whatever this association between them is, it will be over the minute I find out about it. If I can't convince Liza of that fact, then I'll make sure Wrenn understands what will happen if he doesn't walk away. I've taken from him before, and I will do it again without a moment's hesitation.

LIZA

IS THIS WHAT MY LIFE has come to? I wonder glumly as I pop another M&M into my mouth and try not to think about the number of calories in the little chocolate piece of heaven. The ten pounds I've added to my ass tells the tale, though. Why, oh why can't I be one of those women who stops eating when they're depressed? But no, I eat to deal with my problems. I take a hefty drink from my wine glass and giggle as I imagine the look of horror on my sister's face if she could see me now. I swear, I'm not sure that Jacey even eats. When we go to a restaurant, I see her holding a fork but have never actually spotted anything going into her mouth other than a random piece of lettuce. That probably explains why she weighs one hundred pounds soaking wet. My mother affectionately told me I was big-boned like the women in her family. My dickhead cousin Chad nicknamed me J-Lo after the famous actress with the *well-proportioned* ass.

Truthfully, I've spent my entire adult life feeling frumpy and awkward. Only one man made me feel beautiful and

desirable, and he's the reason I'm packing on the pounds.
Lee Jacks—the very thought of him is like a dagger to
my heart.

I hear the front door open, and I panic, quickly tossing
the candy under a sofa cushion. Jacey comes sailing into
the room and stops just inches away from me. I see
the look of disapproval on her face as she takes in my
appearance. Obviously, the yoga pants and sloppy T-shirt
I'm wearing don't quite meet with her approval. She's
dressed in a form-fitting pencil skirt, high heels, and a
blouse so sheer I can easily see the outline of her bra. We
share long, blond hair, but that's where the similarities
end. Mine is piled into a messy ponytail and hers an
elegant French twist. She puts her hands on her slim hips
and releases a long-suffering sigh. "Exactly how long is
this pity party going to last?" Wrinkling her nose, she
asks, "For God's sake, when's the last time you took a
shower and washed your hair?" That I must think about
my answer tells her all she needs to know. She plasters
on her best concerned-sister look and eases onto the other
end of the sofa. "You've got to snap out of this." Then
she goes for the ultimate low blow. "Do you want to end
up like Mom?"

I pull the pack of M&M's from their hiding place and
wave them in her face defensively. "I'm eating chocolate,
not drinking myself into a stupor. I think there's a
difference here."

She leans over and pulls the candy from my hand as if to
save me from myself. "I'm referring to the fact that you
aren't dealing with life very well. Food may be your drug
of choice, but it still boils down to an inability to cope."

Crossing my arms over my chest, I roll my eyes at her
because I know she hates it. It's petty, sure, but this
therapy session is pissing me off. Why can't my family
just leave me alone? It's because of them that I'm so damn
miserable. When will I ever stop letting them tell me

what to do? For God's sake, I'm thirty-four years old. Shouldn't I have grown a backbone by now and learned to stand up for myself? "Was there something you wanted?" I'm so tired of this familiar conversation.

Her mouth tightens, and I can see her struggle to hold back the tirade she's dying to unleash on me. She's probably afraid she'll send me off into an alcohol-fueled tailspin. After all, it's certainly in our genes. *Thanks, Mom.* I wait, wondering which route she'll take today. I watch in fascination as her inner struggle plays out before me. Finally, I see the moment she plasters on the good-sister face, and I'm almost disappointed. An argument would have at least gotten my blood pumping and given me something else to focus on besides the dismal shape my life is in. Hell, if I got really worked up, I might even burn a few calories in the process—winning! She does manage to catch me by surprise when she hands my pack of candy back to me. "Here, honey. You probably really need this. I know this has been hard on you."

She looks almost faint when I pour a handful of the brightly colored goodness into my palm and pop them loudly in my mouth. It's probably more carbs than she's consumed in the past month, much less in one sitting. I make a production of rolling my eyes back into my head and smacking my lips. She runs her hands nervously down her thighs as if she's afraid the calories I'm consuming will rub off on her. That's one thing about being sisters. We learned how to push each other's buttons long ago. When I'm finished with the pack, I'm almost sure I have chocolate somewhere on my face by the way her gaze is glued there, but I refuse to give in and wipe it away. It's too much fun watching it irritate her. "Man, those were good," I groan. "I may have to make a run to the store later for more." Giving her a sweet smile, I ask innocently, "Do you think you could pick up some for me the next time you're coming over? It would save me a trip."

I bite my lip to keep from laughing out loud as she shudders. "Absolutely not," she snaps. And just like that, the good sister is gone, and the familiar, snippy one is back.

Oh well, it was nice while it lasted. "Is there a point to this visit?" I ask, more than ready for her to leave now. If not for her almost daily impromptu drop-ins, I could be left in peace to die alone and be eaten by my cat, Rufus. I've started locking him out of my bedroom at night, though, because I'm afraid of that very thing happening.

"Dad is worried about you. He said you refused to ask for your job back at Falco." *Yes, sis. I was there last night. I know what he wants from me.*

Ding, ding! We've got a winner, ladies and gentlemen. My father is no more worried about me than my sister is. They've both spent most of my life trying to pretend I don't exist. But now with their sights set on Lee Jacks, I've suddenly become useful. I left my job with him before I was supposed to and failed them. I lost the man I love out of some insane, misplaced loyalty to a family who couldn't care less about me. And now they want more. *Well, fuck them. I'm finished. Done. It's over.* "I'm not going back. Ever," I interrupt Jacey's attempt at coercion. "I never should have done it in the first place. The whole thing was crazy, and exactly what would it have accomplished in the end?" Before she can answer, I continue. "You have no idea what type of man you're dealing with. Lee plays in the big leagues. He eats people like our father for breakfast. If he ever found out what I was attempting to do, he'd destroy us all."

She looks as if she can't believe what I'm saying. "I realize you've always been different, but surely, even you care about what he did to our mother. He's the reason we were raised by a nanny while our father grieved." She jumps back to her feet as if pulled upright by an invisible set of strings held remotely by our father. I literally feel the blood drain from my face when she taunts, "Why don't you just admit this has nothing to do with fear and everything to do with the fact you're infatuated with the bastard. I found you a job and a new guy, yet you still cling to this crush you have on that monster. What more does he have to do for you to wake up and see the light? I told Dad you were the wrong choice to work at Falco, but he said that no one would ever suspect someone like you being a Wrenn. Well, I was certainly right about that, but a lot of good it did us. We were so close, and you tossed it all away. I'll even admit that he's a handsome devil—hell, more than that. I would have looked the other way while you slept with him for the greater good. I'd have probably been impressed."

Now that the initial shock has passed, I'm pissed. *How dare she judge me?* I glare at her, then realize she still has the advantage while she towers over me. *Fuck that.* I get to my feet and do something else she hates. I move closer and invade her personal space. Her eye twitches, but she stands her ground. "How dare you presume to judge me," I grind out through tightly clenched teeth. "I'm the one who spent over two years of my life doing exactly what was asked of me. Regardless of what you say, I don't recall you trying very hard to take my place. On the contrary, I believe you mentioned repeatedly that you were needed as Dad's right-hand. There's no way you could have made the sacrifices I have, and you damn well know it. So save me the lecture."

She's momentarily taken aback, but she recovers quickly. She is truly the female version of our father and always manages to land on her feet. Her lips curl into a sneer of disgust as she runs her gaze up and down me. "I knew this would happen. You've never been around a man like Lee Jacks. I mean really, you've barely even been on more than a handful of dates. I had to call in some favors with Harry to take you out. I believe he said he wasn't interested in a chubby blonde who ate more than he did. Luckily for us, Dad holds the lease on his building, and the threat of a sharply escalated monthly payment was enough to change his mind. It's not all bad, though," she adds in a falsely encouraging voice. "He says you do a fair job of answering the phones, and he's not constantly tempted to chase you around the desk like his last assistant. Plus, we're paying your salary, so it's a win-win for him."

My stomach clenches as her words sink in. It's not that I'm attached to Harry. Heck, I'm not even remotely attracted to him. He'd seemed kind, though, and when he began asking me out shortly after I started working for him, I'd agreed. He was pleasant company, and it took my mind off my dismal life for a few hours. Of course, now I knew he was simply a Wrenn minion. Even though I didn't care about the loss of a date or the job, it still stung that my sister had been paying someone to go out with me. *He* never made me feel that way. Lee had wanted me. I felt the proof of his desire the few times he kissed me. *If only he'd done more.* Suddenly, I'm tired. More exhausted than a woman my age should be. The fight leaves me, and I want her gone. I can't deal with any more today. "Get out," I say wearily. I turn my back on her and begin walking away. This may not be a backbone move, but I refuse to be belittled in my own house. *As I so often am.*

"I'm not finished," she snaps, but I ignore her. Unhurriedly, I make my way toward my bedroom and close the door. For good measure, I turn the lock. Rufus is sitting in the center of my bed giving me a pitying look as if to say, *your sister is one hell of a bitch.* I nod my agreement—we understand each other perfectly. I slump down next to him, putting a hand on his soft fur and gently stroking his back until he begins to purr. I expect to hear Jacey pounding on my door, but there is nothing but silence until I hear a car starting in the distance.

"Wow, I can't believe that worked," I murmur. But I know with a certainty that this isn't over. There is no way my family will let me walk away. The irony is that we both want the same thing—me back with Lee—just for different reasons. To them, I'm the key to taking down their enemy, which is exactly why I left. And it was almost too easy. I used the one tool at my disposal guaranteed to make him let me go. I pressed him for more. Amazing how simple it was to make a powerful man literally run in the other direction. Just have the "relationship talk" and they quiver in their damn shoes. Even though it had been horribly embarrassing, I knew he'd see right through anything else. Don't they always say that the trick to pulling off deceit is to add as many elements of the truth as possible? Well, that much had been easy because I'm in love with him. I have no idea what my backup plan would have been had he given in to my demands to have a real relationship, but sadly, that hadn't been necessary.

I shift until I'm more comfortably settled on the stack of pillows behind me. Images of our last moments together flood my mind, and this time, I don't attempt to stop them. Because even if it changes nothing, I need to be with him again. *Even if it's only in memories.*

It had been an unusually quiet day at Falco. It was casual Friday, and I was wearing my favorite pair of Levi's and a green fitted blouse. I was also more exhausted than I could ever remember being. I hadn't slept eight hours straight since I began working for Lee. At first, it had simply been a case of nerves. Pretending to be someone else wasn't easy, and I was constantly on guard, afraid I'd say the wrong thing. After all, I was Jade Wrenn, not Liza Malone as I had pretended to be for the past two years. I have no clue how my cover managed to hold up under Lee's intense scrutiny, but it had. I probably owed a huge debt to his former security chief who'd been more interested in chasing skirts at the office instead of digging for the truth. I never expected to make it past the first week, much less be there long enough to fall helplessly in love with the man I was supposed to hate.

On that last day with Lee, I'd reached my limit. My sister had been pushing me to sleep with him so I'd have access to his apartment, which I realized was as stupid as it sounded. I'd been there on a few occasions, but I'd never had the freedom to look around. I'd found no evidence to suggest Lee was as evil as my family suggested, and I had access to many confidential files for quite some time at the office. I knew I wouldn't find anything in his apartment.

Lee is brilliant, and he's beyond gorgeous to look at with that blond hair, blue eyes, and holy hell, what a body. He might be in his forties, but he could pass for someone years younger. One of the key things that always turned me on was his intelligence. Everything he touched turned to gold, and it had nothing to do with luck. He was insightful and driven. He knew which struggling companies he could turn around and sell for a fortune as easily as some knew what brand of toilet paper they preferred. I suspect that if tested, he would have the IQ of a genius. Move over, Stephen Hawking, Lee Jacks could make you look like a toddler with a box of crayons.

It was after four in the afternoon. Lee had been absently rubbing his temple because he'd been staring at his computer screen for far too long. His mind never shut down for long, and as a result, he sometimes suffered from tension headaches. A weakness he hated. I didn't like to dwell on how he likely blew off steam when things became too much for him. He kept his sexual exploits out of Falco, which I was grateful for, but I knew a man like him had a healthy appetite for all things, including women. In my time as his assistant, I'd never so much as caught him looking twice at any of his attractive employees. And some of them were so pathetically obvious in their attempts to get his attention.

He'd surprised me that day by suddenly glancing up as I was arranging a stack of papers on the corner of his desk. "You should take off early, Liza. You've been here late every night this week."

I'd shrugged, not really interested in leaving since I had nowhere to go other than my quiet home. "That's life when your boss works eighteen-hour days."

Normally, the personal conversation would end at this point, and he'd shift his focus back to whatever he was engrossed in. Instead, he'd leaned back in his leather chair and studied me until I became so nervous I'd damn near swallowed the paperclip I'd put between my lips while sorting the last stack of paperwork. I pulled the silver metal from my mouth and saw him quirk a brow in amusement before shaking his head. "I've told you not to do that. It's dangerous. I have nightmares about having to dig one of them out of your throat."

Before I could think better of it, I'd joked, "Well, at least you're dreaming about me. Even if it's a far cry from what I'd prefer you think about when you're asleep." *Oh shit!* I'd cringed, wanting to take back what I'd said. I'd lowered my head, hoping he'd missed it, but no such luck. Lee, it seemed, was in the rare mood to have a non-business-related chat.

He surveyed me lazily, bringing to mind a cat playing with a mouse before it moved in for the kill. "And what exactly would you prefer, Liza?"

I'd dropped my gaze, attempting to break the connection. "Er . . . nothing. I was kidding." I'd forced a laugh out that sounded far too shrill even to my own ears.

He shifted the conversation suddenly. "What's bothering you? Don't bother to lie, because you haven't been yourself all day. Aren't you feeling well?" It was that note of concern in his voice that was almost my undoing. I felt the overwhelming urge to crawl on his lap and confess everything. If only that were possible. But he wouldn't pull me closer and make it all better. No, he'd have me kicked out of Falco and probably arrested. Those things would be bad, but it was the thought of him hating me that I couldn't tolerate. I'd rather walk away and lose him in that manner than to have him know who I was and what I'd done.

This was what it had come down to. Say goodbye on my own terms or let my family push me into destroying any fond memory that Lee might have of me. So I'd forcibly swallowed past the huge lump in my throat and looked at him. Then I'd rocked his world, but not in the way I'd always longed to. "I'm tired of this game we've been playing. You know I have feelings for you, and I believe you have some for me as well. You've kissed me before, then pushed me away and acted like it never happened. Do you realize that I've only been on a couple of dates the entire time I've been working for you?" When he'd opened his mouth to say something, I'd waved him off angrily, no longer having to pretend I was pissed. "You think I don't know that when I mentioned needing to leave early in the past, you made damn sure we had some emergency that required us to stay late? And the sad part is that I didn't care. My heart wasn't in seeing anyone else. You gave me the perfect excuse not to have a life outside of Falco. I blamed it on our hectic schedule, but in reality, no one else interested me. After all, who could possibly compare to you? And dammit, you gave me just enough encouragement to keep me coming back for more."

"Liza"—he exhaled sharply— "don't do this. You know there can never be anything more between us than the relationship we have now."

"What exactly do we have?" I snap. "You're my boss, and I'm your assistant. We flirt with crossing the line occasionally, but that's it. And regardless of what you tell yourself, you don't want me to move on. You want me right here mooning over you. Is it some kind of ego rush, or are you simply oblivious to how I feel? Heck, for all I know, you have a mean streak where I'm concerned, and you enjoy seeing me suffer." He looked pained as my words hung in the air between us. For some reason, that made me even angrier. How dare he pretend to be the one suffering here? He had no idea what I'd been going through since this whole damn charade started. Granted, a big part of that was the fault of my family and not him, but dammit, they're not here and he was. I pointed at myself then to him. "Really, no explanations are necessary. I'm the frumpy secretary, and you're the mega-hot boss. Naturally, you're not interested in me in a personal way. We both know you have women who look a heck of a lot better than I do throwing themselves at you daily. And I've certainly never seen you in the tabloids with anyone approaching chubby. Most of them look as if they've never walked in a McDonald's before in their lives. I bet they force themselves to throw up if they even drive within a mile of a fast-food restaurant." Then it happened . . . something beyond comprehension. His shoulders shook, and for just a moment, I feared I'd made the great Lee Jacks cry with my hurtful comments. But no—the bastard was actually laughing. Without thinking, I grabbed the first thing within reach and threw one of his expensive pens at his head. As if anticipating the move, he plucked it effortlessly out of the air. "You're such an asshole," I hissed, no longer caring that I was committing career suicide. That was what I wanted. *I thought*. A way out of the mess I'd gotten into.

He raised a brow, twirling the pen in his fingers. "I always knew you had claws under that calm exterior," he murmured.

"And I was certain you were a dickhead beneath the whole iceman persona. Looks as if we were both right, huh, boss?" I smirked. At that point, I didn't even know the woman spouting insults at the man she loved anymore. I'd never been so disrespectful to anyone before in my life, and it was both scary and strangely exhilarating. I'd opened the gates, and it was hard to stop the flow of catty comments, so I didn't even try. I perched on the corner of his desk and began shifting items around on the immaculate surface. I knew well how much he hated disorder, and I grinned inwardly as his eye twitched slightly at the mess I made. I was tempted to knock his half-empty cup of coffee over, but I wasn't quite that brave. He would've probably strangled me for that offense. "This gangster vibe you're rocking might turn all the other women on, but I've always felt it was a little absurd. I mean, *The Sopranos* have already been done to death. Couldn't you have come up with something more original?"

He was out of his chair so fast I barely tracked the movement. I was pulled from his desk and slammed into the hard wall of his chest. "You have no idea who you're playing games with, little girl," he gritted out. "I could show you a monster so fucking ugly that you'd never be able to close your eyes in the dark again. Is that what you want? For me to poison every part of your life until I've destroyed you? Because you're naïve if you don't think it would come to that. You don't have a goddamned clue what I've done without blinking a fucking eye or what I'm capable of doing." I expected him to be rough, but when he took my face in his hands, he was gentle as if I was made of glass. "You've been closer to me than anyone other than Pete. But unlike him, I've sheltered you from the real me. And maybe that was a mistake." He ran a finger across my lips, and they parted almost of their own violation. "You're a beautiful woman, and I've always been attracted to you. I have no idea where this absurd and inaccurate opinion that you have of yourself came from, but it's bullshit. You have no clue how tempted I've been to throw caution to the wind and give us both what we want."

Drowning in the desire in his eyes, I whispered huskily, "Then do it. Stop trying to protect me. I'm not who you think I am." That last part was as close to a confession as I'd ever been, but he didn't know that. He thought I was saying I was some sort of closet bad girl who was up for whatever he unleashed. Maybe he was right about that, but sadly it didn't mean that, and I wasn't brave enough to go any further with my revelations. I couldn't live in a world where he hated me. I wasn't that strong.

He lowered his mouth to mine and kissed me angrily. He was tempted. I felt it. It was also impossible to miss the bulge of his hard cock pressing into my stomach. Knowing he desired me was a heady kind of power. Regardless of everything else, he wasn't lying when he said he wanted me. I moaned, attempting to get closer. And for a moment, he allowed it. We were both lost as his lips devoured mine and his hands on my ass pulled me tightly against him. The ache inside me was sweet agony. I was ready to beg him to take me, but before I could make a total fool of myself, he pulled back abruptly, putting distance between us. "Fuck," he gritted through clenched teeth. "Fucking hell! I can't think when I'm touching you." He sounded bewildered, as if I'd cast some type of spell on him, which was absurd since it was the exact opposite.

"Don't stop," I whispered shamelessly, still holding on to a shred of hope that this could work out. I stepped forward and went up onto my toes to wrap my arms around his neck. "If you want me, then for once, show me. I can't keep going the way we have been. I deserve more than this."

I knew I'd said the wrong thing when his eyes closed briefly before opening again. The sad resignation broke my heart. I'm not sure how I could lose something that I never really had, but it happened. He brushed a kiss onto my forehead in a gesture so tender that it slayed me. "You're absolutely right, little bird. You should never settle for a man like me. You're goodness and light, and I'm nothing but darkness. Even if I turned over a new leaf today, it wouldn't matter. My soul will always be tainted black from the things I've done. And I refuse to let that seep over onto you."

"That's where you're wrong. I've never been who I appear to be. I'm closer to the color of night than you could imagine." He probably thought I was lying to get what I wanted. What he didn't realize was that this was in fact my truth. If I said my father's name right then, would it have made a difference? After all this time, would he even know the man who hated him so very much? People came and went from Lee's life every day. Even a man as intelligent as he was would have to lose sight of some after a while. Especially ones he didn't label as a threat. To him, it would have only been business, but to my father, it had been anything but. I'd been around long enough to know that for every big winner in corporate America, there must be a loser. Every positive needed a negative. It is the balance of most things in life. My father was simply on the wrong side of the equation. When I'd gone to work for Lee, I'd expected to find the very monster he proclaimed himself to be. And he was single-minded when he wanted something. But he was also fair. More so than my father ever would have been. He weighed the odds and impact of acquisitions very carefully before he pursued them. Heck, most of the companies he'd taken over still retained their original board members and they spoke in glowing terms of Lee. And why wouldn't they?

He made their broken corporations profitable again, in turn lining their pockets along with his. I must admit, it had been damned confusing for the longest time. I'd expected one thing, but had gotten another. Hence my initial crush, then my unrequited love for the complex man before me.

"I believe we have very different opinions on what constitutes good and bad, sweetheart," he said ruefully. "I don't think your occasional use of profanity and borrowing office supplies qualifies you for hell."

My face colored as I remembered the pack of pens I'd taken home the week before. In my defense, I mostly used them for work I did after hours, but still . . . damn. The man truly knew everything. "I'll have you know those were the cheap plastic ones, and I used them to proofread those contracts." I rolled my eyes before pointing at the stack of papers in his letter tray.

He grinned as he tweaked my nose. "I was kidding, but the fact you confessed so easily just proves my point. You'd never be able to handle the pressure of my world."

I jab a finger in his chest and smiled when he winced. "We're hardly dodging gunfire up here, Lee. And as far as I know, your penthouse hasn't been so much as robbed since I've worked for you. What exactly am I supposed to be frightened of? Have you stiffed your cleaning lady? Is she going to beat me with her vacuum cleaner? Will the window washer attempt to drown me in a moment of madness because you left a smudge on the tinted glass in the lobby?" Snapping my fingers, I add sarcastically, "Oh I know, the security guard is pissed because you didn't ask about the newest addition to his family. Dammit, how could you have been so rude! He'll probably slug me with that handheld scanner now. Or maybe Lia is tired of having a gangster for a daddy? That's totally understandable. If she's going to send someone after me, I sincerely hope it's her hot hubby, Lucian. Mmm, do you think he'd use handcuffs? I bet he could take the light right outta me."

Lee's mouth dropped open, and he looked downright shocked and a tad offended. Maybe I'd gone a little too far in objectifying his son-in-law, but really, he deserved it. Plus, Lucian was a stud, so it hadn't been a lie. I didn't bother adding that I found Lee far more attractive than his daughter's husband. The man had a big enough ego already. He reached out and gripped my arm. His hold was firm but not enough to be painful. He glared daggers at me when he snapped, "So, you fancy Quinn?"

I had started that train wreck so I bravely plowed on. "Who wouldn't?" I winked. "You should think of using a better word than fancy, though. That's a bit outdated. These days, we prefer something like smoking or yummy. Of course, after a few drinks, they get a lot more descriptive. I guess that's not something they cover in your AARP newsletter, though. You're so lucky you have me to help you out."

"Oh, really now?" he purred. The voice in my head was screaming for me to shut the hell up, but when had I ever listened to that annoying bitch? If I had, I wouldn't be in this mess now. "How fortunate for me indeed. Thanks for showing this old man the error of his ways. That's so thoughtful of you, Liza. Granted, I've never had an occasion to need such a descriptive overview of Lucian's appearance, but it was nice of you to so thoroughly provide one for me."

I grin uneasily, determined to see this through no matter how badly it's bound to go. "No problem, dude. We're pals, right?" *Dear God, had I actually called him dude and pal?* He blinks rapidly a few times as if unable to believe the shit coming out of my mouth either. I attempt to give him my best seductive smile. "Don't worry, I've always been attracted to older men. You're plenty hot enough to me." I narrow my eyes, looking at him closely. "It's hard to tell, considering the color, but I don't think you have any gray hair yet. Plus, you easily pass for late forties."

There went that twitch again. For a man who I'd always believed above such things, he seemed sensitive about the whole age thing. Which was laughable, considering he could be mistaken for a thirty-year-old. "I'm forty-five," he gritted out. "It's kind of you to say that I only look a few years older than that." He released his hold on me to put a hand behind his head, rubbing his neck. "Again, I must ask, what in the hell has gotten into you today? If I didn't know better, I'd swear you're not the same person who walked in the door this morning. Did you have a few drinks at lunch? Hell, did you smoke a joint in the stairwell? I won't even lecture you; it would be a relief to have some sort of explanation."

I pat his muscular arm sympathetically. "Sorry, buddy. None of the above. Although I might do both of those things later." And that was a strong possibility. How else would I deal with my soon-to-be unemployed state and the loss of the man I hated leaving? Not that he'd ever been mine to start with, but at least there had been mutual respect. By the time this was over, that would be out the window as well. "I think I have suffered some kind of breakdown brought on by my years of being strung along by you. Have you ever stopped to consider what that can do to a woman? You dangle your sexiness over my head, then when I'm all in, you pull it back and list all the reasons why we're not compatible. Can't you just admit that you're simply not that into me? Wouldn't honesty be the best policy here?" *Oh brother, I'm preaching to him about being honest? Heck, I have a hard time not lying to him about what I had to for lunch. Deception has become second nature to me now.*

"Liza, you know that's not it. I'm extremely attracted to you. You're also aware why it can go no further than a business relationship between us." He's frustrated again.

What man wants to have this kind of talk? Naturally, he'd rather throw himself out the window than endure this hell. I almost feel sorry for him and start making excuses.

I wanted to back down; I really did. I didn't want to quit my job and walk away from Falco—or Lee. But hadn't this been inevitable since the beginning? We'd always been on borrowed time. Admittedly, I thought it would end another way, so going out on my own terms— even if they were insane—seemed better than having him discover my true identity. No one played Lee for a fool and got away with it. He might have some type of complicated feelings for me, but those would all go away in the blink of an eye when he discovered what I'd done. So I square my shoulders, clear my overly dry throat, and say, "I'm over all this drama. This job is entirely too demanding, and if you have nothing to offer along with it, then I'll need more time to get a life. I'll even make the arrangements with a staffing agency for someone to fill in until you've decided on a replacement."

His eyes drill into me, and his mouth moves, but no sound escapes for what seems like an hour. I'm shifting uncomfortably on my feet, ready to wrap myself around his feet and beg him to forgive me. Finally, he says, "You're not talking about a long vacation, are you?"

Again, he's given me the perfect out, but I can't back down now. "No, I'm not."

And then he absolutely crushed me. I know it was just the stubborn part of his personality, but instead of begging me to stay, he turned his back and walked behind his desk. His blank mask and air of control perfectly in place as he simply nodded. "As you will, Liza. Take care of things, then submit your official resignation. I'll see that you're compensated adequately." He took his seat and appeared engrossed in his computer. I know that move well. I've seen him do it time and again when he wants rid of someone. He's dismissing me, and it fucking hurts because he's never done that to me before. It's as if a stake has been driven through my heart. I'm no longer in the inner circle. I'm an outsider, and I've made it happen. *It's better this way*, I try to convince myself. Wouldn't I rather be ignored than hated? I knew this would be hard, but I hadn't realized until this exact moment how much it would hurt. *He kissed me, and even that changed nothing. How can he say he's attracted to me, touch my skin, kiss my lips, and then moments later, show me the door? How?* A stranger would soon sit at my desk and spend hours a week with the incredible man before me. He'll eventually get comfortable with her, and they'll form a bond as we have. She'll be a part of Falco, and I'll be a distant memory. The crazy assistant who fell for the boss, then left after having an emotional breakdown.

Before I embarrassed myself by crying in front of him, I left his office. I made a note to call the staffing agency on Monday morning, but it never happened. Lee made arrangements for Kara to fill in, and I never returned to Falco. I never returned to see his handsome face, hear his voice that could make my heart race, or marvel at his brilliance beside him. I lost my job at Falco, but in reality, I lost much more. *Apart from my dignity.* It had been sweet torture working for Lee Jacks, but it was him I truly missed. *I still do.*

I don't need to work. I have plenty of money in my bank account thanks to my mother. But I've never been good with idle time. I'm already a freaking basket case, so I know I need to do something. I just need to figure out what. *Die of a broken heart and eventually be eaten by Rufus?* Yeah, right now that's the front-runner. I sleep with my bedroom door closed, not trusting the furry animal that I outweigh by . . . well a lot. The way my luck is going, the bastard probably has a shitload of friends waiting by the back door to help a brother out.

CHAPTER TWO

——— ✦ ———

LEE

"**W**HAT THE FUCK DO YOU mean, you don't know?" I snap. Jenkins, my head of security, shifts uneasily in his chair as sweat begins to dot his forehead. "How complicated can it possibly be to get a goddamned background report on someone? She worked here for two years, and she lives in the area. Her fucking barista at Starbucks probably knows more about her than you do." I toss the report across my desk and roll my eyes when it lands on the floor. Kara will be pissed if someone doesn't pick that shit up, so I glare at Jenkins until he lumbers awkwardly to his knees and gathers the useless information.

"Something's not right with her, boss," he stutters uneasily. "It's like she didn't exist until she came to work for you. None of her bank accounts, credit cards, or anything go back longer than two years. She simply appeared out of thin air, took this job, then came to life. Before that, there's not a trace. No tie-ins to anything or anyone." It pisses me off further that he seems so damned impressed that my former assistant is essentially a ghost.

"Was she fucking vetted at all before we hired her? I know that Sears was an idiot, but I assumed he'd at least done some part of his job."

"I checked her security clearance, and it's um . . . well,

there's not really much in it. Just her authorization for the background search. I don't see the usual backup paperwork where it was conducted."

"She was getting a paycheck, so trace that back to her social security number," I point out slowly as if talking to a child. Why do I bother to employ people to do this shit if it falls back on my lap? I wonder idly if Kara will be interested in taking over that department as well. She'll certainly do a much better job. But even I don't have the balls to suggest it to my niece. She's still ticked at me over running off the last assistant. Is it my fault the woman couldn't handle a little constructive criticism? The world is literally full of pussies now.

His face flushes as he says, "I already thought of that, boss. That's one of the first things I did, but that's a dead end as well."

When he doesn't elaborate, I clench my fists to keep from planting one in his fucking face. Is everyone around me deliberately obtuse? Maybe this is *fuck with your boss* day, and I wasn't told. "And?" I inquire mildly. Anyone who knows me would be pissing his or her pants right about now. Weirdly enough, *grouchy, loud* Lee is almost always better than *agreeable* Lee. I go into some freakish Zen-like zone when I'm truly angry. It's lethal. Like the way the winds die right before a tornado strikes. The back building of energy. "Explain." I stare at the paperclips on the corner of my desk, thinking I could kill him with one and he'd never see it coming. The idea is so tempting that I firmly talk myself out of it. *Mentally. You know Pete and Kara will be disappointed if you do something so stupid in the office. I'd guess that goes firmly under the heading, don't shit where you sleep or, in this case, work.*

He looks away before mumbling something that I only catch pieces of. I'm beginning to think he's got a death wish, because what other excuse can there possibly be for him to continue to jerk my chain? Before I can further plot his death, he appears to grow a pair and sits up straighter. His voice is shaky when it comes out, but at least I can understand it this time. "Her social security number belongs to someone who died in a car accident five years ago. The information has been tweaked, but *Liza Malone* is dead. Her driver's license is also linked to the same person. I haven't finished going through everything yet, but I feel certain I'll find that to be the case with most everything else."

I'm stunned as I collapse back in my chair. Who in the hell has been working for me, because apparently, it's not who I thought it was. What reason could there be for this type of elaborate cover-up other than deliberate deception? If not for her being spotted at Hunter Wrenn's, I might suspect some kind of witness protection program. But not now. I may not see Wrenn as a threat, but there's no such thing as a coincidence, especially if a man you've wronged is involved. My gut clenches as the unwanted image of Liza as Hunter's lover fills my mind. What other possible reason could there be? "I want you to refocus your attention on Hunter Wrenn. He's the key here. If we sift through his background, I feel certain we'll also have the answers we need about Liza. I want to know everything you can dig up on him, especially in the time right before Liza came to work for me. And make damn sure she doesn't leave home without being followed. I want answers—*yesterday*—so don't even think of going home until you've got something concrete for me."

"Yes, sir." He nods as he gets quickly to his feet. "I'll let you know as soon as I have something."

After he walks out, I pick up the phone and place a call to the one man I know is likely to uncover information quicker. "Quinn," I hear as my son-in-law answers.

"How are my daughter and granddaughter?" I ask without exchanging pleasantries. This is the relationship we've always had, and it works for us.

"You see Lia about as often I do," he says sarcastically. "But they were both fine at breakfast a few hours ago. So what can I do for you? I assume this isn't just a wellness check."

"Smartass," I mutter ruefully. He's an insolent shit, but I couldn't have picked a better husband for the daughter I hadn't known existed until a few short years ago. Since Lucian's investigators managed to put the pieces of Lia's past together, I hope they can do the same with Liza and Hunter. So, without further delay, I explain the situation and gather by his indrawn breath that he suspects this won't end well.

"Damn. Liza?" he asks in a stunned voice. "She's been with you forever, hasn't she? Lia really likes and trusts her."

"She's well respected at Falco," I agree. "I'd never have guessed that she wasn't who she pretended to be, and I consider myself a good judge of character."

"Something doesn't add up." Lucian doesn't believe in coincidences any more than I do, and that's why I called. He understands threats, and when to look for one, and when not to.

"Agreed," I say dryly. He laughs. "Lia says I always believe the worst, so I've been trying to be more positive, but it never pans out. This is the world we live in. And when you have anything in life, there's always someone hiding in the dark that wants to take it away. We can't afford to think otherwise."

"The fact that Lia can still see the good in people after going through everything she has is a testament to the person who she is." My daughter lived through years of abuse at the hands of her mother and stepfather, but she survived and came out on the other side stronger than should be possible. I couldn't be prouder of the woman she is. I only wish I'd been there when she needed me. But I'd made damn sure that they could never hurt her again.

"You're right," Luc says proudly. He loves his wife and doesn't care who knows it. I'll never have to worry about kicking his ass for screwing around on her, because she is his life. He's so besotted he couldn't make it without her by his side. And for one moment, my heart twinges, and I feel envy that I'll never know that type of love. I let myself develop feelings for Liza and look how well that's turning out. No, I simply need to stick with fucking when the urge hits and leave the emotional attachments to those who can afford them.

"So you'll have someone investigate?" I ask, ready to end the call and brood in silence.

"Yeah. I'll have Max put his guy on it. I'll expect something soon."

"Thanks. I appreciate it," I say before disconnecting. My head is reeling, and I'm so fucking angry that I'm on the verge of feeling out of control. I know I need to wait until I have something concrete to go on, but the urge to go to Liza and demand answers is overwhelming. I don't believe she'll hold out on me if I confront her. I get to my feet and begin pacing my office. I'm buzzing with wild adrenaline that demands an outlet. I want to tear someone apart. *How fucking dare she deceive me? If she were anyone else, she'd be as good as dead.* The thought no sooner crosses my mind than I discount it. Fuck that, there will be no easy way out for her. She stood right here in my office months ago and all but begged for a relationship. Thinking I was saving her soul, I turned her away. Well, apparently hers is just as black as my own so all my good intentions are no longer valid. I'll make sure she regrets ever wanting that. Hell, she'll fucking wish she was never born. I'll ruin her life and Hunter Wrenn's. It will be easier if she is in love with the bastard. She'll be willing to do whatever it takes to protect his sorry ass. Either way, it doesn't really matter to me. She sealed her fate the moment she walked into Falco under false pretenses. Now I need to know exactly what else she's been involved in. I know I should wait, but fuck it. I can get further in person than all the investigators behind the scenes. So I quickly shut down my computer and grab my cell phone from my desk. Kara has already gone for the day, which I count as a stroke of good luck. She'd take one look at me and know something wasn't right. Damn, I love my family, but they were meddling pains in the ass sometimes. And you can't simply kill them. You *have* to live with it.

I don't bother calling for my driver. Instead, I make my way to the underground garage where my personal cars are kept and ask Denny for the key to my Aston Martin Vanquish. Yeah, the older guy in a sports car is a bit of a stereotype, but if the car costs more than three hundred thousand, that puts you in a whole different category than a dude driving a Corvette while wearing a gold medallion. Tonight, I need to burn off some excess energy before I see Liza or whoever the hell she is. And driving fast is one way to do it. Asheville has plenty of backroads where you can plunge to your death with one false move, and I'm in the mood to try them all. If I live through it, then the urge to go strangle my former assistant will have either passed or I'll at least be calm enough to let her live a life of torture. Fuck, I do sound like someone from *The Sopranos* at times. For a moment, I want to share the joke and the laugh with the traitorous bitch, but I realize with a pang that'll never happen again. The relationship between us has been forever altered. Even if she's innocent of a serious infraction against me, she's still guilty of lying, and I have no room in my life for someone I can't trust. Plus, there are no innocent scenarios that require you to assume another person's identity. No, she is in this up to her pretty little neck, and I simply want the fucking dots connected for me now. It's absurd that I must demand answers from her instead of having people on my payroll provide them, but apparently, Falco still has a few incompetent people on staff. I'll be rectifying that problem soon enough. I think briefly about calling Pete and filling him in on what I've learned, but I hesitate. He's always liked Liza, and he'll be conflicted. He and I were raised in a world where you did what you had to do whether it was distasteful or not. But I know it's gotten harder for him to deal with our past sins, and I don't want to heap new ones on top of them. He deserves the life he has now. I'll at least spare him for as long as possible. That's the dynamic between us. I can count on him to have my back in any situation, but I try to shield him from the shit show that occasionally lands on our doorstep.

Before I know it, an hour has passed, and I'm at Liza's. It's early evening, and I have no idea if she's home, but I'm prepared to wait it out if I have to. I stick a finger over the peephole and ring the bell. If she's smart, she'll at least question who's there, but that's not the case. We're both blinking in surprise when the door is wrenched open and an irritated voice says, "That's so not funny, Jacey. I thought this discussion was—" She finally stops her tirade long enough to notice that I'm clearly not who she was expecting. Her mouth opens and closes like a fish out of water before she finally squeaks out, "Lee, what're you, um . . . doing here?" She's uncomfortable now, downright nervous. Her hands flutter to her hair, and she attempts to smooth the tangled strands into some type of order. She's wearing black pants that fit like a second skin and a T-shirt several sizes too big. The fact that I think briefly that she's never looked more beautiful just pisses me off further. I must get past this attraction I've always had for her. Nothing can ever come of it—especially now.

Without answering her question, I push past her into

the foyer before she can panic and attempt to close the door in my face. "I was in the neighborhood," I begin pleasantly, almost believing it myself. "I remembered you lived here, and thought I'd drop by and see how you've been." She closes the door behind her and approaches me warily until we're once again looking at each other.

For some absurd reason, she's always been self-conscious about her body, and I see that hasn't changed. She pulls the shirt down further until it's brushing her knees. She's not model-thin and probably never will be, but it only adds to her appeal. She has curves where a woman should have them, and it's made it damn hard to keep my hands to myself in the past. That plump ass of hers has been the inspiration behind more jack off sessions than I care to admit. "Er . . . what a surprise. I was just going to bed. Well, actually I was already there, but I got up for a glass of water and heard the doorbell."

I look at my watch, then back at her. "You go to sleep before seven? Do you have to get up early?"

She flushes, then shakes her head. "Not really. I'm a little tired. It's been a long day. I'll probably sleep late tomorrow as well. It's not like I have anything to get up for since—"

Once again, her sentence ends abruptly. It's not an unusual habit for her. I'd gotten used to her thinking aloud at the office in much the same manner. The difference was that I could usually read her thoughts, and it didn't bother me. We no longer have that connection so it's more of a challenge. "I thought you had a job now," I prompt, feeling irritated for some reason. Apparently, I'm still a little sore than she quit Falco so abruptly for no good reason—or so I thought. *How the fuck did this happen?* I can't think of any other time when someone slipped so seamlessly through my wall of defenses. *Both physical and emotional.* But new walls can always be erected, and seeing her tonight won't change that. I need to know how . . . *I need to know why.*

She looks at the floor, avoiding eye contact. Another classic Liza move. She did that when our conversation became uncomfortable and she wanted to change the subject. *Too fucking bad, sweetheart.* "Oh, I do," she says weakly. "I've really been enjoying it. But . . . I think I have the rest of the week off."

"You don't know?" I ask, injecting just the right note of doubt into my voice.

Suddenly, she yawns loudly, not bothering to muffle the sound. I can't tell if it's real or fake, but it doesn't matter. I'm not leaving. Maybe she'll crack faster if she's sleepy. "Sorry about that," she says sheepishly. "It was good to see you again. I'm glad you stopped by." She's lying through her teeth, but I must give her points for trying to politely dismiss me. *Not gonna happen, though.*

Again, I step around her and find myself in a comfortable living room. I take a seat on her sofa and hear something crinkle beneath me. Moving my leg, I pull out a brown wrapper and inspect it. M&M's. A grin tugs at my lips at the mortified look on her face. She's always had a sweet tooth. I lay the empty pack on the table, and she stands there uncertainly, darting her gaze from me to it as if wanting both of us gone so badly. "So other than working, what have you been doing since leaving Falco? Anything new?" She's unnerved by my attempt at small talk because she knows it's not something I engage in. I'm a very direct man, and I hate wasting time with unnecessary words. She finally lowers herself to the edge of a chair the farthest away from me. One sudden move and she'll jump through the fucking ceiling. As angry as I am, this is faintly amusing. I'm torturing her by being nice. Imagine the possibilities should I unleash my evil side. *But fuck if I'm worried about her seeing that tonight. Maybe that's what she knows best.*

"Um, no," she mutters. "Same ole, same ole. Nothing

exciting here. Well, unless getting a new dishwasher counts. Rufus was downright riveted by it."

Who the fuck is that? "Rufus?" I ask, keeping the same pleasant tone. Why was there no mention of this person in the last report? Oh right, I employ a bunch of idiots. How did I forget that? She could be screwing the entire city, and I'll never know about it. Jenkins had better pack his shit; he's history as soon as I leave here.

I'm still steaming over the other man's incompetence when her words register. "He's my cat. I guess I never mentioned him at the office before."

The game that I was enjoying has lost its appeal. She looks at if she's going to bolt at any moment, so I need to decide how to proceed. Fuck, this would be a lot easier if it were anyone but her. This is what happens when you allow yourself to develop feelings for others. You become a fucking indecisive pussy.

———◆———

LIZA

WHAT IS HE DOING HERE? I try to keep my expression neutral as my thoughts race frantically. Something is definitely off. Lee isn't the "I was in the neighborhood" type. He doesn't do anything without a purpose. And considering he didn't rip my clothes off when I opened the door, I feel safe in ruling out a booty call. I can't see him begging me to come back to work for him, so that doesn't leave many options. And the few I can think of aren't good—at all. Heck, if I thought I had a shot at making it, I'd run for the door right now. He is seriously giving me the creeps. It's been several minutes since I explained who Rufus is, and he hasn't said another word. He just continues to stare at me. "So how's Kara doing?" I ask to break the uncomfortable silence.

He shrugs his broad shoulders, but a smile softens his lips. *Oh my God, that mouth. Down, girl, down.* I force myself to blink and attempt to stop drooling over my former boss. "She's good. She's been giving me hell for going through another assistant, but it's not my fault that they're all completely incompetent."

I try not to show it, but I'm thrilled at that. It's been agony for me to think of someone taking my place in the company—and with Lee. I study my nails as I ask, "So how many exactly have there been since I left? Assistants, I mean," I add quickly. I certainly have no desire to hear about the number of women warming his bed. *He probably can't count that high.*

"A few," he says vaguely. "No one has any type of work ethic anymore. And the few who managed to show up on time couldn't take direction if you stapled a detailed list to their damn forehead. Do you know that I asked one of them for the Camden file, and she came into my office with a purse the size of the Grand Canyon and dumped it out on my floor? When she started crawling around down there going through the debris, I asked her what she was doing and she said that she didn't know what name brand her nail file was, but she figured it would do the job."

I can't help it. I laugh until tears are rolling down my face. I can so easily imagine Lee's expression when that happened. "That's hilarious," I manage to croak out as he shakes his head at me. When I get myself under control, I ask, "So I take it that she didn't make it long after that?"

"Hell no," he grunts. "As soon as she put all that shit back into her bag, I had HR inform her that her services were no longer needed. I was half afraid that she'd find that damn nail file and stab me with it, but according to Pete, who was close by, she actually hummed on her way out."

"She was probably thrilled to get away from you," I joke. Lee wasn't an easy man to work for, especially if you couldn't read his mind. Luckily, we connected from the beginning, and it had never really been a problem for me.

"I just want people to do what I pay them for," he states, making no apologies. And why should he? Yes, he can be a bit abrupt, but he works just as hard, if not harder, than anyone there. Plus, the pay scale at Falco is far better than most businesses in North Carolina.

"I agree with you," I say softly. Then as quickly as the moment of familiarity that only comes from working together is there, it's gone, and I'm on edge once again. I want to know why he's here, yet I'm terrified to ask. But this strange impasse that we're at must end, and he doesn't seem to be in a hurry to do it. Therefore, it's up to me. So, squaring my shoulders, I ask point-blank, "Why are you really here, Lee? You and I both know this is completely out of character for you."

He smirks for a moment, then inclines his head to acknowledge the truth of my words. "I'd like you to come back to work. Seeing as you're currently unemployed, it shouldn't be a problem. You can start in the morning. Kara will be more than happy to turn everything back over to you."

I gape at him in shock. "I—er . . . what?" I manage to get out. He's completely unruffled, while my hands twist in my lap as I try to decide if he's joking or not. *Since when have you known him to joke? It's time to make that run for the door.*

He gets to his feet abruptly as if everything has been decided. "I'll see you at the usual time tomorrow." When I open my mouth to protest, he adds softly, "Don't even think about not showing up. Because if you aren't there, the first place I'll look is Hunter Wrenn's home, and I know you don't want that."

My vision blurs as I stare at his retreating back. For the second time that day, the front door is slammed as another angry person leaves. "Oh, my God," I whisper as I collapse in my chair. *He knows. Dear God, he knows!* The voice in my head is in full panic mode, but outwardly, I've fallen into some kind of weird trance-like state. If I felt pain, I'd suspect I'm having a heart attack and passing on from this life. Just a calm acceptance. I should be losing my shit right now. Packing my bags and running for my life. But it's almost a relief. I've been carrying this secret for so long . . . Did I really expect that Lee would never find out? He must have been furious, yet he remained in perfect control. He even left without stuffing me in the trunk of his car—something I more than deserve.

I get to my feet unsteadily, take a deep breath, and then pull my cell phone from my purse to call Jacey. My fingers are hovering over the keys when I make a decision that will surely end in disaster. But hadn't the course of my life been altered the day I agreed to spy on Lee Jacks? I toss the phone aside and lock the front door before returning to my bedroom. I need to get some sleep if I'm going to return to Falco tomorrow. *I'm working at Falco tomorrow. With Lee Jacks.* The main difference? The reason I think I will be able to sleep tonight? This time, I'll be going there for myself and not my family. He came here, knowing who I am, knowing who my father is, and didn't . . . *kill me.* I can only hope that contrary to everything I know, Lee has a modicum of mercy inside him *and* that I'm able to find it. I shouldn't feel at peace. I know this, yet for some reason I feel more calm than fear. *Hope.* I'll finally be free of playing the starring role in a two-year deception I never really wanted. And that is more hope than I've had in a long time. My only question is whether or not I will enter Falco Corp. tomorrow morning as Jade or Liza?

LEE

IT'S OFFICIAL. I'VE GONE SOFT, I think in disgust as I step off the elevator and into my penthouse. I didn't do anything I set out to do tonight. Her face went deathly pale when I mentioned Wrenn, which turned my stomach. I wanted to believe that her visit to the other man was random. Even though I damn well know it wasn't. But her reaction gave me the proof of her guilt I needed. The only thing to be determined now was their exact connection and what she hoped to gain by working for me.

I checked with Jenkins on my way home and wasn't surprised that he still had nothing for me. Instead, he whined about the layers he had to dig through. He can spend tomorrow pissing and moaning in the unemployment line. I am so fucking tired of incompetence. Hopefully, Lucian will have more luck because it doesn't look as if I've accomplished anything on my end, and that makes me furious.

What do I tell my family about bringing Liza back to Falco? I hate keeping secrets from them, but it's necessary for now. I want to concentrate on Liza and that means not having to deal with my family's questions and concerns over her. Perhaps I'll tell them she's come back as a temporary until we can hire and she can train a new assistant. *At least things will get done properly for a while.*

Has there ever been a time in my life, even in the earlier years, when I've been this undecided on a course or action? *Why did it have to be her, of all people, to betray me?* I've always known that love is a weakness, but this is certainly bringing that home to me in the most painful way possible. I've made and discarded a dozen plans where she's concerned, but none of them seem right. Hence my demand she come back to work. A stall for time so I can make up my damn mind. It infuriates me even more that I'm looking forward to seeing the little traitor in the morning. *If she was anyone else* . . . How many times have I thought that very thing in the past few hours? It's running on a fucking loop inside my head. I care about her, I desire her, but I also want to destroy her. Where does that leave us? Fucked—that's where, and not the good kind. Although, if this progresses like I think, that'll no longer be off limits. No need to save her soul when it was likely compromised long ago.

That very thought sends a shaft of desire through me. I've always wanted her, and finally, I'll have her. I'll fuck this weakness out of my system and then dispense justice for whatever the hell her crimes are. In a twisted way, being betrayed has never held so much promise. I stepped into the unlikely role of her protector years ago, but that's no longer necessary. Instead, she'll need someone to save her from me—and a person like that doesn't exist.

The disgust I felt earlier is gone as adrenaline fills me instead. She is mine now. Whatever claim Hunter Wrenn had is over. I'll deal with him soon, but in the meantime, beautiful Liza will take the brunt of my anger for them both. Soon, she'll find out what it is to dance with the devil and lose. Ironically, she begged to do that very thing months ago. *Careful what you wish for, beautiful.* I'm about to make all her dreams come true—and likely most of her nightmares.

CHAPTER THREE

LIZA

IT'S SURREAL TO WALK THROUGH the doors of Falco once again. As nervous as I am, it's also akin to coming home. The familiar surroundings comfort me as I step off the elevator on Lee's floor. I've barely rounded the corner when a blur of movement has me freezing in place. Kara pulls me into an excited embrace, literally rocking me on my feet. "Oh, my God! I couldn't believe it when Uncle Lee said you were coming back. You have no idea how much we've all missed you." She pulls back, dropping her hands to intertwine with mine. Her eyes are sparkling, and she looks the picture of health, which makes me so happy for her. "He's been such an ass without you. We've gone through so many temps that they've stopped taking our calls. He got rid of the last one for stapling papers in the wrong corner. They were absolutely terrified of him. They kept leaving, and then I'd have to come fill in again because no one at Falco wanted to."

"I'm so sorry, Kara," I say sincerely. I can well imagine how difficult her uncle has been. And I hate that she's had to bear the brunt of my departure.

"Oh, who cares?" She shrugs off my apology. "You're here now, so that's all that matters. I'm sure you'll have him tamed again in no time." We both laugh for a moment at the absurdity of her statement. Lee is and will always be Lee. And no amount of trying will ever tame the beast.

"How have you been?" I ask, genuinely interested in the woman I grew fond of while working here.

"I'm great." She literally glows, and I feel a momentary twinge of envy, which is absurd. After battling cancer, she deserves to be happy. "Aidan is ready to get married sooner rather than later, so I'm expecting him to abduct me any day and fly us to Las Vegas. The only thing stopping him is trying to explain it to our parents afterward."

"I'm so glad things are going well," I say sincerely. Fanning myself, I add, "And Aidan . . . you're one lucky lady. He's absolutely gorgeous."

"You have no idea." She wiggles her brows suggestively. "I almost want to hate the man for looking so good, but as long as I'm the one benefiting from it, then I'll just have to suck it up."

Before I can respond, a door opens, and Lee steps out of his office, trailed by his brother, Peter. I've always liked Pete—as everyone calls him. He's the nice Jacks brother—at least outwardly—but I'm not fooled. I have no doubt he can be as ruthless as Lee, but he's more civilized about it. After all, he's married and has two kids. I've been to some gatherings at his home before, and it's straight-up suburbia. Pete's wife, Charlotte, is hysterical. She watches a lot of reality television and tends to lapse into ghetto speak at times. She is also obsessed with the internet and finding out the dirt on all her neighbors. Sure, maybe it's a bit nosy to those concerned, but it's certainly funny to the rest of us. "Liza!" Pete's deep voice booms out as he pushes by Lee to reach my side. He pulls me into an affectionate hug that I return without reservation. "Damn, it's good to see you. I'm happy you've decided you can put up with my brother again.

The place certainly hasn't been the same without you. I barely get anything done every day for listening to Lee complain about his latest temp. Plus, I'm afraid that Kara may kill him any day for dragging her back to fill in when he runs yet another one off."

Lee stands to the side with his arms folded over his chest. His expression is blank as he stares at me. Is he surprised I showed up? Surely not. Who in their right mind ever turns down an order from him? "Wait . . . what?" I turn to look at Kara, only catching the last part of her whispered words.

She puts an arm around me and murmurs, "I said I couldn't believe it when Mom told me you quit on Lee during a meeting. And called him a blind fool, or something like that." She laughs on the last part, but I hear the genuine note of admiration in her voice and feel like shit over it. I'm not the brave person she thinks I am. Nor is that the way that I left. Apparently, someone has embellished the truth along the way, but it does paint me in a better light.

"It wasn't quite like that," I offer. "But I guess the result was the same. I want to thank you for calling me. It meant a lot that you were thinking of me and missed me here at Falco." Kara had reached out to me on more than one occasion, but eventually, I stopped taking the calls, because what else could I say? The truth sure wasn't an option, and I didn't want to keep lying to someone who I had come to consider a friend.

"Well, if the welcome wagon has finished circling, Liza and I have a lot to do." My spine stiffens when Lee speaks. Kara literally skips to the desk and grabs her purse. She gives me a wave before calling out that we need to have lunch soon. Pete touches my arm on the way out with what looks almost like sympathy in his eyes. For a moment, I consider running, but where is there left to go? Lee knows about my family, so he could certainly find me with ease. At this point, it's best not to piss him off further. First, I need to find out exactly what he knows—then I'll find the biggest rock I can and hide under it for the next twenty years until he forgets I exist. *Great plan—this will totally work.* Even the voice in my head thinks I'm doomed. Great.

I force myself to calmly approach my old desk and stow my purse in the bottom drawer before turning to face the lion. That's how I've always secretly thought of him. The deadly animal, one that can pounce at any moment. A predator you never cross or turn your back on. And I've done both. *I am so fucked. I should hope my damn cat eats me before Lee tears me in two.*

"Good morning, Lee," I say as I have so many times before. *Just act normal. Maybe he'll go along with it.* And weirdly enough, that's exactly what happens. We spend hours going through correspondence, contracts, and an array of other paperwork piled on his desk. He makes no mention of my father or his visit to my home last night. It's almost as if I never left Falco. By the afternoon, I'm exhausted, but almost happy to be back in my element, a place where my skills and mind are stretched and challenged. I always felt so alive within these walls— with this man—and today is no exception. Around five, he tosses his glasses aside and rubs the bridge of his nose. I recline back in the chair in front of his desk and sigh. "Well, I think we made a dent in everything," I say, giving him a rueful smile. "No wonder you got rid of the last temp. Did she do any actual work?"

He rolls his eyes and snorts. "She worked full time at annoying the hell out of me. Oh, and she worked overtime at texting on her damn phone. And her laugh"—he shudders— "sounded like someone torturing a fucking hyena."

I start giggling as he attempts to imitate her. "How long was she here?" I ask, thinking of the amount of work still left to go through.

"Not long." He shakes his head. "But things have just progressively backed up as they came and went without accomplishing much. If not for Kara, Falco would have probably ground to a halt. What are they teaching them at the temp agencies? Incompetence? How to turn a computer on and off without knowing how to operate it?"

I take both him and myself by surprise when I murmur softly, "I'm sorry, Lee. Regardless of my reasons, it wasn't fair to leave you until you had a competently trained replacement. You've always been good to me, and I owed you more than that. It was completely unprofessional and well—kind of an asshole move," I add sheepishly.

He picks up a pen from his desk and begins twirling it in his fingers. I wonder if he knows that it's one of his few nervous tics. He uses it to stall for time while he thinks. "Thank you for that," he finally says. "It's not all on you, though. I have—on occasion—confused the ground rules between us. Something I regret."

My shoulders slump as disappointment fills me. I should be grateful he's so cordial, but a part of me had hoped something would change between us. That he'd realize he missed me as more than his assistant. *Oh right, that's so likely now that he knows what a liar you are.* Okay, maybe that is asking too much. I should be praying instead that he doesn't kill me and bury my body underneath my desk so I can never leave Falco again. The absurdity of that thought has me biting my lip to keep from laughing. *Wonderful, now I'm hysterical.* "I'm sure you do," I acknowledge, knowing it's a true statement on his part.

Then he shocks me by getting to his feet and saying, "Let's go have dinner. I'm starving."

Wait. What? Talk about mixed signals. Isn't this blurring the lines? It's not as if Lee and I have never shared a meal, but they were mostly business dinners. He wasn't the type to take me out to eat after a hard day at the office. He had plenty of bimbos for that type of thing. *Maybe he's tired of having to cut their food up for them.* Okay, I don't know for sure that all his dates are young with a low IQ, but it makes me feel better to assume I'm at least superior to them in some areas. I certainly have no problem with anything related to eating. "Er . . . really?" I ask doubtfully, wondering if perhaps he worded his vague order—*invitation*—wrong.

"I'm in the mood for Italian, so let's go to Leo's. Lucian and Lia have me hooked on that place. And if I show up alone again, the owner will attempt to set me up with his daughter." With a grimace, he adds, "Trust me, it's not good. She has buck teeth, hair like Morticia Addams, a nose longer than any I've ever seen on a human before, and reeks of garlic. I swear she hugged me the last time I was there, and I had to shower three times to get the smell off me. I tossed my fucking suit in the trash."

I laugh, captivated once again by his rare display of humor. This day has been so different from what I expected. For Lee, he's positively mellow—which is atypical. I should probably skip dinner, but I can't refuse the opportunity to spend some time with him away from the office. After all, he's sure to broach the subject of my family soon. Although I can't imagine why he'll do it in an informal setting rather than here. *At least he's not likely to make a scene in public.* I'm not sure Lee cares about his image to that degree, but it makes me feel better to assume that he does. "Let me get my things. I know where Leo's is, so I can meet you there. That way you won't have to bring me back for my car."

"I live here." Lee shrugs. "It's not as if it's out of my way. Besides, I thought we'd walk. It's not that far from here."

This is getting stranger by the minute. Lee Jacks walking to dinner? "Um . . . sure." I nod. He follows me out to my desk, and I quickly collect my purse, then he waves a hand for me to precede him to the elevator. We're silent on our descent. Lee calls out to the employees we pass by name and wishes them a good evening as we make our way through the lobby and out onto the sidewalk. We've taken a few steps when I stumble over a crack in the pavement, and he reaches out to grab my arm. "Thanks," I murmur, feeling heat flood my cheeks. Naturally, I embarrass myself. To my surprise, he doesn't release me. Instead, he moves his hand downward until it's curled around mine. *Holy shit, he's holding my hand. I've officially died and gone to heaven. Maybe he's giving me one last wish before he adds me to his hit list. Even prisoners on death row get a last meal. Oh crap, is that what this is?* The voice in my head is going crazy as we stroll down the street looking like any other normal couple. By the time we reach Leo's, I've imagined every scenario of how the evening will end. Most of them aren't good. I can't help but feel that he's lulling me into a false sense of security before lowering the boom.

Lee opens the door to Leo's for me, and I take an appreciative sniff. The air is heavy with the scent of herbs and spices. We are inches from the hostess desk when a female voice shrieks, "Lee! So good to see you again. I didn't know you were coming in tonight. I would have saved a special table for you." Dear Lord, he wasn't exaggerating. This must be Leo's daughter. She does look like Morticia Addams, with a huge nose.

"Zola," he says smoothly, as he leans down to kiss each of her proffered cheeks. "This was a spur-of-the-moment decision. I hope you can find room for us."

Zola cuts her eyes at me, then narrows them. *Uh oh, someone's not a happy camper.* "And who do we have here?" she asks in a thick Italian accent.

I open my mouth to answer her question, but Lee beats me to it. He slides an arm around my waist and says,

"This is Liza." He finishes the introductions, and the other woman gives me a bland stare. Apparently, there will be no greeting for me.

She leads us to a small table in the back of the crowded room, then hands us our menus after we're seated. She smiles warmly one last time at Lee but doesn't bother looking my way. "Wow, she's so friendly," I say dryly as I study my menu. "Couldn't you have told her that I'm your assistant? She's likely to spit in my food now before it comes out. Maybe I should stick with bread and water."

Shrugging, Lee says, "Zola isn't that brave. If word got back to her father, there would be hell to pay. She'll have to settle for sulking instead."

Shaking my head, I say dryly, "You know nothing about women, do you?"

He pauses in the process of raising his glass of water, a smirk twisting his lips. "I know how to make them scream. Isn't that what's important? I don't concern myself with the rest."

My mouth drops open as his provocative statement stirs something inside me. Lee has never been one to filter his comments, but normally, they aren't sexual. He's probably always been afraid I'd lose control and pin him to his desk if he did. "I—um . . . right," I manage to squeak out.

Instead of changing the subject, he seems intrigued by my incoherent response. He sets his glass down and asks, "Don't you agree? Or do you have a different set of priorities where a man is concerned?"

Oh, my God. We are talking about sex, right? My mind races as I attempt a reply that doesn't make me sound like a blubbering idiot. Or worse yet, someone fresh out of the convent. "Well . . . I've never given it much thought. I mean—it just happens, right? You can't script those kinds of moments ahead of time." He doesn't say anything, simply stares at me as if waiting for more. So I stumble on, thinking I haven't made myself clear. "Don't get me wrong, it would be—nice to have a man who knew what he was doing. You know, who could take charge and make me—er . . . give me—the big finish."

He appears positively confused now. His brows are raised, and he's tapping a finger on the table. Finally, he says, "You're talking about being brought to orgasm? You've never been with a man who can make you come?"

You have, you just weren't physically there. I have no doubt that my face is a flaming shade of red as I think of the many times I've gotten myself off while thinking about him. "I don't really think we need to discuss this," I protest weakly, desperate to change the subject. "You couldn't possibly want to know stuff like that."

He places a hand on my knee, and I almost swallow my tongue. I assume it must have been accidental . . . then he slides it higher up until it's only inches away from my now throbbing core. "On the contrary, I'd love nothing better right now," he purrs.

"Good evening, Mr. Jacks. It's a pleasure to serve you again." I nearly jump from my seat when our server picks that moment to approach. I don't know whether to be relieved or disappointed at the interruption. Lee, however, doesn't seem fazed at all.

"Thank you, Julian, it's good to see you." They have a brief discussion about the wine list, then Lee turns to me. "What would you like, Liza?"

You, always you. Then it hits me that I'm supposed to order. I manage to ask for the spaghetti, which is sure to be a disaster. I'll probably get it all over myself, but nothing else comes to mind. When the server is gone, a tense silence falls over us. His hand is still on my thigh, and I wonder if he even realizes it. "So . . . it was nice to see everyone today," I say lamely, attempting to get the conversation back on more neutral ground. Truthfully, I'm a little sad to leave the sexually charged one behind, but what good could possibly come from it? *I'll go home turned on, and he'll probably find a willing and available girl and make* her *scream. Men are such assholes.*

To my surprise, he ignores my comment and says, "I'm still waiting for an answer to my earlier question."

What if he's talking about something at the office? "And that was?" I ask, then hold my breath in anticipation. *Please talk dirty. No, wait, don't. Shit, I don't know.* As the voices in my head argue it out, I try not to stare at the man who's once again running his fingers dangerously close to no-recent-man's land. *I need to get laid.* Finally, a thought that every part of me agrees with. I wouldn't be acting like a horny teenage boy if I'd had sex anytime in the last three—make that five years.

He leans closer as he carefully enunciates each word. "Has. A. Man. Ever. Made. You. Come?"

Holy wet panties, Batman. I feel like one of those people you see in movies who have an asthma attack and start clawing at their chest while wheezing for breath. *Do you think his* partners *act like this? Say something clever. Act like you've at least seen a naked man.* "Of course," I manage to get out. "Isn't that the norm? I mean, you guys have one job in the bedroom, and that's it." *Oh God, did I just say that?*

"Trust me, sweetheart, pleasuring a woman isn't a 'job.' And as it appears you've discovered, many men don't know or care about making sure the person they're with comes . . . again and again. That's not the case for me. A woman will always get hers first, even if I don't get mine. I'm not an inexperienced boy and can go without. I'd just rather not."

I pick up my wine glass and take a big gulp—and then another. "Is it hot in here?" My voice sounds high and squeaks as I fan myself with my other hand. I'm in danger of going up in flames. *Am I too young to have hot flashes? Maybe I'm in early menopause.* I feel Lee's intense gaze on me as I attempt to gather my composure. Damn him. He's always known how to find peoples' weaknesses and move in for the kill. *But why is he bothering with me?* He's probably laughing inside at how easily he's shaken me. Somehow, that thought gives me a surge of strength, and I lift my head to glare at him. "How do you know that you actually get women off like that? Considering most of your . . . dates are paid by the hour, they're not likely to do anything other than scream your name like a porn star. You do realize that women can fake that, right?" I clear my throat, before channeling my inner *When Harry Met Sally.* "Ohhh Leeee, oh my God! Yes! Yes! Yes!" I add a few more moans before flopping back in my seat as if I've just had the orgasm of my life. Then I pick up a piece of garlic bread from the basket in the middle of the table and take a bite as if I didn't just pretend to come in front of my boss.

I hear a sound that shocks the hell out of me. Lee is laughing—and it's not the usual cynical laughter. It's a full-on booming sound of genuine humor. I stare at him as his shoulders shake. When he catches his breath, he says, "That was both the hottest and funniest thing I've heard lately." He doesn't appear in the least insulted, quite the opposite. Then he turns the tables on me. "You'll say those very words to me one day soon, amore mio, and it won't be an act. Your fingers will be curled into the sheets as sweat drenches your body. My face will be buried between your legs, and you'll be coming so fucking hard that you'll be on the verge of passing out." His voice lowers as he adds, "And that, sweet Liza, will only be the beginning."

Medic! Someone call 911; I think I'm having a heart attack. Wait, on second thought, the discomfort is well below that area. I wonder if anyone has ever been caught masturbating in the bathroom at Leo's? The thought of being caught in the act by Zola is enough to give me some measure of self-control. No. Scratch that. What if I caught Zola in the act after serving Lee? *I think I'd vomit.* Our food arrives, and I'm given a temporary reprieve. I half expect the verbal foreplay to continue after that, but it doesn't. I'm not sure if I'm relieved or disappointed. Lee returns to the safe topic of business, and soon, I'm relaxed from the wine and the familiar conversation. When I can eat no more, I push my plate away. "That was wonderful."

Lee seems distracted now, and he simply nods before signaling for Julian to bring the check. All too soon we're walking toward the door. Zola manages to give Lee a goodbye embrace that stops just short of a lap dance before turning to glare at me. "I trust your meal was satisfactory," she says stiffly.

Lee wraps an arm around my waist and answers for me. "We both enjoyed it very much, Zola. Give my compliments to your father."

"Of course." She gives me a simpering smile but doesn't bother to look my way again. "Until next time," she adds, and I hear the double meaning behind the words. *This is Lee Jacks's world. We're all just dancing around his feet, begging for crumbs of affection from him.* It's not as if I haven't known this for some time. And in the scheme of things, I'd rather see Zola throw herself at him than one of his bed buddies. After all, I'm certain he's never slept with her and isn't likely to.

"Thanks for dinner," I say softly as we step outside. Once again, he shocks me by taking my hand as we walk toward Falco. *The man is either stoned or on some new medication. I wonder if he'll share?*

He shrugs. "I have a feeling we'll be spending a lot of time together soon."

I laugh. "Is this your way of saying that we'll be working overtime until we're caught up?"

He doesn't reply. Instead, he takes his cell phone from

his jacket pocket with his other hand and presses a button. I hear a voice on the other end before Lee says, "Denny, I'll need you to take Ms. Malone home. Move the car around front please. We're almost there."

I pull against his hold, and he immediately stops. "I don't need a ride, Lee. You know that."

He sighs, and I hear the fatigue in his voice as he says, "Honey, you had wine with your meal. There's no way I'm letting you drive. Please don't argue with me. You know it's the responsible thing to do."

An objection is on the tip of my tongue, but he's right. I'm certainly not drunk, but my reflexes are not what they should be after a few glasses of wine. Plus, his use of yet another endearment has me incapable of putting up a fight. Instead, I'm close to melting in a puddle of sappiness. Before I do something insane like call him my little Jacky Wacky, I shall go—quickly. I bite my lip to keep from giggling as I picture his face should I utter a pet name for him. It would almost be worth it just to witness his reaction. After all, it's not a hardship to ride in a Rolls Royce. Even with my family's wealth, I've never owned a flashy car. My father didn't believe in spoiling his offspring. I'm still making payments on my Honda CRV. I have a sneaking suspicion Jacey couldn't say the same for her Mercedes, but I'm fine with that. I don't want all the strings that go along with extravagant gifts, and with my father, nothing is ever free. "Sure, I'll call a cab in the morning," I say as I see Lee's car up ahead.

"I'll pick you up around eight tomorrow," he says impatiently. That's the Lee I've come to know. Always in charge of every little detail. I can only imagine how impossible he'd be to live with. He'd probably have his wife line up next to the bed each morning and evening for a military inspection.

Rolling my eyes, I say, "You're so anal. You know that,

right?"

He stops so suddenly that I slam into his side. He catches me easily before pulling me closer. Then his mouth drops to my ear and the feel of his breath against my sensitive lobe has shivers racing down my spine. "I had no idea that you were into that, amore, but thanks so much for letting me know."

Blinking up at him, I manage only, "Wh-what?"

He shifts until he's looking down at me. "It's nothing to be embarrassed about. In fact, it's very mainstream now. And although it's not something I do every day, I'd certainly be happy to accommodate you."

I'm completely lost. I haven't a clue what he's talking about, but the gleam in his eyes and the seductive stance of his body lets me know that it's sexual in nature. I consider running for his car without further comment, but once again, I'm too damn curious for my own good. So, I ask, "Um . . . what exactly are we discussing here? I've missed something."

He waves his driver away and opens the backdoor of the car for me himself. He motions for me to get in, and I reluctantly comply. I've barely settled against the buttery soft leather when he lowers himself and murmurs, "You indicated that you wanted to try anal. That's what I was referring to." He straightens back to his full height on the sidewalk while I stare at him with my mouth hanging open. Before I can protest, he shuts the door and claps his hand on the roof.

I shake my head as the car pulls into the late evening traffic. This has quite possibly been the weirdest night of my life, and that's saying a lot. The man I just left looks like Lee, but that's where the similarities end. My boss isn't the type to use endearments so freely, or to do something romantic like hold my hand, and he certainly wouldn't be discussing anal sex with me. Not that I doubt he's experienced in that area, but other than a few minor blips along the way, he's never so openly blurred the lines with me before. *So why now?* He indicated last night that he knew about my family, yet instead of being hostile, he's gone in a different direction. *He's playing games with you.* But why? What could he possibly hope to gain from this? Lee doesn't take backroads to his destination. And that same logic applies to those who cross him. There's more in play here than I'm seeing. If I were smart, I'd go home, pack my bags, and leave the country. But I'm so fucking tired of being afraid all the time. I haven't had a decent night's sleep in two years. Deceiving Lee was compounded by feeling disloyal to my family for loving him. There was no way to win. I knew and accepted that. My only solace is understanding that the collateral damage will be limited to me. Because I'm finished trying to destroy Lee. I'm not sure I would have ever gone through with it even if I had found a smoking gun in his hands.

Now it's just a new mess and seems hopeless to me. Again. When it's finally over, I'll be lucky if either side allows me to walk away.

LEE

I'M IN A PARTICULARLY SHITTY mood as I stalk through my home. I'm also on my second glass of bourbon and a third isn't far behind. Why in the fuck is it so damn difficult to find out who she really is? I've never given much thought to the abilities of Hunter Wrenn, but if I had, I certainly wouldn't have expected him capable of crafting such an ironclad cover. Truthfully, it shouldn't have held past the first inspection, but it did, and according to Lucian, it's still firmly in place.

Despite my irritation, I'm intrigued. This is bigger than I originally thought. It had to be, or none of this would have been necessary. I'm not a man prone to games. I'm far too impatient for that. So my first instinct is to go to Wrenn's home and demand some fucking answers. And if that doesn't work, kicking his ass would be next. The thoughts of the second option fill me with so much adrenaline that I have a hard time controlling the beast inside me. If I give the monster free rein, no one in the vicinity will be left standing. I may not be that man often anymore, but there's no escaping the fact that I'll always think of ways to solve problems that most normal people never will. I'm wired differently. It's neither good nor bad to me—simply a fact.

The only thing stopping me from getting my answers in any way necessary is *her*—Liza. This hold she has on me is truly puzzling, which angers me even further. I'm not in complete denial. I do have feelings for her beyond a mere sexual attraction. And that's something I've never allowed myself. The last woman I let under my skin turned out to be the insane cunt who abused my daughter.

Maria Adams.

She's rotting in jail now, and if I have my way—and I usually do—she'll never live in the outside world again. That she didn't end up face down in a river like her asshole husband is something I regret. Maria's life might be hell now, but does she deserve to even draw a breath after what she did?

How can a mother not only inflict pain upon her own flesh, but allow *and* encourage another to do the same? She is beyond evil. She should have been put down like a rabid dog. Instead, I forced her to turn herself into the authorities for her role in my daughter's brutal attack by her stepfather, Jim Dawson. Had Victor or Draco still been alive, I would have been overruled. Any insult or attack upon a member of our family demanded retribution. If the person wronged is unable to carry it out, then another steps in. Anyone who says there is no honor among thieves is dead wrong. In fact, we live by a strict code. Because without it, such a volatile group will quickly fall into chaos.

I met Maria in the middle of a busy street. Both distracted, we crashed into each other. I'd been irritated at first—until I saw the sexy blonde with the endless legs in front of me. As I apologized, she blushed prettily before admitting she hadn't been paying attention to where she'd been going either. She'd just broken up with her boyfriend and was distraught—supposedly. The flirty smile on her face should have been my first warning, but I'd fallen victim to a hot girl with big tits. Oldest story in the book.

And then she committed her second sin against me. The bitch kept me from *my* baby girl. Seeing her so many years later, when I went to confront her about Lia, she'd barely resembled the girl I once knew. Thin, pale, and frail looking, I doubt I would have recognized her on the street had I walked past her. Her beautiful blond hair, which had easily been her best feature, was gone, and dark hair hung limply down her back. She had the look of someone who'd long used and abused drugs. I had been completely taken with her for months before Victor wanted me to oversee one of his business ventures in South Carolina. I had even pondered taking her with me, but where I was going was no place for a woman. Victor wanted my head in the game. There had been no room in my life then for a long-term relationship, and it would have ended eventually. I'd noticed her conniving side—that she tried to hide— but I'd put it down to a simple survival instinct. *Then.* Now, I knew differently.

Sometimes, the atrocities people commit are so evil that death is simply too good for them. Death as an escape from

punishment when there should be one. She will suffer
for many more years before meeting an untimely end.
Retribution. She'll plead for the Lord's divine intervention
with one breath, then curse His very existence with the
next. Maria isn't capable of loving anyone other than
herself. She is a cruel, sadistic, cowardly shrew who
deserves to be buried in a hole six feet under. She isn't,
though, because of my need for revenge.

I've second-guessed my decision countless times—which
I rarely ever do. Of course, leniency is not something I
practice. To me, that goes together with being a spineless
pussy. You're either the alpha in life or the bitch.

My thoughts circle back to Liza and our dinner. Even
I don't understand what I was playing at. Talking dirty
had come naturally because I was almost always in the
mood to fuck when she was around. But holding her
hand to and from the restaurant? What the hell had that
been about? It had literally happened before I knew what
I was doing. I could kid myself all I wanted and pretend
it was part of the game, but it hadn't been planned. None
of it had. Bringing her back to Falco was the only thing
I'd been certain about. Truthfully, I figured I'd know
what in the hell I was dealing with by now and could go
from there. But it appears I'll be flying blind for a while
longer.

Liza had been on edge at the office, that much was
obvious. She'd been waiting for me to confront her
about what I eluded to knowing. Fuck, that had been
the only amusing part of the day. She flashed one wary
look after another, and I pretended not to notice any of
them. Another week of this behavior, and she'll confess
on her own. She might be up to her neck in something,
but she isn't a hardened criminal. Whatever she got
herself mixed up in, there is a reason she felt it absolutely
necessary. If I know nothing else, I firmly believe that.
I also believe that the guilt of it is eating her alive. *What*

have you done, amore? How do I break you? She may not know specifics, but she's been with me for long enough to realize I'm a dangerous man. So the likelihood of her breaking is slim to none. And it's going to be damn difficult to threaten Wrenn when I don't know what in the hell he is to her. So that only leaves two options. Well, three if you want to get technical. I can build on the whole romantic bullshit I started unwittingly tonight. Or there's the opposite direction of attempting to scare the hell out of her until she cracks—which doesn't appeal to me nearly as much as it should. Or I can pick apart everything Wrenn owns until I get to the fucking truth.

The last option appeals the most to my dark mood, but in doing that, I'll be limited to playing only that hand with Liza. Because she's likely to bolt when he alerts her. So I circle back to the safest course of action for now. Surprisingly, I feel a sense of unease at the thought of pretending to be Prince Charming. It's so far out of my element that I may need to google it to know where to start. I've fucked more women in my lifetime than I can count, but I've never deliberately set out to get one to fall for me. Fuck, I've tried to avoid that. Don't get me wrong. I love women. I'll even go so far as to say that innumerable women are our superiors in many ways. Their capacity to give, nurture, and multitask is awe-inspiring. And even though my mother was a less-than-stellar example, I've never harbored a grudge. Nor can I allow my opinion of Maria to taint my view. There are plenty of bad people in the world. If you're lucky, you avoid the worst ones, and if you're not, then you deliver your own brand of justice and move the fuck on. But it appears that I'll have to delay my verdict on Liza until I've unraveled the mystery surrounding her involvement with Wrenn.

Just thinking of them together again has me longing to throw my glass through the window or do something childish like punch a fucking wall. I long ago learned to control such impulses because they accomplish nothing and hurt like hell. Okay, so occasionally I give in and blow off some steam, but not often. I hate giving my brother the satisfaction of laughing at me when I'm forced to have the drywall patched in my office again. Pete gets way too much pleasure from my bouts of temper. *Bastard.*

Back to the issue at hand: how to alter my relationship with Liza without her becoming suspicious. If I suddenly appear with flowers tomorrow, she's likely to run screaming, and I wouldn't blame her. We both know I'm not that type of man. With a sigh of resignation, I set my glass down and pick up my phone from a nearby coffee table. I pull up his contact information and wince before typing a text message to him.

BREAKFAST AT SERAPHINA'S AT SEVEN? Before I can set my phone aside, it chimes.

LUC: I'LL BE THERE.

I like the fact that no questions are asked. He knows that any invitation from me that doesn't involve my daughter and granddaughter is usually something important. No doubt he'll laugh his ass off when he discovers the purpose of the meeting. Hopefully, he has enough survival instincts to wait until I'm gone before he does it, though. Shaking my head in disgust, I fix myself another drink. Has it really come to this? I'm asking the arrogant Lucian Quinn for advice on women? *Fuck me.* Google might have been a better way to go, after all. At least it wasn't likely to tell every damn person at Quinn Software about my dating woes. *You'll pay for this, my beautiful Liza.* For the first time in hours, I smile. I might be out of my element, but what man doesn't relish the thrill of the hunt? The goal might be different this time, but the rules of the game remain the same: winner takes all. I will fuck the woman who tried to fuck with me. I don't lose—ever.

CHAPTER FOUR

LEE

L UC IS SEATED AT A table on the patio when I arrive. He knows I'm a stickler for punctuality, so I admire the fact that he's fifteen minutes early. It also irritates me because I like to arrive first, even for informal meetings such as this. No doubt the whelp did it on purpose. "Morning," I say as I take a seat across from him. A nearby server hurries over to fill my coffee cup, and I flash her a smile of thanks. Caffeine is one of my few vices. Although I can do without it, I enjoy the kick of energy in the morning.

Luc gives me a look of amusement before asking, "So is this a male bonding thing or is there a reason for this last-minute meeting? Your daughter was a little offended she wasn't invited until I assured her that you probably needed some sexual advice." I choke on a drink of hot liquid and scowl as I grab a napkin to blot my expensive dress shirt. He continues as if oblivious. "She turned a rather sickly shade of green before walking away. Actually, it was more like running, but you get the idea."

He's so close to the truth that I wonder if I'm doing something as insane as blushing for the first time. This may have seemed like a good idea last night after a few drinks, but in the light of day, it feels wrong. I need to abort this plan and come up with something else, fast. "Considering Lia has been married to you for a few years now, I'm certain she's quite aware that you're not an expert in that area. I believe if I had that need, I'd turn to Google first."

"Touché." He smirks as he raises his cup to his mouth. He places it on the table before prompting me once again. "I'm sure you'd benefit greatly from a few pointers. Things are done differently now than they were back in your day. You can use this thing called email or send a text from phones that you carry around with you. Plus, there's Facebook, Twitter, and Instagram." He snaps his fingers together. "Why don't we walk to the bookstore and pick up some of those instructional books. Don't be offended that most of the titles end with 'for dummies.' They're not talking about you personally, it's just a generalization."

"Fuck off," I say, but my words contain no anger. In fact, I'm amused by Luc's humor as I almost always am. I try not to dwell on the fact that my daughter married a younger version of me—with a few key differences, of course. Luc has experienced his moments of darkness. Most at the hands of his psychotic ex-fiancée. Luckily, she did the world a favor and died in a final fit of insanity while attempting to kill Lia. He has also beaten a long-term cocaine addiction, which I doubt very seriously he would have even attempted to stop had he not fallen in love with my daughter. His nature doesn't run to the extremes that mine is capable of, but I know that if pushed, he would do whatever necessary to protect his family. Most believe that all men are capable of violence in the right circumstances, but that is simply not true. There are those who would sacrifice a wife or a child to protect themselves. But it's only by their gender that they're considered a man. In all other senses of the word, they're complete failures to what their sex should be—

the protector. The head of the household. I'm all for equality, but in times of danger, a man should be the protector. There should never be a question about that.

He laughs off my response as we place our order. We both opt for eggs, bacon, and fruit along with a refill of coffee. "There's still nothing on Liza," he offers, assuming that's what I want to discuss. Rolling his eyes, he adds, "Our investigator is intrigued. He said he's never seen so many dead ends before. Just when he thinks he's onto something, the trail stops, and he has to consider something else. He says whoever set the whole thing up is a mastermind." Luc shakes his head ruefully. "I swear, I think he wants to find out who it is so he can either get their fucking autograph or marry them. At this point, I'm not sure if it even matters if it's a man or a woman."

This should make me feel better about the fool, but it doesn't. I pay him enough to be better than the best, and just because someone else can't find the answers either doesn't mean jack shit. Incompetence is simply that. I drain my cup once again as I process his words. Finally, I admit, "I never would have guessed that Liza, of all people, would be at the center of such an elaborate cover-up. Not once did I suspect that she was anything other than a dedicated employee." *And the woman I've been dying to fuck.* I don't bother to verbalize the last part. Luc has probably guessed as much anyway.

"You and I both know that things aren't always as they appear." He nods. I know he's referring to Lia and the life she once led. Will I ever get over the fact that she was forced to make a living as an escort to pay for her schooling? Even though it appalls me that it was necessary, it also makes me absurdly proud of her. How many could survive an abusive home for years and still have the determination to do whatever necessary to make their dreams come true? Again, I marvel at what an amazing woman she is and feel a lump in my throat.

I love her more than I ever thought possible. I'd give everything that I own to have those lost years back with her. To save her from what she suffered, but I can't. The only thing I can do is make sure that neither she nor my granddaughter ever want for anything again. Of course, with Quinn for a husband, I imagine there is little extra they'll need. He's fiercely in love with and overprotective of his wife and daughter. A fact that makes me like him as much as I can any man who's sleeping with my daughter.

"I'm aware of that," I agree. "But I also know that where there's smoke there's a fucking fire. And is there ever a good enough reason to deceive someone?" He opens his mouth to answer, but I wave him off before adding, "A deception that requires that many perfectly placed layers and roadblocks? That's what bothers me the most. I can possibly buy into a different scenario that doesn't make Liza into a traitorous bitch if not for the intrigue surrounding her. This isn't small-time shit. It's elaborate, which tells me that someone has put a great deal of time and money into hiding her intentions and more than likely her identity."

"All true," Lucian concedes. "So what do we know about Hunter Wrenn? If he's at the center of this, she may well be the pawn and he the mastermind."

I shrug. "He's nothing to me, so I haven't tracked him through the years. I took over a company his father founded years ago for Victor and Draco. It was a seamless process, and in the scheme of things, it was almost cordial. After that, I didn't look back."

"You and I both know that there's no time limit on the thirst for revenge. It may have been an ordinary day for you, but perhaps, it stayed with Wrenn well after the fact." He takes a bite of his food, chewing thoughtfully before asking, "Are you thinking that there's a romantic connection between him and Liza?"

"Meaning has he fucked her into stupidly doing

his bidding?" I ask harshly, not bothering to hide the revulsion I feel at that very thought. *He's fucking thirty years older than Liza.*

"Stranger things happen every day," Lucian says wryly. "We need to also look at the family angle. She could be a wife, daughter, or some other blood connection. I think we should shift our focus to him for the moment and go from there."

"I concur. I'd like to go demand answers, but I don't want to panic him into running." I don't mention that I implied threats to Liza to get her to return to Falco. For all I know, she could disappear along with Wrenn at any time. But my gut tells me otherwise. This whole thing was too well organized for them to flee at the first sign of trouble. I think Wrenn is probably thrilled that Liza is back. Maybe she'll try to do whatever the hell she was supposed to do before she left. *Before I pushed her away.*

"It's not like you to wine and dine me for a little chitchat, and you certainly don't need me to confirm what you already know. What gives?"

"Maybe I simply wanted to spend some quality time with my son-in-law." I smirk. My repeated delay in answering his question is annoying the hell out of him. Fuck, he really is too much like me.

He settles back in his chair and eyes me curiously. "If that's true, then I'm either dying and I'm the last to know or this is something that you find embarrassing—and if that's the case, I'll make it doubly painful for this fishing expedition you're taking me on."

Fuck. I have a business to run, and I'm behind schedule. "Unfortunately, I've heard no news of your impending departure from the world, but I'd be happy to change that for you if you'd like." He grins, not looking in the least intimidated. I release a long-suffering sigh, then prepare to be laughed at for the first time in my fucking life. Hell, I can't even kick his ass for it without my daughter's wrath coming down on me. "I have a backup plan in mind where Liza's concerned." I pinch the bridge of my nose before adding, "I thought I'd . . . get her to fall for me and hopefully confess in the process."

Lucian studies me for a moment. "I guess the added advantage of getting her away from Wrenn never figured into it. All right, before you pull me over the table and cause a scene at one of my favorite restaurants, what do you need me for if you have this all figured out?"

Fuck, this is going to hurt. I brace myself for his amusement. "I—um, might need a few pointers in that area."

He gives me a blank look. "You're not asking for advice on sex. Because if you are, then your reputation is certainly a lie. And porn is pretty much an instructional video, so you should start there, and we'll pretend we never had this conversation."

"I don't need you to tell me how to fuck," I snap, then lower my voice as a table of women nearby turn to stare in our direction. "I meant with the whole romance thing. I've never had to put that kind of effort into it before. And I want it to appear genuine."

He smiles, giving me a look of commiseration. "I was about as experienced as you in that area before I met Lia. I'm still not great at it, I'm sure, but the mushy stuff comes more naturally when you're in love with someone."

Exasperated, I say, "Well, since I'm not, I'll need a little more insight here."

"You realize you could have saved yourself a lot of embarrassment by googling this shit? You do use the internet. You see, there's this icon of a big G on your desktop. You click on that and—"

"You have no idea how badly I want to hurt you right now. Be glad I walked here. Otherwise, you'd end up on the bumper of my car."

He clicks his tongue. "You should really talk to someone about these violent tendencies. You can't solve all your problems that way. Plus, if you touch me, I'll tell your daughter." I get to my feet, ready to put an end to what was clearly a mistake. I've had enough heckling for one morning. "You have no sense of humor," he deadpans. "I'll attempt to rein it in, if you'll have a seat. I mean, you must give me a few here. You certainly would have a little fun with me if the positions were reversed."

"Without a doubt." I grin. *Asshole.* I hate to admit even to myself how much I like him, though. I couldn't have chosen anyone better for my daughter. His arrogant self doesn't need to know that, though. I take my seat once again. "Can we get back to it then, or do you have any other smart remarks to add first?"

He holds his hands up in a sign of surrender. "I'd suggest that you toss her on the desk and go for it, but I wouldn't want you to throw your back out. So possibly something a bit more PG-rated first. Some lingering looks. A touch that lasts longer than necessary. Compliments are also generally appreciated. In other words, go in the complete opposite direction from what you've been doing for two years. Because that doesn't appear to have gotten you anywhere. You can ask her out to dinner, but I'd also invite her over to your place. That's more intimate than a crowded restaurant." He gives me a knowing smile before adding, "Don't leave her alone with the silver or your checkbook. We could be giving her too much credit. She may simply be your regular type of criminal. Old Hunter might be broke and in need of some cash."

"I wish it were that simple," I say truthfully. Hell, I'd rather her be a thief any day than a traitor. A large amount of those types of crimes were of necessity—and that was something that I understood.

"So do I. I'd ask that you go easy on her, but in your position, I'd have a hard time doing that. I'll simply say that when you do finally have your answers, listen to her side of the story as well. Make certain she isn't being forced."

"If that were the case, why wouldn't she come to me? She knows I'm more than capable of protecting her."

Lucian takes his wallet from his suit pocket and peels off some bills before tossing them onto the table. Then he levels a serious look my way. "When your back's against the wall, your judgment can become impaired. It isn't always easy to determine who's your savior and who's your executioner." *And that's why I called Luc.*

"In my experience, they're often one in the same," I say solemnly as we part company on the busy sidewalk. I turn toward Falco, and Lucian goes in the opposite direction where Quinn Software is located. I have an uneasy feeling that before this is over, that statement will describe me perfectly to Liza. And I wish to fuck I didn't care. That I could shut down as easily as I always have. No emotions—no feelings—no regrets. That mantra has never been harder to achieve than it is now.

CHAPTER FIVE

———◆———

LIZA

I'VE ALMOST CONVINCED MYSELF THAT the sexual undertones from the previous evening were all in my head, but now I'm not so certain. Because for the first time in two years, Lee is perched on the corner of my desk watching me take a sip of the coffee that he'd arrived with this morning. It's not that he expects me to fetch refreshments for him all day. He usually takes care of that himself. But he's certainly never stopped at Starbucks— for me. He didn't even bring a cup for himself. He's mentioned on more than one occasion that he hates the crowds that tend to hang around at the trendy coffee shop, so there is no way he had his own cup there. I take a cautious sip of the beverage and look at him in surprise. It's a white chocolate mocha. How does he know that's my favorite? As if sensing my unspoken question, he quirks a brow at me in amusement. "I've read the label on your cup before."

Of course, he has. I'm not even a little surprised at this revelation. Lee is the type of person who takes in even the smallest of details. I have little doubt that he could tell me the contents of my desktop without looking. He rarely misplaces anything. In fact, I hazard a guess that if he doesn't have a photographic memory, it's close. He can skim a legal document in an absurdly short amount of time and answer any questions accurately. *He probably has my cycle memorized as well.* My lips twitch at the thought. That would explain why he tended to steer clear when I had my period. I always believed it a lucky break, but now I'm not so sure. "Thanks for this." I smile as I set the cup down.

I fully expect this bizarre encounter to end, but he makes no move to go to his office. He shuffles uncomfortably, then begins twisting one of his cufflinks. This type of fidgeting is so out of character for him that I find myself staring—waiting to see what he'll do next. Then without looking up, he says quietly, "You look . . . nice today. I like the purple on you. It makes you look—bright."

Bright? My mouth is hanging open in surprise, and I close it with a snap. Just when I think things couldn't possibly get weirder . . . First the dinner and handholding last night, now a compliment. A strange one—but still. "Er—thank you." I tug at the snug-fitting sweater uncomfortably, remembering how it outlines every curve of my body. I don't often wear it because of that, but I was in a hurry this morning, and it hadn't required ironing. "I know it's a little tight. I should probably get rid of it." His eyes zero in on my hands, and I freeze. *Way to draw attention to your stomach.*

His brows draw together with a look of confusion. "I have no idea what you mean. It fits perfectly. Much better than those sheet-like dresses you seem to prefer. You have a beautiful body. Why do you hide it behind something so shapeless?"

Why didn't I keep my mouth shut? Lee takes everything entirely too seriously. It's obvious he considers this a puzzle to solve instead of a woman complaining about the fit of her clothing. I take a breath and decide to go with the truth. If I don't, he won't let it go. Surely, at some point he'll act like all men and run from any discussion that alludes to the age-old question, 'does this make me look fat?' "I'm not exactly thin," I point out. "I have more than my fair share of boobs and backside. I also have a stomach that isn't flat and hips that are a nightmare. If my pants fit me there, then they gap at the waist. So I end up having almost everything altered. Dresses are easier because they're more forgiving. They're not as likely to draw attention to my flaws."

He appears positively riveted by my explanation as his gaze moves over every inch of my body. Finally, he says, "You look like a real woman, Liza. Or the way one should look. There's nothing worse to a man than feeling like you're fucking a scarecrow. A pointy tailbone is a mood killer. Do you have any idea what a turn-on it is to explore all those curves? What you hate, we revere."

Before thinking better of it, I snort inelegantly. "Give me a break, Lee. I've seen some of your supermodel dates in the paper. They look like they only eat on special occasions. So if you prefer fluffy women, then why are you hiding them? Is it that they're good enough to sleep with, but not to be seen in public with?"

"I wasn't aware that you followed my social life so closely." *But he doesn't deny who he's normally seen with. Hypocrite.*

I literally feel the heat rushing into my cheeks as I stumble for something to say. "I—er . . . don't. I may have seen a picture once—or twice. Quite by accident," I add quickly. "I don't have an alert set up or anything. That's something a stalker would do." *Shit!* "Which I'm not. I was simply pointing out the difference, you know—for your information." *Shut up! Dear God, stop the insanity.*

He laughs, he actually laughs, and it's not a polite gesture to make me feel better. No, it's a deep sound that fills the office and reverberates from the walls. Even to my ears, it sounds faintly rusty, as if he doesn't do it very often. "My little bird," he says almost fondly. "You're an endless source of amusement. Why has it taken me this long to notice?"

I don't think he expects an answer as he almost appears to be asking himself the question. "Possibly because you and I rarely discuss anything that isn't business related. No offense, but your office doesn't exactly inspire a lot of humor. Terror for some, maybe—but laughter—not so much."

He stares at me for a moment before nodding slowly. "Then perhaps it's time to make some changes. This isn't a prison camp and I don't want you to feel as if it is. I realize that I become engrossed in work and often block out things around me, but I'll strive to do better."

If he drops his pants in front of me, I'll be more surprised than I am at his declaration. Okay, well maybe a little bit, but still—he's shocking the hell out of me. Why is he attempting to turn over a new leaf? People generally only did that when— "Oh my God, you're dying, aren't you?" I blurt out as I spring to my feet. "Is it cancer? Your heart?" Then I look wildly around the room. "Has someone put one of those hits out on you?" I grab my purse with one hand and his arm with the other. "Come on, we'll find somewhere to hide." When he remains seated, giving me an incredulous look, I pull harder. "Lee, get your ass in gear! Do you want to be blown away? There could be a sniper rifle trained on you right now." A surge of panic shoots through me. "A bomb, of course. They'll take you and Falco out with one blast." *And he still doesn't move.* He's clearly in shock, which makes it even worse. If Lee is scared, then it must be bad. I snap my fingers in his face. "Get it together. I can't carry you." I motion toward the door, saying slowly, "Come on, we're wasting too much time." Wrinkling my nose, I ask, "How in the world did you ever make it as a gangster? Pete must have been the enforcer."

I'm still muttering complaints under my breath as I once again tug on his arm. "Liza, what in the fuck are you talking about?" he asks, sounding exasperated as he gently shakes me off. He picks up my Starbucks cup and sniffs it. "It will explain so much if they put alcohol in there," he adds ruefully.

I put my hands on my hips in frustration. "If you're not dying or anything along those lines, then why are you being so—nice all of the sudden?" I'll probably regret it later, but while I'm going, I decide to ask the question that has been driving me insane. "You practically blackmailed me to get be back here, and since then, you have made no mention of—well, whatever you think you know." Eyeing him warily, I ask, "Is this some kind of game? Keep me guessing and kill me with kindness? You're usually a little more direct than that, so I don't understand this at all."

He appears surprised by my jumbled rant. But other than that, his face gives nothing away. He simply shrugs and gets to his feet. "Maybe you need to lay off the caffeine, little bird. It's making you paranoid. I'm simply attempting to improve the work atmosphere. After all, it was apparently bad enough for you to walk out before. I'd like to avoid that happening again." Without waiting for a response, he walks into his office and shuts the door behind him.

"That's such bullshit," I say to the empty room. He couldn't care less about my job satisfaction. Something else must be at play here, and I need to remain on guard. I swear if he breaks out a picnic and a blanket at lunch, I may well kill him myself. After spending a lifetime with a father who loved to play mind games, I've learned that it pays to be suspicious of unusual displays of kindness. Because men like Lee and my father don't suddenly change unless it's with motive, an attempt to get what they want. And I refuse to be a pawn in this particular game. If he doesn't want to be straight with me, then I'll push him until he cracks. There are two things Lee absolutely detests . . . *Ha.* I'll give him both and see how long this act of his lasts. *Buckle up, Mr. Jacks, it's going to be a bumpy ride.*

———◆———

LEE

I GRIN AS I CLOSE MY office door behind me. Why have I never realized just how damn funny Liza is? I swear I almost lost it when she went into a tizzy about protecting me. I had been tempted to play along just to see what she came up with. Although I was a little offended when she insulted my skills as a gangster. *If only she knew.* As far as romancing her went, that whole scene may be considered a failure. Instead of swooning at my feet, understanding I was coming on to her, she jumped from one conclusion to another. Again, a tad insulting, but she is unlike any other woman I've known, so it stands to reason that her reactions are different. I'll have to adjust my methods and try again. I'll start by finding excuses to keep her close for the rest of the day. Maybe a little touch here and there and she'll come around. I walk around my desk and take a seat. I log onto my computer and open my email. Perfect. I'll have her come in so that we can deal with the replies together. My finger is hovering over the intercom when the door suddenly flies open and slams back against the wall. *What the hell?*

"Whoops." Liza giggles as she steps into the room holding her Starbucks cup and a notepad. "My bad. I don't know my own strength sometimes." She crosses to a chair in front of me and sets her cup and legal pad on my desk before plopping down into a chair and crossing her legs at the ankles. Then I stare at her incredulously as she smacks her lips frantically before blowing a huge bubble.

"Liza," I warn, "that's going to—" Before I can get the words out, the bubble pops and covers her face. I see her eyelids blinking against the pink gunk before she raises a hand and attempts to clean the mess off. I release my breath on a hiss as we both realize that she has some in her hair. "What were you thinking?" I snap in irritation as I stand and move to her side. I spend the next five minutes picking out pieces of the sticky mess from her blond locks while she blinks at me like an owl. "That's about the best I can do. It'll probably take a few days and some shampoo to take care of the rest of it." I know how women are about their hair, so I'm prepared for a freak-out, but as usual, she never does what I expect.

"No biggie." She waves me off. "It's not as if I have some big event to attend." Then she winks at me. "Thanks for the help though, Tony."

"Tony?" I scowl down at her. "Who in the hell is that?"

She grins, then wiggles her brows. "You know, Tony Soprano. The mob boss from *The Sopranos*. I'm kinda digging that as a nickname for you. Whatdaya think? Maybe shorten it to Ton?"

"He's old and dead," I point out, not liking the comparison at all. Naturally, she has to pick someone unattractive to group me with. *Do I look that fucking old?* And seriously, the man had a huge gut on him. I glance down, making certain that I do in fact still have the chiseled form I've had for so long. I run and work out daily. Partly to stay in shape and I've also discovered that it's a great stress reliever.

Her eyes widen as she asks, "In real life? I hadn't heard that."

Rolling my eyes, I say, "I believe Kara told Pete and

me at a family function a while back." At that time, I'd found it amusing because she was calling her father Tony. Somehow, it wasn't as funny to be on the receiving end of it. She eyes me for a moment, then I see her mouth move. "For fuck's sake, Liza, you're still chewing that damned gum after having it on your face and in your hair? Do you know how nasty that is?" I suddenly feel like I'm dealing with a child as I stomp around to pick up my trash can and hold it in front of her. "Spit it out." She pouts before doing as I ask. *Unbelievable. She needs a good spanking.* And with that thought, she's certainly no longer a child in my mind. Time to get things back on track before I completely lose it. So I settle into my chair and open my email program. "I need you to call Mark Isner and schedule a meeting for tomorrow afternoon." I hear a thump that has me looking up. *No way, really?* She has her feet on my desk. There are papers crinkled under the heels of her sandals as the pointy soles dig into them. And as bad as that is, it's not the most alarming part. No, that would be the fact her chair appears to be leaning backward as she hums under her breath.

"You don't happen to have Mark's number handy, do ya?" she asks. "That would save me from looking it up. Do you know how much time I waste on crap like that?"

I shake my head. I'm dreaming. *This can't be happening.* Liza would never be this unprofessional. Hell, this is worse than the idiots who were filling in for her and that's saying something. "Please remove your feet before you make a mess," I say stiffly.

She huffs as if I've asked her to change the fucking oil in my car. Just when I think she's going to ignore my request, she moves one leg before disaster strikes. I watch in horror as she kicks the Starbucks cup and it wobbles in slow motion. My hand shoots out—but it's too late. The cup turns over onto its side, and naturally, the damn lid pops off and what looks like enough liquid to cure the drought comes rushing out. Within seconds, my desk is covered, and it's trickling off into my lap. "Oh shit," I hear muttered as I jump to my feet. My hands clench and release at my sides as I strive to control my temper. I seriously want to lose it, but I'm not even sure where to start.

Somehow, Liza is in front of me mopping at my crotch with one hand while the other plops a stack of paper towels onto the now ruined stacks before me. Then she has the audacity to say, "Look what you made me do."

"How in the hell is this my fault?" I shout as my control snaps.

The hand that had been wiping my crotch pauses, then resumes with a little too much force so I step back before she rips my dick off next. "Because you startled me. I was doing fine until you demanded that I move. From the tone of your voice, I knew if I didn't do it quickly you'd spaz out."

I pinch the bridge of my nose, counting to three under my breath. "You shouldn't have had your fucking feet there to begin with. This is my office, not your living room."

She sighs, then points at the mess that was once perfectly dry and organized. "If you chill and stop fussing at me, I can get this cleaned up. After all, it's probably not a good idea to have liquid under your laptop."

"For fuck's sake!" I hiss as I grab the three-thousand-dollar laptop purchased last week. The screen flickers as coffee drips from the underside. *This isn't happening.* How has this day gone off the rails so quickly? She's lost her mind. *Un-fucking-believable.* Plus, I've probably also broken my own personal record for saying or thinking the word "fuck." I must get out of here before I do something I'll regret. I tensely say, "Either take care of this or find someone who can." I toss the laptop back onto the carnage and add, "Call IT and have them get me a new computer within the hour." Then I leave the room at a near sprint. Instead of wanting to fuck her, I'm trying to talk myself out of organizing a hit. There's no doubt if I were the real Tony Soprano, she'd be swimming with the fishes tonight. And as fucked up as it is, I feel a smile tugging at my lips at that thought. Then it hits me with the force of a sledgehammer. Liza has far more power over me than I ever realized. Because there's no way I'd let anyone else get away with the shit she just pulled. Not only that, but I'm also grinning like an idiot about it not two minutes later. *I'm fucked if she ever discovers how easily she can get to me.* And with that thought, I'm once again frowning. This feels far too much like vulnerability, and that could easily be the death of me and everyone that I hold dear—including Liza. *Although right now, I have no fucking idea why I'm trying to romance her. What just happened?*

CHAPTER SIX

———◆———

LIZA

I ATTEMPT TO HIDE MY SMIRK behind the paper napkin that I use to wipe my mouth. When my sister called to demand I meet her for dinner, I informed her that I was already inside Fuddruckers. I felt like a treat was in order after surviving Lee's wrath earlier in the day and what better reward than a delicious hamburger from one of my favorite places. I didn't expect Jacey to meet me here. That could ruin the moment for me if I wasn't enjoying her attempt at trying not to stare in revulsion as I take big bites of my burger. Naturally, she ordered a salad and had done little more than shift the lettuce from one side of the bowl to the other. "I'm glad you could join me," I mumble around the bite of food in my mouth. Normally, I have better manners, but I simply can't resist yanking her chain a few more times. And I realize why I am finding it so easy to rile Lee. I've had years of experience pushing buttons. Poor Lee. He never really stood a chance.

Her lips purse together tightly as a fleeting look of disgust crosses her face before she can control it. "Really, Jade? Are you surprised Harry wasn't interested in you? Your table manners are deplorable. You look as if you belong in a truck stop wolfing down a ten-dollar steak."

I refuse to take the bait. I managed to all but run Lee

out of Falco earlier, so why stop there? Jacey shall be simple in comparison. Although I'm full, I continue to eat. At one point, I wipe my mouth on the back of my hand, and for a moment, I think she's going to pass out from the horror of it all, but she stands her ground. This next step may be going too far, but what the hell. I let out a burp that admittedly is much louder than I planned it to be. Luckily, no one is nearby, so Jacey is the only witness to my rather gross display. "Whoops." I smile broadly. Rubbing my stomach, I add, "More room out than there is inside, though, right?"

"Dear God," she snaps. "You weren't raised in a barn. If Dad hadn't told me numerous times that you weren't adopted, I'd swear that you were."

Okay, that dig stings. "I wish." I shrug indifferently. "I'm nowhere near as anal as you are, so I've questioned the same thing before. And if you're so worried about Harry, then you should hook up with him." Giving my best wink, I reach out and cuff her on the shoulder. She's so damn skinny that I nearly knock her off the chair. "If you're expecting anything impressive down below, you'll be disappointed. The few times he kissed me, I was close enough to tell that there's not much going on in that area."

She's clearly appalled by my crass comment, and I resist the urge to do a victory dance around the table. *This is too much fun.* She visibly swallows, then takes a breath. I seem to be having that effect on everyone today. I'm disappointed when she doesn't comment on Harry. "So I understand you're working for Lee again? I'm glad to see you took my words to heart. Dad was thrilled when he found out. How did you manage to get back in so quickly?" *Why am I even shocked that she knows?*

"You should really consider cutting back on the Botox. Your eyebrows are so high now they're practically touching your forehead. You have this look of surprise all the time."

She tosses her fork down and says, "It's called maintenance, and most normal women do it. I'll still look young when I'm eighty, but you won't be around to see it." She points at my side of fries and sneers, "Because you'll die of some obesity-related disease way before then."

And the gloves are off. I have no idea what's gotten in to me, but I'm enjoying taunting her far more than I normally would. It's just so damn easy since she doesn't approve of a single thing I say or do. I pop a fry in my mouth and roll my eyes in exaggerated bliss. Again, I display horrendous manners by talking with my mouth full. "So, if you already have me dead and buried, explain to me why I should do the dirty work for the family?"

"You know this is for our mother," she says as if speaking to a child. "Aren't you in the least bit angry that she's gone because of Lee? Can you forgive and forget that easily? This has nothing to do with what Dad and I want."

By this point, I've had more than enough. Normally, I'm quiet and go along with whatever so she says—but not tonight. Her Botoxed brows get even higher when I push my plate away and get to my feet. "Good talk, Jacey," I say sarcastically. "See you around." Her words of protest follow me as I leisurely stroll out the door and to my car. I resist the urge to leave a trail of rubber in the parking lot and instead calmly maneuver my car to the exit and out onto the street.

I think about everything that's happened today and begin to laugh. I have managed something that not many have accomplished before: I've gotten the better of Lee *and* Jacey. And I simply did it by not giving a shit. Okay, so maybe I added a few theatrics, but it has been worth it. It's amazing how easy it is to get to people who are so damned anal. And after a while, it was less of an act and more about freeing myself from the prison I've lived in for my entire life. I've spent far too many years trying to make everyone happy, and where has it gotten me? I'm the outcast of my family yet still willing to do their dirty work—even though I don't agree with it. The only time I'm treated like a Wrenn is when either Jacey or my father need something from me. Otherwise, I'm invisible. *If only my mother was still here.* Even amidst the sorrow I feel when I think of her, I don't blame Lee. I know my father well enough to understand that there are two sides to every story, and naturally, his would be the one that makes him look like the good guy. It's past time I learn the actual truth and not just the pieces that they hand-fed me. I will no longer do their bidding. Even if I discover Lee is guilty, I will decide the best recourse—and no one else. I'm thirty-four years old, and dammit, I'm not a puppet on a string for everyone to pull. It's time I stop thinking about stepping out of the shadows and do it. Regardless of what happens when this is over—at least I'll finally be able to look at myself in the mirror and know that although I'm not perfect, I'm free.

LEE

NOT ONLY HAVE I CONTINUED to say "fuck" a lot, but I am also tossing back booze like it's fucking water. I can't remember the last time I got drunk, but I am damn close to it now. When my buzzer sounds, I feel myself weaving as I cross the foyer to toss the door open. So much for security—no one bothered to let me know that someone is on their way up. When I see Pete standing there, my question is answered. He has free rein in my building. They don't bother to let me know when he is here. Hell, he has a key to everything that I own, so it's hardly necessary for him to ask for permission. "Did we have plans?" I ask as I wave him inside. *Maybe this is what a senior moment feels like.*

"No." He stares at me in disbelief before shaking his head. "But since you referred to Kara as Kate, and you called me Luc at least three times while we were talking on the phone an hour ago, I figured I'd better stop by and see if you were either drunk or having a breakdown of some sort." He points to the near-empty glass in my hand. "Thankfully, it appears to be the first option. What's brought this on?"

I lean against a nearby wall and toss the rest of the whiskey back, grimacing as it burns like fire on the way down. Then I clear my throat and say, "She blew a bubble the size of my fucking car, then continued to chew the gum even after I'd pulled it from her face and hair. Next, she put her feet on my desk and knocked her coffee over my papers. But that's not the worst of it," I slur. "She completely ruined my new computer, then had the nerve to blame it all on me. Said something about me yelling at her." I look at the ceiling as if praying for divine intervention. "Pete, I had to get the hell out of there before I lost it. You know how I feel about any kind of disorder. I simply can't function in that type of environment. And my whole desk was swimming in coffee. It dripped down onto my crotch, for fuck's sake. And she tried to clean it off, but nearly emasculated me in the process." *I swear I can hear a whiny voice, but surely that isn't me.*

"Let's go sit down," he replies as he motions toward the living area. It pisses me off that I must concentrate to navigate my own apartment, but it's either that or face plant on the marble floor. After what seems like an hour, I find myself sitting in my favorite chair. I think I may have drifted off for a moment at some point. A quick glance at my brother's amused expression confirms that suspicion. *Fuck.* "So now you've rejoined me, let me see if I can make sense of what you were saying earlier. Someone spilled coffee on your desk and sent you into a drunken spiral?" Before I can answer, he adds, "But I have no idea what the gum part was all about. Is that even related to the coffee incident because it was all a bit jumbled?"

I take a couple of deep breaths and attempt to clear the cobwebs from my mind. Then I say as clearly as possible, "Liza lost her fucking mind today. She made a complete mess of my office and of herself. And apparently, it was all my fault." I snap my fingers together. "Oh, and she said something about me causing her to waste a lot of time looking up numbers or some such shit. Can you believe her nerve? Isn't that her job?"

He laughs until he notices my murderous expression. Then he takes it down a few levels to simply a broad smile. "Lee, I know you can't abide disorder, and I, of all people, understand why. But I'm almost certain that Liza has no clue about that part of our past and the issues that it left both you and me with. Granted, the fact that I've raised two children has helped me tremendously in dealing with that phobia. Otherwise, I'd have been off the rails every time they made a mess. And believe me, my wife was always quick to point that out to me. But you've lived alone for all your adult life, and you've never had to confront that particular issue as I have."

"That has nothing to do with it," I deny weakly, but we both know I'm lying. We grew up living in complete filth with our druggie mother, who was too stoned on any given day to care about the condition of our government housing. When I got older, I did my best to clean up so my brother didn't have to live in complete squalor. But with mold covering so many surfaces and the place practically crumbling around us in disrepair, it was the equivalent of putting a fucking Barbie Band-Aid over an amputated body part. It did little good. And Pete was right. It had left me with issues that I've never had to deal with. I simply make sure that everywhere I stay is pristinely clean, and if it isn't, then I make it clean. Even as lazy as Maria had been, it didn't take her long to make sure her tiny apartment was spotless when I was there. Not that I ever complained—I didn't have to. Just a few times of me staying up all night to do the cleaning was enough.

"You can't punish Liza for our mother's sins," Pete says softly. "So she was having an off day. Things like that happen. But she doesn't have a clue what something that simple does to you unless you tell her. I put Charlotte through hell even before we had kids. I couldn't admit that I was traumatized by our past. But it didn't take her long to figure out that I needed my surroundings to be clean and orderly—although she didn't get the full scope of the problem. One night, I completely lost my shit when I went into the kitchen at midnight, and she hadn't loaded the dishwasher as she'd said that she would. I started banging dishes together so loudly that it woke her. When I looked up and saw her standing there in my T-shirt looking scared out of her mind, it hit me what I must look like to her. Even though it was one of the hardest things I've ever done, I left the rest of the mess where it was and asked her as calmly as possible to take a seat at the table and let me explain. She didn't want to, I could see that. Hell, for a moment, I thought she'd bolt. But she finally agreed to hear me out. And after that, we worked on dealing with my hang-ups together. The kids, of course, brought a whole new level of chaos, but by that time, Charlotte was secure enough in our love to speak bluntly to me. She'd let me know when I was out of line, and if I needed to walk off for a moment and regroup, she understood."

I stare at my brother in shock, surprised by his revelations. I know I'm fucked up because of the shit from our youth, but I tried so hard to shield him from the worst of it. My hope had been that he was too young to know that others didn't live the way that we did. It's like a punch to the gut to realize he's just as messed up as I am. *I've failed to protect everyone I love.* "Why didn't you tell me?" I ask softly. It's a testament to my level of intoxication that I feel like fucking crying. First, I find out that my daughter has lived through hell, and now I discover that my brother is more fucked up than I'd imagined. Is there some kind of dark curse that plagues the Jacks' bloodline? Do all who cross our path risk living a life of hell?

Pete shakes his head before giving me a smile that doesn't quite reach his eyes. "Because you're battling your own demons, brother, and they're much worse than the few I live with. You did unimaginable shit to provide for us when you were nothing but a kid yourself. And I know that even now you're sitting over there drowning in guilt because of what I said." He sees the truth of his words as I drop my gaze, staring at the now-empty glass in my hand. "That's what I thought," he adds wryly. "You're like a sponge, Lee. You've always absorbed all the bad stuff and attempted to make it clean again. But at some point, you must realize you can't continue to do that without losing yourself in the process and everything else good in your life. You've worked so hard to turn away from Victor's way of life and make a new one for all of us. One where we don't have to be afraid of ending up in prison—or worse."

I stare at my brother in silence. "I've never known those types of fears. I could give two fucks about any of that— but I never had anything to lose like you do."

"Maybe not before, but you have a daughter and a granddaughter now," Pete points out. "Somehow, I don't think you want them visiting you behind bars or in a funeral home. You may feel like no one would grieve your absence from this world, but what about me? Do you have any idea how that would feel? You might pride yourself on being a hard-ass, but you and I have been joined at the hip for far too long to sever that connection now. Maybe we both have families now, but for so many years, it was just you and me. We're the only people we could ever rely on. So we no longer have to worry about where we'll sleep or when we'll have another meal, but the bond those things created cannot be broken. In a strange way, you and I are not only brothers, but we're also soul mates."

"We're what?" I ask, thinking surely, he's lost his mind. When did Pete start thinking like a woman? *Soul mates? What the fuck?*

Pete laughs at my expression of disbelief. "A soul mate isn't always a romantic connection. Oftentimes, it's a family member, a friend, or someone else you've connected with. Simply put, we've lifted each other up through all our hard times and made a life for ourselves that wouldn't have been possible alone. Don't get me wrong; you would have succeeded financially without me. You're too fucking smart not to have. But you might not have managed to retain your humanity without having to include me in the equation. You are the man who you are because of the love you have for me."

I don't bother to argue, because even in my alcohol-induced haze, I see the truth behind his words. Some men might attempt to shrug it off as bullshit, but Pete and I have had what I'd call deep discussions for most of our lives. We're both people who think through every angle of all scenarios, so his reasoning isn't surprising to me now that I've got past my initial reaction. "I might have worded that a bit differently," I concede, "but it makes sense in a weird way. And you're right, I'd probably be more of a monster than I am if not for you."

He grimaces in distaste before saying angrily, "You know how I feel about that. Fuck yes, we've both done some bad stuff, but where we come from, it's called survival. We never took pleasure in it, nor did we bully the innocent to get our rocks off. You're not some kind of demon, Lee. If you were, I wouldn't be here now. You'd have left me with our sorry excuse for a mother and never looked back. Your life would have been much simpler if you had. I was a noose around your neck from the moment I was born. You were both my father and my mother when you weren't even old enough to care for yourself."

"I was never a child, Pete." I hate that this is true. "You know that as well as I do. Don't make me out to be a hero because I'm anything but."

"You are to me," he states firmly, then raises his hand to ward off my objections. My brother has seen the worst sides of me, yet he absolutely feels no fear. He speaks bluntly, corrects me when he feels I'm wrong, and laughs at my OCD tendencies when others wouldn't dare. I respect him immensely. But we'll always disagree on the subject of me. I'm jaded and weary from the burdens I've carried for years. But I also accept that I can't go back and make myself into something I'm not—nor do I want to. Every good and bad decision in my life has made me who I am. I'm Lee Jacks, and I've worked my fucking ass off to acquire all that I have. I've built an empire through hard work, being ruthless when necessary, and always staying one step ahead of everyone around me. While others were sitting around reading the *Wall Street Journal*, I was reading people. With one glance, I know how they think, and better yet, I know their weaknesses. It's all there for anyone to see—if you know where to look.

You couldn't read her. She fooled you.

Liza—she is the exception to it all. The one person who is not as she seems, and I missed it.

He sighs, knowing that, as always, there is no winner in this disagreement. He'll always believe one thing and me another. And if I'm being truthful, I rather like the fact that my brother sees some good in me. I'll even take it so far as to hope that my daughter does as well. With that thought, I feel a pang in my chest. If I weren't drunk, I'd go see Lia tonight. I've wasted years that I yearn to have back. I'll see her tomorrow, though, at the board meeting for the company we run together. I'm so fucking proud of her. I've stayed in the background unless she solicits my advice, and the business is already turning a profit. She and her friend, Rose, are doing an amazing job, and I find myself bragging every time the opportunity arises. I'm quite sure that everyone at Falco is tired of hearing it—but I'm their boss, so they'll grin and bear it. I squint at my watch and am shocked to see that it's after nine. "Shouldn't you be getting home? I'm surprised Charlotte isn't looking for you." I smirk. Making fun of Pete's tendency to be hen-pecked by his wife is one of my great pleasures. He knows it's true, so he simply shrugs and grins. I'd never admit it, but at times like these, I'm almost jealous of what he has waiting for him. I've made my choices—but as with everything, it has come with a price. One I've never spent a lot of time questioning—until her. *Why is she the exception to everything?*

He gets to his feet and shakes his head when I attempt to get to mine. "Just stay there. I know my way out." Then he gives me a look of concern. "Are you good? I can always stay if you need me to." He raises his hand and points behind him. Years ago, that was our unspoken sign for "I've got your back." It's something we still randomly do after all these years and neither of us has ever forgotten it. As much as he loves his wife and kids, I know he'd give his life for me as I would for him.

"I'm fine, Pete." We share a brief hug, and I feel strangely forlorn when the quiet surrounds me once more.

Shaking it off, I manage to stumble to the bathroom, and then make it to my bed. As the room spins around me, I think of her—*why is it fucking always her?*

CHAPTER SEVEN

———◆———

LIZA

"I SWEAR I COULD SIT HERE and look at hot daddy all day." Rose sighs as she stares at Lee. I'm grinding my teeth and fighting the urge to do something crazy like pull her hair for gawking at my man when she suddenly switches her attention to me. I can tell by the smirk that settles over her face that she's picked up on my jealousy and is amused by it. "Remind me again why you're not all over that." She shakes her head as if I've gravely disappointed her.

"Remind me again why you're lusting after Lee when you're engaged to Max," I snap.

Lia laughs softly before bumping her friend on the shoulder with her fist. "I guess she told you, Perv. Haven't we discussed how creepy it is that you're constantly ogling my father?"

Rose rolls her eyes before pointing at the object of her obsession. "Give me a break. Your daddy looks like freaking Brad Pitt—only hotter. It might be weird for you to notice it, Lia, but I'm betting you haven't missed it, Liza—am I right?"

The anger drains out of me, and I find myself giggling and no doubt blushing. *Yep, guilty as charged.* "It would be a little hard to miss it," I admit. "And he's way more attractive than Brad Pitt."

"You're damn right he is." Rose nods. "Can you even imagine how he'd be in bed?" She fans herself quickly. "I get chest pains thinking about it."

Lia makes a gagging noise, and I put a hand on her arm in sympathy. I remember what a surprise it had been for all of us to find out Lee had a grown daughter. I had watched him closely, wondering what he'd do. After the initial understandably shock, he threw enormous effort into being there for Lia. Some men would have turned a blind eye and believed it wasn't worth the bother, but not Lee Jacks. The love I've seen in his eyes toward his daughter has not only impressed me but also has, at times, almost made me jealous. My dad has known about me since birth, but I've never seen the pride and affection in his eyes that Lee has toward Lia. Buying the company that they now run together was just one of many things he's initiated to connect with her. He's so very proud of the beautiful, intelligent woman before me. His eyes light up when he talks about her. In a strange way, it's given me hope to know that he is capable of that type of love. Before I can comment, Lee walks up and raises a brow in inquiry when we all look at him with varying degrees of guilt. He drops a kiss on Lia's forehead before asking, "Have I missed something important?"

"God, no." Lia shudders. "Trust me, it's nothing you want me to repeat."

He shrugs, giving her an affectionate smile. "If you say so. How's Lara? I was hoping you'd bring her with you this morning."

Lia beams at her father as they discuss her daughter. "She's teething, so she would have probably raised holy hell during the meeting. You know you're always welcome to stop by, though, Dad. She loves seeing you."

I see Lee swallow audibly when Lia calls him Dad—and

he's not alone. I'm battling a lump in my throat as well. I couldn't be happier that he's no longer on the sidelines while his brother has a family. I realize that it was a choice he made, but life has a funny way of changing all that when you least expect it. "I'll drop in soon, honey," he promises. He shoots me a wary look before adding, "If everyone is ready, let's get started. I have a lunch meeting after this."

I fight the urge to laugh as Lee reluctantly pulls out a chair at the conference room table for me before taking the one next to it. Since the whole fiasco in his office yesterday, he's been treating me like a ticking bomb he expects to go off at any second. I'd love nothing more than to jerk his chain, but I'm not sure how he'd react if I were to crawl onto the table and start stripping. He certainly lost it over the coffee spill. I've worked for him long enough to understand how he is about order, but he freaked out a little more than I expected. Not that it would stop me from doing it again—but still, watching him struggle for control was as fascinating as it was scary. I set my phone in front of me and push the recorder application on it. "Boy, do I love this sucker," I say enthusiastically as I point at my iPhone.

"Liza, you're supposed to be taking notes instead of texting," he says in disbelief as he stares at the neon-pink case with the black zebra stripes across it.

I shake my head. "Nah, that's old school and a complete waste of my time. You see, this baby can be used like you would a cassette recorder." I point at the image of a cassette tape on the screen. "Plus, I don't have to listen to any of this because I can do that later. And I can send the recording to you as well if a question arises."

His mouth moves in a way that's comical, but no words come out. Finally, he pinches the bridge of his nose in the way that he always does when he's frustrated. I can just imagine him counting to three in his head as he struggles for control. "Taking notes is your job. I realize it's asking a lot, but surely, you could focus in on the meeting for an hour."

"Sure"—I nod— "but what I'm trying to tell you is that it's not necessary." I give him a bright smile and turn away from his glare only to lock gazes with an amused Rose.

"I totally underestimated you," she murmurs. "It's not exactly the route I would have picked, but you've certainly got his attention."

"I don't know what you're talking about," I mouth back, then ruin the denial by winking.

"If he doesn't kill you first, this might just work." She wiggles her brows. "Let's do lunch soon so we can make some plans."

The meeting is called to order, and despite what I told Lee, I follow every word as usual. Although when he looks my way, I pretend to be studying my nails. At one point, I even draw a tic-tac-toe board on a nearby legal pad and put a big X in the middle square before sliding it in front of him. He freezes for a moment before shocking the hell out of me by putting an O in a nearby box. We finish that game—and three more—and I admire the fact that he never misses a beat again—following along with the meeting while beating me in every single game. It's a sad commentary on my romantic life that this is one of the coolest things to ever happen to me. I would have never believed Lee capable of participating in something so silly. If I wasn't already in love with the man, I would be now. I take a sip of water just as he passes the notepad back to me and then begin to choke when I read what he's written below the game board. "I want to lay you out on this table, bury my face between your legs, and lick your pussy—right fucking now. Circle Yes or No." Rose thumps me on the back, craning her neck to see what I've hastily put my hand over. "Are you okay?" Lee whispers in my ear, sounding vastly amused at my dilemma.

"I'm fine," I hiss back. He begins to pull back, no doubt thinking he's won this round. I reach out and grab his tie, halting his progress. His eyes widen in surprise as I mouth one word: yes. Then it hits me that the room has gone quiet. *Please don't let them be looking at me.* Naturally my inner plea has fallen on deaf ears because when I glance around, everyone is focused on the interaction between us. *This is why you don't mess around with the boss.* I'm considering crawling under the table when Lee tugs his tie from my hold and asks Lia for some figures as if nothing unusual has occurred. I sag back in my chair in relief only to feel his hand squeeze my knee briefly. *And this round belongs to him.* I might have pushed his buttons yesterday, but Lee has changed the game today, and he knows it. My body is still throbbing from his naughty words, and I'm honestly hoping he means them. *What would it be like to be so sexually overpowered by a man like Lee?* To be devoured? I'm not brave enough to fall onto his desk with my legs spread to see if he follows through, though. *But I'm thinking about it . . .*

Then the meeting is over and Rose pulls me aside as we get to our feet. "Whatever you're thinking, I say go for it. You two were obviously doing some type of dirty note play, and trust me, he was into it. I've never seen Lee be anything other than professional during these things, but you had him acting like a horny college boy."

"He wasn't rattled at all," I say. "He picked right up where he left off, which is kind of insulting."

"That's where you're wrong." Rose smirks. "He'd already asked Lia for those exact figures once. And that's not a mistake he's ever made before."

"Really?" My eyes widen in shock because she's right. Lee doesn't forget anything. And he's far too impatient to repeat himself. Of course, if I'd been listening at all, I would have picked up on it myself. Hell, I wouldn't have noticed if someone had stripped naked and started pole dancing in the corner. I'm beginning to really suck at my job.

I nearly jump out of my skin when a hand settles on my waist. "I'm running late for my next meeting," Lee murmurs. "I'll take a cab and leave the car for you."

"I'm going in that direction, so I'll drop Liza," Lia offers. I give her a grateful smile and wait as Lee hugs her goodbye. He glances in my direction, nodding his head before leaving the room at a fast clip. Rose gives me a thumbs-up that has Lia laughing as we walk toward the elevator. She pushes a button for the parking garage, then shakes her head. "I can only imagine what advice Rose was giving you. Do yourself a favor. If she ever suggests going shopping, run for your life. Otherwise, you'll probably pay a few thousand dollars for something a prostitute would be embarrassed to wear."

She fills me in on the latest funny stories about Lara, and before I know it, we're sliding into her Mercedes. "I love your car." I sigh in pleasure as I run a hand over the soft leather interior. "It's like the much prettier cousin to my Honda." I laugh.

Lia rolls her eyes before shaking her head ruefully. "It's one of the few battles I've managed to win with Luc. Throw in my overprotective dad, and I usually don't stand a chance. Luc wants me to use Sam for everything, but that's just absurd. At the most, I run a few errands and come to work. Luc spends a lot of his time in the car, and he's always used it to return calls and prepare for meetings. Now I ask you, who needs the driver and who doesn't?"

"I see your point. I don't know your husband that well, but I understand the reasoning behind it. They're both afraid of something happening to you." I hesitate, but decide not to add the last part to my sentence.

"You mean again, right?" I nod, before reaching out

to briefly touch her arm. "I'm so sorry about that. I realize you didn't know your father at that time, but I want you to know that he nearly lost it when he found out. He's usually so calm and controlled—but not then. I had never seen him so enraged. Furious. He was yelling abuse and firing anyone in his path. Pete was the only one able to calm him. If you call it that."

"I really despise that we all have to live with those memories," Lia whispers as she stares forward. It's clear her mind is elsewhere as her hands tighten and release on the wheel. I wonder if she's even aware that we haven't left the parking deck yet. "Luc still has nightmares about finding me." She lets out a laugh completely devoid of humor before adding, "He finally stopped having night terrors about Cassie, and they're replaced with ones about me. The poor man can't catch a break."

"Have you thought about seeing a therapist?" I ask gently, not wanting to offend her. *You should probably take your own advice.*

She nods. "We do see someone, and it really has helped a lot. It's going to be a long process, though. If only he hadn't been the one to find me that day. You have no idea how much I wish I could change that. He'll get better, I know, but he'll never get that image completely out of his head." She finally appears to notice that we haven't moved, and she visibly relaxes before putting the car into gear. "Sorry about that. I didn't mean to be such a downer. It's just—I don't really have anyone neutral to talk to about everything. If I bring it up, I feel like everyone is mentally putting me on suicide watch."

"You can talk to me anytime you need to, Lia. I know I work for your dad, but anything you say will be between us only. I'd never betray your confidence unless it was a life and death matter."

"Thanks, Liza." She smiles before adding, "Now what in the world is going on between you and my dad? Dare

I hope he's finally pulled his head from his ass, and you two are seeing each other outside the office?"

It doesn't occur to me to be embarrassed. Lia has a way of making everyone around her comfortable. Plus, after what she just shared with me, could I do any less? "I don't have a flipping clue what's going on," I answer truthfully. "He's been acting completely out of character toward me."

Lia shoots me a quick glance of inquiry while we're stopped at a red light. "How do you mean? I did notice that whole distracted thing he had going on during the meeting. It's not like him to lose his train of thought. I'm almost certain he has a filing cabinet for a brain. Everything is always so well organized, and he doesn't forget anything. So I was a bit surprised when he asked me the same thing twice."

Before I can think better of it, I blurt out, "We were playing tic-tac-toe."

Her jaw drops, and her eyes widen in shock. "I know I didn't hear that right. Because I thought you said my dad was playing a game during a meeting."

Heck. I've gone this far; I may as well confess and hope she won't spill my secret. "All right, I have to admit that I've been intentionally rattling his cage a little. You know, acting out of character to get a reaction." I tell her about the previous day and smile as she giggles. "So I drew the game board today and then put it in front of him. For a split second, he froze, but then he started playing along—which I still can't believe." I don't add the part about the dirty message. I feel certain she doesn't want to hear that about her father.

"He might not be able to admit it, but he's been lost without you. No one was ever good enough. In his defense, he did have a few weird ones, but it wouldn't have mattered. He would find fault with anyone who wasn't you." I see her lips twitch before she adds, "I personally thought he was too hard on the one with the nose ring. She did have on black and white every time I was there, so I can understand him saying she looked like a bull. I tried to point out that cows come in a variety of colors, but he was adamant that she was too distracting. Plus, she accidentally shredded a whole folder of current financial statements and mailed a signed contract to the wrong customer. And he caught her making out with her boyfriend—in his office."

"What!" I shriek, then lower my voice. "You've got to be kidding. She was getting it on in Lee's office? His pristine sanctuary?"

"Yep, that's the one. I'd have given anything to see my dad's face. Can you even imagine?"

I'm laughing so hard that tears are rolling down my cheeks. "Oh my God," I wheeze. "I bet he called in a Hazmat team to check for bodily fluids. Please tell me they were doing it on his desk. That would be priceless."

Lia giggles as she too wipes her eyes. "Dad wouldn't give me any of the details, but according to Kara, who got it from Pete, they were going at it like jackrabbits on his leather couch. I'm willing to bet if you look closely, he has replaced it. There's no way he'd keep it after that."

"I should have asked for more money," I deadpan. "I'm better at my job on my very worst days than all the others put together."

"You're damn right you are, sister," Lia says readily. "And you're good for him. He's . . . different when you're near. Not as rigid. Don't get me wrong, I've really come to love my father, but I'm sure you've noticed he's a tad uptight—like a lot. He needs everything around him to be just so. I swear when he comes over to visit, he casually walks around picking up Lara's toys. I'm not even certain he's aware of it. I sense it's more of a reflex than criticism. Heck, you can eat a meal off any surface at his place. It's that clean. I'm not offended by it, though.

Luc even jokes that if things are messy, we should just invite my father over and let him take care of it." She gives me a stern look of warning when we stop at the next red light. "You'd better never tell him, but Luc has nicknamed him Hoover—after the vacuum cleaner."

I smile as I reassure her that all her secrets are safe with me. "Do you have any idea why he's like that?" I ask, curious despite myself. "I know that some people are naturally neat freaks, but there is generally something from their past that causes it."

Lia shrugs, looking sad for a moment. "I wish I knew. Considering I've only had him in my life a few years, I am virtually clueless about his past. I've attempted to ask him a few times, but it's clear he's not comfortable discussing it. What little I do know mostly came from Kara. From what I gather, they never knew their father, and their mother was a druggie who didn't take care of them. Dad and Pete left home when they were young and ended up working for Victor Falco. I guess he took Dad under his wing, and when he died, he left everything he had to him."

"Victor was in the mob, wasn't he?" I blurt out, then cringe. "I could have worded that better. I'm going strictly on rumors here. Lee has never confirmed that to me."

Lia appears pensive. "Little is known about Victor, considering the amount of wealth he amassed. I asked Luc once to look into it for me, but he refused. I mean I know that he checked out my dad when he found the link to him in my background, but he's very vague about the extent of what he learned. I think he wants to protect me, but he also doesn't want to influence my opinion of my father one way or the other—which I find strangely touching. And of course, like you, I've heard plenty of rumors. There's no way you can live in Asheville and not. Lee Jacks is practically a legend here. The shadowy figure who resides in the ivory tower. I'm guessing they came up with that catchy name from the color of the Falco building."

"I think a lot of it has to do with the fact that he is single, rich, and refuses to hang out with his peers at the country club. Jealousy breeds pettiness."

Sounding wise beyond her years, Lia says, "No truer words were ever spoken. Don't get me wrong. I know that he hasn't lived a . . . normal life. There are things he doesn't want me to know. But considering the shit I went through growing up, I'm the last one to judge. I understand better than most the things that are sometimes necessary to survive. Life isn't always pretty and whitewashed. Sometimes, it dark and ugly."

"It is," I murmur as we both become lost in our thoughts. I'm surprised when the car comes to a stop, and I see that we're outside Falco. I turn to face her, saying sincerely, "Thanks so much for the ride and the talk." Looking at my hands, I admit, "I don't really have many friends, so it's nice having someone to talk to."

"You know what?" she says excitedly. "We're going to have a girls' night. I'll get Luc to stay with Lara, and Rose is always up for an evening out. I'll talk to her when I get back to work and see what we can put together. You're in, right?"

"Absolutely." I nod enthusiastically. I feel like the ugly kid being asked to sit with the cheerleaders. I lean over before I can think better of it and hug her before quickly exiting the car. *I probably lost major cool points for that, but fuck it.* I wave as she pulls away and walk in the doors of Falco with a smile on my face. This has certainly been a day to remember. Lee wrote me a dirty message during a meeting, and I have an evening out to look forward to. In my boring world, that's some dear diary shit right there.

The rest of the day passes by quickly with Lee in business

mode. He leaves while I'm on a call with nothing more than a wave of his hand. *So much for some after-hours sex on his desk.* I'm beginning to think he's either a tease or in the midst of an identity crisis.

It's after six when I reach a stopping point for the day. I am in the process of clearing my desk when my cell phone sounds with an incoming text. I finally locate it under a file and groan as I see my sister's name on the screen. I debate ignoring her, then figure she'll probably call next if I don't respond. DAD WANTS TO SEE YOU. COME BY THE HOUSE AT SEVEN. I pick up a nearby paperclip and stare at it longingly. I'd rather shove it under every single fingernail than see my family tonight—or most any night, for that matter. I'm pondering a valid excuse to get out of it when my phone sounds again. THIS IS MANDATORY.

I release a frustrated sigh before flipping my middle finger in the air. It's childish, I know, given Jacey isn't here to see the gesture, but it does make me feel the tiniest bit better. What kind of family uses words like *mandatory* when they issue an invitation? *My father is more like Tony Soprano than Lee could ever be.*

A quick look at my watch shows that fifteen minutes have passed. I know better than to be late, so I race out the door at a near jog and hop into the elevator. I wave at the security guard who looks confused as I run past him. Luckily, I have a reserved parking spot near the building, and within moments, I'm in my car and driving toward the outskirts of Asheville. My father's home is in the prestigious Briar Cliff area. The sprawling mansion is a mixture of stucco and glass. It's well over ten thousand square feet with six bedrooms and eight bathrooms. There is also a tennis court, an indoor and outdoor pool, and a large guesthouse where my sister lives. One of the best things about working with Falco was that it had been my ticket out of my father's house. I couldn't very well have Lee find out that I lived with Hunter Wrenn. Until then, I had worked in one of my father's companies as the head of accounting. Of course, that hadn't been listed on my résumé. My father and Jacey had invented my background and money had passed hands to ensure my true identity wasn't discovered.

I arrive at the tall iron gates and smile at the guard posted there. We've had twenty-four-hour security for as long as I can remember. I've never really questioned it, because even at a young age, I knew that my father had enemies. *He's such a sweetheart; how could anyone not love him?* My lips curl at that sarcastic thought as the gates open and I pull around the circular drive. Two visits in less than a month. *Lucky me.* I brace myself as I step out of my car and approach the large front door. My finger is inches away from the bell when the door opens, and my sister stands there looking as if a stiff wind could blow her over. I automatically feel fat and sloppy but refuse to grant her the satisfaction of smoothing my clothes. She gives her watch a pointed look before saying, "Nothing like waiting until the last minute."

I make a production of rolling my eyes, not wanting her to miss the sarcastic gesture. "Do you mind?" I ask as I wedge past her and into the foyer. The double staircase and the marble floors look even more impressive with the light of the chandelier gleaming upon them. I lay a hand on my stomach as it growls. I had a sandwich at my desk for lunch, but that was hours ago. "What's for dinner? I'm starving."

"Aren't you always?" she says snidely. "But unfortunately for you, we've already eaten. I realize you aren't used to depriving yourself, but surely you can make it a little longer without food."

I refuse to let her insults get to me. So I simply shrug, saying, "You mean you don't have a leaf of lettuce you could spare? You must have really pigged out." Smacking my lips, I tease, "I bet you even used some of the dreaded ranch dressing, didn't you?"

"Certainly not." She shudders. "That stuff is loaded with fat and calories. I wouldn't even consider it."

I bet she has nightmares about it tonight. Unfortunately, my humor is short-lived as I hear footsteps to the right a minute before my father appears. He's still a handsome man who could pass for someone much younger than his years. His blond hair shows just a hint of gray if you look closely, and like Lee, he's also devoted to working out and staying in shape. He probably had a salad along with Jacey. He gives me a smile that, as usual, doesn't reach his eyes. "I'm glad you could make it," he says as if it were an invitation instead of an order. "Let's talk in my office." Without waiting for a reply, he turns on his heel, and Jacey immediately follows behind him, leaving me to bring up the rear.

If not for the sheer size and the large windows, the mahogany walls would make the space feel like a cave. In the first surprise of the evening, my father takes a seat on the leather sofa instead of behind his desk. Jacey settles in a nearby chair, which leaves me hovering before them uncertainly. My father gives an impatient sigh before waving to the space beside of him. *Oh, shit.* There is nothing informal about my family, so the fact that they're doing something out of the ordinary has warning bells going off in my head. Against my better judgment, I perch on the end of the sofa and wait for the other shoe to drop—because it always does. My sister makes a production of crossing her legs before saying, "We'd like an update on the situation at Falco. Have you regained Lee's trust?"

How did I not see this coming? They're nothing if not predictable so I must be slipping. "Er . . . I'm not sure I ever lost it." *You can't lose something you most likely never had.* "It's pretty much business as usual. Just—you know, doing the assistant thing."

My father snorts. I swear the man actually does something as undignified as snort. Maybe it was an accident. "I really couldn't give a damn about your work there. Have you been able to find anything useful? You've been with him for over two years, yet you've turned up nothing. I know you have knowledge and access to much more than you're admitting."

I roll my eyes. "Trust me, Lee's not an idiot. He doesn't leave incriminating evidence lying around for anyone to find. Nor does he issue invitations to his staff to drop by his home and go through his things. I've told both of you before that I'll never be able to get anything on him. He's too smart for that. Plus, have you ever thought that maybe he doesn't have anything major to hide? Not everyone is like you," I finish in disgust.

My father moves faster than my eyes or my brain can track him. One moment, he's sitting beside me, and the next, he's in front of me with his hands around my neck. I hear what I think is a gasp from Jacey—or maybe it's from me. I claw at his fingers as they tighten their hold until I see stars. His breath is hot on my face as he leans closer. "You'll watch your fucking mouth around me. I will not tolerate this type of disrespect from my own blood. You've been a disappointment since the day you were born. You were supposed to be a son to carry on the family name and not a spineless halfwit for me to support."

My vision begins to blur as he continues his rant. I wonder fleetingly why no one is helping me. Where is my sister? I have my answer a few seconds later when his hold loosens as she says impatiently, "For God's sake, Dad, don't kill her. The last thing we need right now is someone else on the payroll. You know how greedy the local police are around here." *The last thing we need is someone else on the payroll? What the hell?*

I sag back weakly, coughing as he releases me. I take

large gulps of air as I attempt to calm the burning in my lungs. Tears roll down my cheeks as I process the horror of what just happened. I want out of here so badly, but I'm too weak to flee. I know without a doubt that my knees will buckle the moment I attempt to stand. I cower as my father once again leans near. He runs a finger idly through one of my tears, then looks almost curiously at the moisture there. He shrugs and straightens to his full height, smoothing down his dress shirt. "I have a late meeting to attend, Jacey. I'll see you at the office tomorrow." He doesn't so much as glance my way as he leaves the room whistling under his breath. *What the fuck just happened?*

I turn my head and stare at my sister, attempting to convey my shock. She heaves a sigh before saying, "How did *you* see that going exactly? You've been around him for over thirty years. You should know by now that if you push him far enough, he'll explode." Her voice lowers as she stares off into the distance. "And you never have any warning that it's coming. So you learn to only say what he wants to hear." She appears to snap out of whatever trance she's fallen into and gets to her feet. She stares at me with what appears to be almost hatred on her face. "Whether you realize it or not, I did you a favor. Working for Lee got you away from here. Thanks to me, you have very little interaction with our father, while I am on the front lines every single fucking day of my life."

"You argued against me being the one to work for Lee," I point out hoarsely as I raise a hand and touch my neck to soothe the pain there.

"Of course, I did," she yells. "Why should you be given the chance for a life while I remain here?" Putting her hands on her hips, she snarls, "I would have done a better job, and when it was over, I'd have taken off. He'd have been so happy about bringing Lee to his knees that I doubt he'd have worried about trying to bring me back.

But now—years have passed, and I'm still stuck in this purgatory while you play the dumb-blonde card for all it's worth."

"Lee isn't responsible for what happened to our mother," I say—knowing in my heart that my words are true. "He may have inadvertently started the chain of events that eventually led to it, but there's no way he went after our family with the intention of destroying her. I think our father did that all on his own."

"Possibly so." Jacey shrugs as if we're discussing the weather. "But that doesn't really matter anymore. I'm not sure it ever did. This is about a grudge that Dad has against him, and whether it involves Mom is of little importance."

"We have to stop him," I say urgently as I stagger to my feet. "You know this can't end well for anyone involved."

She gives me a pitying look. "It was too late before this started. The wheels were set in motion before you and I even knew Lee Jacks existed. This hate has festered for years, and it's out of control now." She laughs, shaking her head. "Lee may have taken Dad's parking space when they were teenagers. Anything could have set the old man off. I really don't need the particulars because they change with our father's mood. And that has gotten a lot worse in the past year. All I do know is that while he's obsessed with the man you love, he has less time to focus on the rest of us—which, as you've probably guessed, is a very good thing. So unless you want to be the center of his attention, you'd better find something for him to use."

"I won't do it," I say stubbornly. "If he wants Lee, then he can damn well go after him on his own."

Jacey's eyes widen for a moment before she gives me a look of reproach. "After what just happened, you're still protecting Lee? He may not be guilty of everything Father accuses him of, but make no mistake about it, he's far from innocent. Do you think he'd walk across the street to save you if it came to it?"

"Absolutely," I say without hesitation. Somehow, I know with a certainty. If possible, he'd come to my aid without question. Not out of love, but because that's the type of man he is. He'd never let an innocent woman be hurt on his watch. *But you betrayed him.* I shake that sobering thought off, desperate to believe that it wouldn't matter. A part of him feels something for me. I think.

"You're a fool," she says quietly and then leaves the room. I hear the front door shut a moment later, and I panic. I don't want to be left alone in this house. I'm in no condition mentally or physically to face my father again tonight. I need to get home and attempt to process what happened.

I reach for my purse on the floor near the sofa and fumble through the contents until I locate my car keys. With one hand on my throat, I make my way out of my childhood home quickly. My legs feel like rubber, but somehow, I reach my car. *I hate him. I hate that he can invoke such fear in me.* My hands are shaking so badly it takes three attempts until I get the key in the ignition. I shift the car into drive and take a deep breath as I approach the front gate. I wave at the guard and feel a moment of panic that he won't let me pass. Thank God that fear is unfounded, and I'm soon on the road headed toward home.

The trip passes in a blur of tears and disbelief. I pull into my garage and cut the engine. *How could he do that to me? His own flesh and blood? And Jacey just sat there.* I stay seated for a moment, hating the tears falling because of that man. I'm almost to the side entrance of my home when a voice sounds behind me. "Where have you been? I've been trying to reach you for an hour." I whirl around, then realize my mistake a moment too late. Lee's eyes flare as his gaze moves over my wet face and then downward. His harsh inhale tells me that the light of the garage has revealed more to him than I want to.

"What in the fuck happened to you?" He moves closer and places a hand lightly on the side of my jaw. When I flinch, his mouth tightens, but his hold remains gentle as he tips my head back. "Are those handprints?" he asks stiffly.

I want to deny it, but how can I? "It's nothing." I attempt to shrug his hold off, but only end up hurting myself with the movement. When I grimace, he curses under his breath, but immediately releases me. My throat is so sore that swallowing is torture. There's no hiding the hoarseness of my voice as I ask, "What did you need?" Even though I'm intrigued that he's paying me yet another house call, I don't have the energy to deal with it tonight. I just want him to leave until I'm feeling stronger and less likely to sob at any moment.

The shaking returns to my hands as I attempt to unlock my door. Without a word, he takes the keys from me and makes short work of the task. He's not going anywhere, so with a sigh of resignation, I walk into my kitchen with him close behind me. He shuts the door and flips the deadbolt, before leaning back against the kitchen counter. With his feet crossed at the ankles, he appears completely relaxed—but I know he's anything but. He's waiting for me to explain what happened, and I'm desperately trying to avoid it. I have no idea what will happen if he finds out the truth—and I don't want to know. One thing I am sure of, though, is it will lead to a lot more questions, and I can't answer them without giving myself away. I'm still trying to decide on the best course of action when he says, "I've got all night, Liza, and I'm not remotely tired. So take your time. But mark my words, you will tell me who dared to lay hands on you." He sounds so calm, as if he's discussing nothing of importance—yet I hear the steely undertone. He's beyond furious—but it's not directed at me. *Thank God.* But how can it not be? He knows who I am, so why isn't he calling me on it? Why isn't *he* demanding I tell him whatever it is he already knows? When will his game conclude and he throws me away as well? That thought is harder to deal with than anything my father could do to me.

LEE

I PUT MY HANDS IN MY pockets, so she can't see me clenching and releasing them. I make a concentrated effort to calm myself—but it's not easy. And as I stare at the marks against her white skin, I feel the rage building inside me. I'm so close to losing it, yet outwardly, I give nothing away. I long ago learned to never show my hand too early, and that skill has served me well. Liza is making it harder and harder to maintain my impassive exterior, though. I feel like a kid around her who has no self-control, and I fucking hate it. A smart remark is on the tip of my tongue when I notice her slim shoulders shaking. She's crying—again. I didn't miss the wetness on her cheeks when I found her in the garage. I put aside my impatience for answers and move to her side. Without a word, I pull her into my arms and sigh as she wraps her arms around my waist and begins sobbing in earnest. "Shhh, amore mio, you're safe now," I whisper against the crown of her head as I drop a kiss there. I rub her back soothingly as the floodgates open. I hate the feeling of the wetness from her tears against my skin, but I don't pull away. Regardless of the reason, holding her close feels strangely right. When her sobs quiet and she's leaning limply against me, I murmur, "Who did this to you?" She stiffens and attempts to pull away, but I hold her firmly as I scold her gently. "Stop struggling. You're going to hurt yourself further."

Her movements cease, but I can feel the tension in her body. Finally, she says, "I can't tell you." She doesn't have to—because I already know. That's why I'm here. Surveillance tipped me off when she went to Hunter Wrenn's home. This time, she didn't attempt to elude them. She drove straight there from the office, but the visit was brief.

"Why did you go see him?" I ask bluntly, and her hiss of surprise gives me a perverse sense of pleasure. It's always better to catch people off guard. They tend to reveal more than they realize even if it is only through their body language. Hers is telling me that I'm right, and that she didn't expect it. She begins to struggle anew, and this time, I let her go. I need to see her face. But when my eyes fall to the marks on her neck, murderous rage fills me again. "Did he do that to you?" I yell, then want to hit something when she backs away, shaking her head in denial. *You're fucking lying to me—but why?* *To protect that piece of shit?* "Goddammit, Liza, enough! Don't insult my intelligence. I rarely ask a question that I don't already have the answer to. So I know you went to see Hunter Wrenn. And it's past time you tell me what is going on. Are you romantically involved with him?" Bile fills my throat at the thought, and I must make a concentrated effort to swallow it down. I've never wanted to kill someone as badly as I do him now. *She belongs to me.*

"It's not like *that*," she says, and strangely enough, I believe her. But there's something there, and I don't intend to leave here until I find out what it is. "We're not . . . he isn't—God, it's not even close to what you're thinking." Even in my anger, I feel a smile pulling my lips as she squares her shoulders and straightens to her full height. My little bird is full of fight, and I fucking love it. "And since when is Falco privy to the private lives of their employees? Come to think of it, how do you even know where I was tonight? Am I—are you having me followed?" she sputters out indignantly.

I go from wanting to smile to almost laughing outright. Forget the bird nickname, she's more like a spitting cat now. I swear even her hair is bristling with anger. It won't surprise me to hear her hiss or see claws pop out. "Of course, I am." I shrug nonchalantly. "It's for your protection as much as it is mine. You're in a position that puts you closer to me than anyone else other than family. So naturally there could be some who seek to discover information you may have."

Her eyes drop, and she shifts as if uncomfortable. "That's absurd," she argues weakly. "What could I possibly know that would benefit anyone?"

"Don't be naïve, Liza," I say impatiently. "Just our contract negotiations alone are worth billions. If our competitors got their hands on that information, it could deal a serious blow to Falco." She appears to mull over my words before finally nodding.

"I guess that's true." She flinches.

"Get some fucking ice on that, Liza. Do you have a Ziploc bag to wrap it in?" She moves her hands shakily to her neck again, and I hate the pain I see in her eyes. Thankfully, she then moves to the freezer to get the ice.

"Do you have everyone at Falco under surveillance, Lee?" She sounds resolved but still a little hurt and angry. "I mean, surely there are many other people there who have access to a lot of the things that I do."

Maybe the cat is a tiger after all. I put my hands in my pants pockets and rock back onto my heels. "You're mine in a way that even I don't fully understand. That makes you different from everyone else. It also means that I need to know who hurt you tonight. Because violence against you is violence against me, and I will not tolerate that."

She shakes her head as she stares at me. "I can't—but it's not—sexual." She appears to shudder when she spits out the last part.

Liza eyes me warily as I pull my hands from my pockets and begin to pace the kitchen. I want nothing more than to take her to bed and fuck the answer out of her. But she looks like absolute hell. What kind of monster will that make me if I give in to my desires tonight? I'll never knowingly hurt her—but I could in her present condition. There's no way I'm leaving her alone, though. I don't know if she's in danger, and if whoever did this will come back for her, but the point is moot. It's easy to have someone watch her house, but that thought doesn't satisfy me. Maybe it's the mixed-up shit I feel at not being there to protect Lia, but I need Liza near me. How can I let another woman I care about be hurt? I'll hire every fucking private eye in the state tomorrow if I must. Regardless of the cost, I will find out what she's hiding. I'm simply amazed that I'm even in the position of letting someone close to me who has so many secrets. It both infuriates and excites me. A mixed-up combination, to be sure. Since when has anything in my life been normal, though? Even I can appreciate the absolute irony of the situation. The master has been outplayed by his assistant. And like the twisted SOB that I am, it only makes her more desirable to me. "Go pack whatever you'll need for a few days. You're coming with me." She opens her mouth to no doubt argue with me, and I raise my hand before she can utter the first word. "Don't waste your breath. Believe me, you're getting off lightly. I'm tired, hungry, and irritable. You don't want to push me any further. So either do as I've asked or I'll assume you want to stay here and discuss your association with Hunter Wrenn further."

She narrows her eyes but pushes away from the counter. "Give me five minutes." She stalks out of the room, muttering under her breath. Again, I smile. Since returning to Falco, Liza has shown me a new side of her that I never knew existed. She's always been so perfectly professional and proper, but that appears to have changed. The old Liza certainly would have never put her feet on my desk or had a wad of bubble gum in her mouth while in my office. And she didn't talk back constantly. Then there was the whole tic-tac-toe episode at Lia's board meeting. If she didn't look the same, I'd swear it wasn't her.

When she returns in what is more like thirty minutes, she's struggling with a huge suitcase and a smaller one that is making some type of sound. "What the hell is going on with that?" I ask warily.

She drops the biggest bag at my feet, barely missing my shoes before bringing the one in question to within an inch of my face. "That's Rufus."

"Rufus?" I question as a scratching noise fills the kitchen. Then it hits me. "Hell no," I say firmly. "If that's a cat, then you might as well unload it. There's no way he's going with us."

"Rufus goes where I go," she insists stubbornly. "Plus, a lot of hotels are pet friendly now if you pay a deposit." She raises a brow at me before adding, "And we know you can afford it."

"That's nice to know,' I say sarcastically. "But you'll be staying with me, and I can assure you, I'm not pet friendly."

She sets the carrier down and puts her hands on her hips. *Here we go again.* "Are you allergic?"

"Not that I'm aware of. But that's of little importance here." The carrier is shaking now as the cat meows and claws at the plastic. It sounds like fucking Cujo is going to burst free at any moment. I fight the urge to take a step back. *Don't be a pussy.*

She narrows her eyes at me. "So you're an animal hater? You know they say you should never trust a man who doesn't like pets. It's un-American."

What the fuck? "Honey, I'm not sure why the fact I don't want a cat that sounds more like a hound from hell roaming through my home makes me unpatriotic."

"It's because Rufus is a cat instead of a dog, right?" She rolls her eyes. "I know some men have a problem with that, but if you're secure in your masculinity, it should never be an issue. Would you rather I have a poodle with painted pink nails?"

My head is beginning to pound. I have rubbed my temples more in the past few days than I have in years. I have never met a more exasperating person in my life. "Liza, for God's sake, this has nothing to do with the type of animal. I just don't do—clutter."

"Clutter?" she echoes in confusion. "He really doesn't require that much. I've packed some food and bowls. We'll need to stop for a litter box—but that's it."

"A litter box?" Now I'm the one repeating her words as I stare at her stupidly. Somehow, I don't think I want to know exactly what it means. I wonder idly which one of my employees will be willing to come over and pet-sit for a while. I have no idea why I didn't already think of it. I'll even throw in a bonus. Money is certainly no object when it comes to avoiding having whatever is in that box under my roof.

"Well, it's this box full of a kind of sand. The cat sits in it and does his business. Then they cover it back up. The next day, you get the shovel and scoop it out."

My mouth drops open in shock. "Wait—what? Let me see if I have this straight. The cat shits in my home, and I'm supposed to pick it up afterward? Are you fucking kidding me? Who in their right mind would do that?"

Liza takes a step closer until we're literally yelling at each other over the damned cat. "Well, what else do you expect, Einstein? The last time I checked, Rufus doesn't sit on the toilet. And what kind of self-respecting mobster is afraid of a little cat poop? You act as if I'm

asking you to line the litter box with one of your suits."
I have no idea how it's possible since I'm quite a bit taller,
but she manages to look down her nose at me—or give
the illusion of it. "You're acting like a big baby."

She did not just go there. How many times in one
conversation can I have my manhood questioned? This
must be a record. Well fuck, of course it is. I've never
let anyone else get away with the shit she does. *I can do
this. How bad can it be? It's just some extra cleanup.* "Get
the damn thing." I point at the carrier. "I've got your
suitcase." When she stands there looking uncertain, I
add, "You'd better hop to it before I change my mind.
I'm sure Rufus will love to be set free. Have you ever
thought of that?" She gives a sniff and picks up the
carrier, somehow managing to wrap her arms around it
in a protective gesture.

When we reach the front door, she snaps, "Dammit,
the keys are still on the kitchen counter. Can you grab
them? Rufus doesn't like being shifted around, so I don't
want to put him down again."

"Well, we certainly don't want *him* to be unhappy, do
we?" I mumble sarcastically before retracing our steps.
She's waiting on the front sidewalk when I lock the door
behind me before sliding the keys into my pocket. I stare
in surprise when my driver gets out of the Rolls Royce
and walks around to open the back door. I forgot he
was waiting. He looks at the cat carrier then over at me
as if to say, *are you fucking kidding me, boss?* I nod, since
no words are needed between us. He attempts to hold
the carrier while she gets into the car, but she stubbornly
refuses.

We both watch as she awkwardly manages to slide into
the seat. Denny shuts the door behind her before asking,
"Where to, Mr. Jacks?"

Before I can answer, Liza rolls the window down and
sticks her head out. "We need to stop at Walmart."

Denny shoots a look in my direction, and I swear the bastard grins before turning away. In all the time he's worked for me, I've never requested that we stop at the discount store. It's not that I think I'm too good for it. I simply cannot handle the crowds and mayhem that those places cultivate. There's no possible way to keep an eye on that many people, and the need to watch my back has been ingrained in me since childhood. I glare at the space where Liza was, then stalk to the other side of the car. As always, Denny manages to have the door open a split second before I reach it. "Thanks," I say automatically as I get in next to Liza.

We ride in silence for several moments before she says, "You can stop sulking anytime. This was all your idea. I'm perfectly willing to go back home, then you won't have to deal with any of this."

Her voice sounds husky and muted. My eyes fall to her neck, and I'm grateful that the dark interior hides the worst of the damage there. I can't think straight where she's concerned. And knowing that someone hurt her is more than I can handle. I'd like to at least make it home before I lose it again. "It's fine, Liza," I say more calmly than I feel. "Your well-being is what's important here."

She sighs and lays her head back on the seat before saying softly, "I want to tell you what's going on—I really do. But I'm . . . afraid." *Fuck. Surely, she doesn't think I'd hurt her.*

Her bravado has deserted her, and she sounds so small and lost that I automatically want to comfort her. I'm also frustrated at her hesitation. I'm not used to begging for information. When I ask questions, they're answered. But she'll retreat if I make demands. The woman is beyond stubborn and has no sense of self-preservation. I'm trying to decide on the best approach when the car comes to a stop in a brightly lit area. "We're at Walmart, sir," Denny says. I can plainly hear the amusement in his voice, and I can't blame him. He knows my skin is crawling, but he just has no idea why. He probably thinks I'm too snobbish to do my own shopping. *If he only knew.*

Suddenly, something is thrust in my lap and I look down in horror at the cat carrier. "I'll go, but you need to hold Rufus. If he feels abandoned in a strange place he might—have an accident."

A what? I look after her retreating figure helplessly. The carrier begins to shake as the cat's howls fill the car. "Denny!" I shout to be heard above the noise. "Do something with—this thing!"

I can barely make out a series of sneezes before he chokes out, "Sir, I'm allergic to cats. My tongue's not going to swell up or anything, but if I get any closer, it will get a lot worse."

"All right, all right," I say impatiently. "I'll just put the damned thing on the floor."

I'm in the process of moving it from my lap when Denny's words halt me. "Sir, I wouldn't do that. I don't know about you, but being in this tight space with an animal who has an accident is the last thing I want to do tonight."

"Fuck," I hiss. "She's talking about it shitting, isn't she? I was hoping she meant it would run into the side of the cage and knock itself unconscious."

Denny lets out another sneeze followed by a laugh. "I think you had it right the first time, sir. I've never known you to have any animals. Are you actually going to let this stay with you?"

"Well, apparently paying you to take it home with you is out now," I say wryly.

Denny opens his door and moves around to help Liza with the bags she's carrying. She gives me a bright smile when she's once again next to me. "Everything okay while I was gone?" she asks but makes no attempt to take her cat back. In fact, she crosses her arms and looks the picture of relaxation. "What a long day. I'm beat."

For once, I wish the damn animal would start raising hell again, but with the return of his mistress, he appears to have gone into some type of trance as well. So I have no choice but to lay a hand on top of the carrier to keep it from falling as the car begins to move again. I hear soft snores coming from Liza and am amazed. After what happened to her this evening, how can she fall asleep so easily? When we reach my building, I use my other hand to shake her awake gently. "We're here, honey. Wake up."

She blinks like an owl in the light of the parking garage. Releasing a yawn, she struggles upright. "Sorry, I must have been out for a moment." Denny opens her door before removing her suitcase from the trunk of the car. I wave her away as she reaches back for the cat. As much as I'd like to dump it off on her, it seems wrong to make her carry it. She picks up the items she bought at Walmart and gets out. We walk toward an elevator up ahead, and Denny sets the suitcase down while he removes his cardkey to the private lift. Most everyone who visits me comes through the lobby of the building so they can be announced. But I prefer to avoid unnecessary socializing when possible and simply go straight to the top-floor penthouse of the building I own.

When we reach my door, I set the carrier on the floor and use my key to open it. I motion Liza in, then pick up the cat and follow her. Denny deposits her luggage in the foyer before asking, "Will there be anything else, sir?"

"No, thanks, Denny. I'll let you know in the morning what I'll need for the day." After he leaves, I turn to Liza, "Have you eaten?"

The prints on her neck appear to glow brightly in the overhead light, and I avert my gaze, striving for calm. There's no way I'm going to bed tonight without knowing how that happened. But first, I need to make her feel comfortable. "No, but I'm fine." She shrugs a second before her stomach growls loudly. I can't resist flashing her a grin. "All right, I'm a little hungry," she says sheepishly.

I point toward the kitchen and flip on the light when we reach it. I put the carrier next to the wall, wishing I left it in another room. What if the thing wakes up and starts raising hell again? She might insist on taking it out—something I hope to avoid for as long as possible. "Have a seat." I point toward the breakfast nook, but she takes a stool at the center island instead. I open the double doors of the industrial refrigerator and survey the contents. "There's some leftover pasta or I can make us an omelet."

"You cook?" she asks, sounding skeptical.

I smile as I begin pulling out vegetables. "Of course. I find it strangely relaxing. But before you get too impressed, I'll point out that this is hardly fine cuisine."

She puts her head in her hands as she studies me. "I'm just surprised. You seem too impatient to wait on a pot of water to boil or a pan to heat."

I chuckle as I wash the ingredients before pulling out a knife and a cutting board. "Is there anything here you don't like?" She shakes her head, and I get started on our meal. I make quick work of chopping mushrooms, spinach, avocado, and parsley. Then I crack some eggs into a bowl and whisk them together with a touch of cream. Liza has gone quiet as she watches me move around the kitchen. She appears fascinated by the sight of me cooking, and I'm surprised at how right it feels to have her here with me in my kitchen. I drizzle some olive oil into a skillet and then pour in half the eggs. I then layer the ingredients onto one side and fold the top over when it's ready. I plate the finished product and add a pinch of parsley to the top before depositing it in front of her.

"This looks amazing, Lee," she says as if I've presented her with a masterpiece. I'm strangely pleased by her praise, feeling almost proud that I've made her happy after her earlier ordeal. *Don't think about that now,* I chide myself, not wanting to ruin the moment. As it is, I find it hard to look at her and see the reminder of what someone did without demanding answers. I know instinctively that if I do, she'll retreat, and I'll get nowhere. She looks up at me with an almost apologetic expression. "I'm not in danger, Lee. I didn't need to come and stay with you. I don't want to put you out."

Even though she has opened a door for me here, I won't ask what I'm desperate to know. Not yet. "Well, as I said, someone hurt what I consider mine, Liza. I would not have allowed you to stay in your house tonight." I'm not sure how to read the small smile on her face, but fuck if I don't like it. I glance at her neck again, and any peace I felt momentarily leaves me. "Would you like some juice?" I ask instead as I turn away. I take some glasses from a nearby cabinet, then a pitcher of orange juice from the refrigerator, placing it in front of her. She splashes a small amount on the island when she pours it, and I twitch inwardly. I need to clean it up more than I need to breathe. I make a pretense out of gathering the items together for my omelet, but sweat dots my forehead before she finally grabs a napkin from a nearby holder and wipes up the spill. *It'll be sticky now. That's not going to do it. Such a fucking mess.*

She's talking, something about the cat—who has picked this moment to begin making its presence known once again. *Please, God. Don't remove that thing now.* I'm disgusted as I notice my hands shaking. What in the fuck is wrong with me?

Pull it together.

Don't want her to see.

To know.

Somehow, I manage to finish my omelet without burning it. When it's plated, I can no longer wait. I get some paper towels and pull a bottle of cleaner from under the cabinet. I'm careful to shield her food as I move her glass and spray a small amount where the spill was. I scrub it vigorously until I'm satisfied that no residual remains. Her voice sounds small when she says, "I'm sorry, I should have done that. I just—wasn't thinking."

I feel like an asshole. She's clearly uncomfortable as she stares at her plate. I put the cleaning supplies down and move to her side. Without thinking, I pull her against me and drop a kiss on the top of her head. "It's nothing, little bird. I guess I've lived alone for so long that I'm a little set in my ways." I force myself to relax even though I want nothing more than to clean up the kitchen before I eat. But I desperately don't want her to realize how fucked up I am inside. I give her shoulders another squeeze before taking a nearby seat and forcing myself to eat. I'm so distracted by the nearby disarray that it almost hurts to force each bite past the lump in my throat.

I pause with the fork halfway to my mouth as she gets to her feet and begins doing the very thing I'd been fighting against. She's humming under her breath, but it sounds strained. The tension begins to leave my body as she efficiently handles the clutter that had been driving me to distraction just moments earlier. I've barely finished my meal when she whisks the plate away and deposits it in the dishwasher with the other items. She then begins to clean the countertops and the island, and even though I'd rather do it myself, I don't say a word. The result is the same as my kitchen is returned to its former pristine state, and I can breathe easily once again. Of course, before I go to bed, I'll go back over it myself—there's no way I can't. I won't rest without confirming that everything is just so. "All good?" she asks softly as she comes to a stop next to my stool. *It's as if she knows. Knows me. Knows what I need and when. But how is that possible?*

Once again, I find my arm encircling her, and for a few moments, we stand there savoring our connection. We haven't been simply employer and employee for a long time, and that's more obvious than ever now. "Thanks, sweetheart." I nod, and before I can stop myself, I lower my head and take her lips with mine. I wonder faintly how she can taste of strawberries after just eating an omelet, but rational thought soon flees as she steps between my parted knees and her arms go around my neck. My body kicks into overdrive when my tongue slips between her plump lips and tangles with hers. I have no idea how long we stay that way. Her mouth is like the finest wine, and I'm drunk on the taste of it. My hands lower to her ass, and I fucking love the softness that fills my hands as I squeeze her firm cheeks. Unable to resist, I move my head and begin dropping gentle kisses onto her bruised neck before licking the pounding pulse I find there. "You taste amazing," I say huskily as I raise my head to stare at her flushed face. Her eyes are glazed, and she's panting for breath as she stares at me. I lower my hand and cup her between the legs. She shudders as I whisper in her ear, "I want to taste your wetness and hear you scream when I push inside you."

"God, yes," she says in a near shout. Thank God. But before I can act on it, a loud noise fills the kitchen. I jerk backward, releasing her in my haste to assess the threat. As my eyes swing around the area, they fall to the carrier against the wall. The damn cat is very nearly rocking the plastic container onto its side. I wouldn't be surprised to see it explode out of the thing at any moment. "Rufus," she says hoarsely. She sounds disappointed when she straightens away from me. "He's probably hungry, and it would be a good idea to get the litter box set up before he has an accident."

That's all it takes to bring me to my feet. The last thing

I want is the beast shitting in the kitchen. Then it hits me that I'm going to have a box of sand somewhere on the floor in my home, and the feelings of unease return. "I don't suppose we can sit the box up on the balcony, can we? Do you think he'd jump off?" I ask it jokingly, but I'm dead serious.

She rolls her eyes at me before saying, "I'm not willing to find out. Maybe we could put it in a spare bedroom or bathroom. Trust me, it's not a great feeling to step in cat litter in the middle of the night, and he tends to spray that stuff everywhere when he does his business."

Holy fucking hell. This is sounding worse by the moment. Why do people have pets if this is the kind of thing you have to deal with? "Don't they have people you can hire to take care of stuff like this?"

She doesn't bother to answer. Instead, she walks over and kneels in front of the animal that is soon to defile my home. "My poor baby. Mama's gonna get you out of there right this moment. Just hold on." She continues as if she's speaking to a child instead of a pet. It appears that both Rufus and I are mesmerized as she lifts him from the carrier and cuddles him against her chest. *I've officially hit rock bottom. I'm jealous of a cat.* I swear the thing smirks at me from her arms as he gets all the attention that I was enjoying just moments ago. The bastard cat-blocked me. Unbelievable. "Can you get the box and the litter? Then lead the way to where you want to put everything."

I wonder idly if she'll see the humor if I walk out into the middle of the street. After all, she did ask where I wanted him. Instead, I move toward the foyer where the bags of supplies are and then grudgingly make my way to the bathroom at the back of the penthouse. It's the logical choice since it's not used. Never in my wildest dreams did I imagine I'd allow an animal to crap in a box that I willingly placed on my marble floors. *This is just plain fucked.* But apparently, the worst is yet to come.

Because seconds later, the cat is deposited in my arms, and she's bent over rummaging through the contents I've just placed on the floor. I hold the wiggling, hissing demon away from me. "Liza, you need to get this thing." *What are the symptoms of rabies?* "It's—there's something clearly wrong with it," I say in a panic as it turns its fucking head like that girl from the exorcist and hisses at me. I'm waiting with bated breath for green stuff to fly out of its mouth. When that happens, no amount of protesting on her part will keep me from tossing it outside.

She barely glances over her shoulder before returning to her task. "He doesn't like the way you're holding him. Put him against you and he'll stop. How would you like for someone to shake you around like that?" I stubbornly refuse to take her advice until she adds, "Plus when he's scared he'll pee."

Holy fucking hell. I pull the bastard close and glare at him as he stops howling and starts doing something that sounds like a motor running. Then I feel something wet and faintly abrasive on my hand. The thing is licking me. Running his tongue down my fingers now as if it's the best thing he's ever tasted. Without thinking, I drop him. Or at least I think I do. But the beast barely falls a few inches before he's latched on to my leg and his claws are inches away from my cock. I freeze, afraid to move a muscle. "Liza," I whisper in panic.

"What?" she grumbles without turning around. "I swear, Lee, it's just a cat. I hate to sound like a broken record, but you're really disappointing me with your lack of mobster badassery. How in the world did you ever intimidate anyone? All the other guy would have to do is sic their dog on you."

I grit my teeth as the cat-from-hell digs in even harder and begins to howl. What in the fuck does it have to sound alarmed about? I'm the one in danger of losing my fucking dick here. "Goddammit to hell, Liza, can I get some help here? If you value my cock, then you'll remove this thing while it's still operational."

That gets her attention. She whirls around so fast she falls against my leg. The good news is that the cat is jarred and loses its hold. The bad news is that he slides down my leg like it's a fireman's pole. "Oh my God." Liza looks from me to her soon-to-be-deceased cat. "Are you okay, baby?"

I open my mouth to answer her, then realize—*in amazement*—that she's talking to the cat. There are snags in my two-thousand-dollar suit, but she doesn't appear to give two shits. My thigh is stinging, but I'm hesitant to even mention it for the fear of being called a pussy. Apparently, I'll need to lose a limb to get any sympathy from her. I turn on my heel and leave the room, knowing it's for the best. Time to regroup before I say something I'll regret—or get attacked again by Cujo. I'm not going to lie. I'm disappointed when she doesn't call me back. I'm not sure she even notices. So I go directly to the bar in the living room and pour myself a generous amount of bourbon. I wince as it burns its way down my throat. My other hand rubs absently at my still smarting thigh as I deliberate what a fucked-up evening this is. Then she's there, standing before me. She says nothing—simply stares at me.

"I do hope the cat is all right," I say, keeping my voice neutral. "It would be a shame if he hurt his claws while he was tearing into my flesh."

Her eyes widen, then drop as if to inspect me for injuries. "Where?" she asks as she moves closer to me.

"It doesn't matter." I shrug away her concern. I know it's childish, but it's too little, too late for me. As far as injuries are concerned, these are nothing. I've had much worse in my life and not given them a thought. I don't want or need comfort from anyone. Shit like that makes a man weak. I learned long ago that to expect anything is to beg for disappointment. Even those rare people with the best intentions will let you down or turn away when things get too tough. It's human nature to choose the easiest route.

She puts her hand on my arm and squeezes it lightly. "I'm sorry." She sighs. "It's been a long day, and I'm making a mess of this."

I feel myself softening as I study her upturned face. *How dare anyone touch her? How. Fucking. Dare. They.* I reach out and cradle her face in my hand. My thumb brushes over her bottom lip, and my breath hisses as her tongue darts out to lick the tip of my finger. "Liza," I whisper. I want to warn her off. To tell her to run and hide, but I don't. It was too late the moment she walked into my lair. I've wanted her for a long time, and despite any noble intentions I had, I can no longer wait. Staying away has gotten me nowhere, and it certainly hasn't helped her either. Decision made, I swing her up into my arms, surprising a shriek from her.

For a moment, I think she'll protest until she all but latches on to me. "I swear if you stop this time, I'll put a hit out on you myself." By the time we reach my bedroom, she has my tie off and my shirt halfway unbuttoned. Every bit of polish and self-control that I have is gone, and I'm just as frantic as she is. Then she's on her feet and the scary part is that I have no recollection of putting her down. *Fuck, I hope I didn't drop her.* I'm not sure what I was expecting, but the sexy black bra she's wearing is fucking gorgeous. I run a finger over the silky material and circle the outline of a nipple clearly visible through the thin fabric. She moans low in her throat before swatting me away and pulling at her pants. Something about her eagerness is a boost to my ego. Hell, I don't even know if that is possible. I've always been more than confident in my ability to turn a woman on. But this is Liza. And holy mother of God, she's wearing a thong. Again, been there—seen plenty of those. But I wasn't expecting it from her. I never have guessed that she likes skimpy lingerie. I feel like a kid at Christmas. The fact that she very nearly trips as she awkwardly kicks off her shoes before sliding her slacks off does nothing to distract me from the beautiful and desirable package she presents when she finally straightens.

"You're absolutely beautiful," I say hoarsely as I put my hand on her hip possessively. *Mine—finally.* We kiss. Tenderly. Slowly. I'm rock hard at the feeling of her soft body nestled close to mine. Then once again, she's a flurry of activity as she undresses me. It's as if she's terrified I'll stop. "Liza," I whisper softly when I'm down to only my boxer briefs. "Slow down, little bird, and let me enjoy the moment."

She stares at me with a pleading expression on her face. "You can do that the next time. I just—need you now . . . please?"

There's no way I can deny her anything right now, not with her looking at me that way. I remove the remainder of our clothing before backing her against a nearby wall. I leave her briefly to grab a condom from my dresser drawer before returning. I quickly sheath myself, then lift her into my arms. Her legs automatically wrap around my waist a second before I plunge into her wet heat. "Fuck," I hiss. I take her lips with mine as her back rests against the wall. My hands curl into her hips as I pull her down to meet each of my thrusts. "So good," I groan against the curve of her neck as I circle my tongue against the rapidly beating pulse there.

"Lee, I love you," she groans. I lose my rhythm for a moment and almost send us both tumbling, but quickly recover. I convince myself I heard her wrong. "Love you so much." There is no more time to dwell on it as she begins to spasm around me. I don't need her to tell me that she's coming, because I can feel every contraction as she cries out. My movements increase in speed, and my jaw clenches as I explode inside her.

I rest my forehead against hers. My legs are like jelly, and I don't have the strength to separate us yet. I start in surprise when her hand runs through my hair. Normally, this type of closeness would be far too intimate, but it's . . . strangely comforting. I close my eyes and allow myself to enjoy this rare vulnerability with a woman. I brush a kiss against her temple in a gesture as foreign as it is tender. *What in the fuck is happening to me?* If I had any strength left in my body, I'd be in a full-on panic, but I'm too tired to fucking care. "You okay?" I ask as I stare into her flushed face.

Her lips turn up into a contented smile as she nods. "Never been better," she adds, then yawns very inelegantly. *Never been better. Yeah, I'm feeling that too.*

I chuckle before lifting her to separate our bodies. She shivers, and my cock stirs to life again. *Down, boy.* I shouldn't have fucked her. But, God, I want her. Once will never be enough. But regardless of how badly I want to, twice is out of the question. Especially until I know the extent of what happened to her earlier. Someone hurt her, and I need to know who and why. I place my hand on her hip before saying, "I'm going to shower in the bathroom down the hall. Why don't you use the one in here?"

She pushes her bottom lip out adorably, and before I can stop myself, I nip it with my teeth. "Ouch!" She laughs as she pushes my head away. "I would suggest that we conserve water by sharing, but it seems like you're on your own, buddy."

I shake my head, before giving her ass a light swat. "Having you wet and naked isn't the way the save water, sweetheart. Hell, we'd probably both drown in there. So be a good girl and do as you're told." Her snort lets me know what she thinks of my words, but she walks in the direction of the master bath without comment. The sight of her full hips and firm ass swaying seductively almost has me following her, but I force myself to turn in the other direction. There'll be plenty of time for that after she gives me some answers.

I started the day with a vengeance on my mind for a betrayal I didn't know much about. Fuck, I embarrassed myself in front of my son-in-law. I played tic-tac-toe in a board meeting. Both screw-ups are because of the luscious woman heading toward my shower. Somehow, some unknown fucking way, the day has ended up off course. The minute I saw her mouth *yes* after I told her what I wanted to do to her on that table, I knew I was in trouble. It's her. For the past two years, it's been her. I've fucked other women, seeing her in my mind, often feeling as though I was betraying her in the process. But right now? I feel as though every moment was leading to this. To making her dinner. To kissing, being kissed, being touched. *God, being inside her.* Yes, I'm pissed that something other than the truth brought her across my path. And I need to know the what and the why. This will be the first of many nights that Liza will be in my bed and in my arms. There's a surprising kind of freedom in giving in to something that you've long since tried to deny. I haven't a clue as to what will happen in the light of day, but for now, we belong to each other. I only wish I could give her more.

CHAPTER EIGHT

LIZA

I ROLL TO MY BACK AND blink rapidly, attempting to shake off the last vestiges of sleep. Something feels different this morning. My throat is sore, and my body feels tender in an unfamiliar way. I glance around the room, barely able to make out the shape of a bedside lamp in the dim light of early morning. The silence is shattered by a loud screech, followed by a meow that will be heard for miles. I sit up quickly just in time to hear a commotion in the hallway. "Goddammit, you mongrel, come back here! How was I to know you weren't finished taking a shit? There was a pile in the box the size of a small building." My mouth drops open as a light flips on outside the door, and I see Rufus run by, followed closed by a nearly naked Lee.

It takes my brain a long moment to register where I am and why, before I gather my wits enough to slide awkwardly from the bed. I look around but see no sign of my clothes from the night before or anything else for that matter. The sound of a crash, followed by curses has me tossing modesty to the wind and hurrying to find out what's going on. I'm brought up short by the sight of Lee, with his hands on his lean hips, staring down as Rufus kneads his claws in what is undoubtedly a very expensive chair. "I think I'm gonna be sick," I whisper as I survey the damage.

I swear, if it's possible for a cat and a person to be glaring at each other, then they're doing it. Rufus appears almost defiant as he works his claws into the leather while Lee stands there doing nothing to stop him. "You do realize that you'll pay for that, don't you?" he asks without looking my way. I open my mouth to assure him that I will, when he continues. "I know you're doing it on purpose, and while I applaud your attempt to show me who's boss, you've made a dire miscalculation." *He's having a conversation with Rufus. Damn, I wish I had my phone to record this.* I remain stock-still not wanting to ruin the moment. "You see," Lee continues, "if you knew me at all, you'd realize that there's only room for one boss here, and that ain't you, pal. I let you get away with covering most of the bathroom in fucking sand and attempting to rip my dick off last night, but it's the end of the line." His voice takes on that commanding tone that I've heard so often at Falco as he raises his hand and points toward the floor. "Now come down from there right now and don't even think about taking off." I grin, waiting for Rufus to ignore him, but I'm astonished when my normally stubborn animal does exactly as Lee has commanded. Even going so far as to sit at his feet as if awaiting praise and his next order.

"Unbelievable," I say to myself, but neither of them appear to know that I'm witnessing this scene unfold.

I'm further shocked when Lee bends down and scratches Rufus behind the ears. The cat begins purring loudly and staring at Lee with a look of absolute adoration. "Well done," Lee praises him. "Since you listened so well, I'll let the chair thing go, and you'll be rewarded at breakfast. But if this happens again, you'll be shitting in the street somewhere."

That's it. I can no longer hold it back. I begin laughing. Lee turns and rolls his eyes at me as if he's known I've been here all along. "I swear you could be the cat whisperer," I gasp out. "I can't believe he did what you told him to. How in the world did you manage that?" Lee stands, and his eyes roam leisurely over me. It's then that I realize that I'm completely naked. "I couldn't find my clothes," I say awkwardly as I cross my arms over my chest. Of course, the bottom part of me is still exposed, and I can't do anything about it without looking like an idiot.

I almost expect him to pretend like nothing happened last night, but when he pulls me against him and lowers his mouth to mine, I feel giddy. He kisses me thoroughly, and when he pulls back, I'm drunk from the taste of his tongue sliding against mine. Sweet baby Jesus, the man is amazing at both kissing and fucking. *Wait, did I just call it fucking?* It's hard to refer to being taken against the wall as making love. Whatever, it was amazing. I came in an embarrassingly short amount of time, but there was no holding back. His big cock, along with his mouth and hands, were enough to drive me insane with desire. I want him again now, and if the hardness pressed against me is anything to go by, then he is of the same mind. "Good morning," he murmurs against the side of my neck, before dropping a kiss onto the tip of my nose. "I trust by all the sounds you were making that you slept well?"

I drop my forehead against his chest in embarrassment. When I'm overly tired, I do tend to snore. "Sorry," I mumble. "I hope I didn't keep you awake."

He rubs my back leisurely before moving lower and squeezing one of my butt cheeks. He does seem to have a thing for my ass. His hands were there several times the night before. And even though I've always been self-conscious about the size of it, I haven't cared. It feels so good that he so openly admires my body—even the parts I don't love myself. "No, sweetheart, you were fine. I can't say the same for the beast, though." He turns his head to where Rufus is still sitting in the same spot watching us. "I'm surprised you didn't hear him raising holy hell. I went in there the first few times thinking he'd hurt himself somehow only to find him absolutely fine."

I press my lips to his chest, kissing him in apology. "It's the new surroundings. I'm sure he was nervous. Other than the veterinarian, he's never been anywhere overnight except for my house." I look around for a clock but don't see one. "I know it must be getting late, and we need to get ready for work. So as soon as I find my clothes, I'll straighten up the bathroom."

"It's already been taken care of," Lee mumbles. He looks uncomfortable now as he stares at some point over my shoulder. "I was up early, and I didn't want you to have to deal with it."

I'm beyond stunned. "You cleaned up? But surely, you didn't scoop the box out? I can do that. I've done it so often; it's almost like second nature to me now."

"Honey, it's been taken care of." He isn't making eye contact, and I'm not sure what to make of that. Then he adds softly, "I've never lived with anyone other than Pete in my adult life. So I'm used to a certain amount of order. If something needs to be done, I do it."

"But don't you have a housekeeper?" I ask, knowing he does. I've met her a few times when she's dropped off stuff at the office that he needed from home.

"I do." He nods. "But she mostly does the shopping and a bit of cooking. Occasionally, she handles the laundry. She's away visiting her sister right now, though." I want to question him further, but he derails me by saying, "Now that we've covered that, we'll have some bagels that were delivered earlier and a glass of juice. Then we're going to talk." *So much for him being tempted by my nakedness. Talk?*

This can't be good.

"Don't we need to get to work?" It must be earlier than I thought, because Lee is never late.

"We're taking the day off," he tosses out as if he's discussing nothing of importance. "There are some things we need to address, and I don't want to wait any longer. Plus, there are too many distractions and interruptions at Falco. Kara has kindly agreed to handle everything until tomorrow."

New strategy time. "But I'm not wearing any clothes," I purr in what I hope is a seductive voice. He's still hard against me, so surely I can tempt him.

He appears faintly amused as his arms tighten around me. "I'm not blind, little bird. I've never been more aware of something in my fucking life." *I've so got this,* I think a mere second before he puts me firmly away from him. "Your clothes are hanging in my closet. Why don't you go do whatever you need to and then meet me in the kitchen for breakfast?" When I simply stand there gaping at him, his hands land on my shoulders as he turns me gently around before swatting my ass. "We're going to have to work on this sulking. I know where the cat gets it from now." I stick my tongue out at him childishly thinking he can't see it, but his chuckle lets me know he does. "I'll find a better use for that later," he murmurs before walking in the other direction. I stop, a little giddy thinking about using my tongue on him. *And now a little wet too.* Damn the man.

"That was an epic failure in seduction," I grumble to Rufus. "And what are you now, a lap dog? Have a little pride." I swear he gives me a look of disdain before following behind his new master. Once in the bedroom, I wander into his closet and blink in surprise. It's as big as my entire bedroom, and everything is organized so well it boggles my mind. The hangers are all pointing in the same direction and the clothing is arranged by color. All the shirts are grouped together as well as the slacks and jackets. There's a separate area for his ties, shoes, and hell, everything really. I wander around the space until I find the items from my suitcase all carefully arranged at the far end of the closet. *Dear Lord, he's anal retentive.* I'm almost afraid to touch anything. I have a feeling he'll notice if a hanger is moved. *He even hung up my yoga pants.* I grab a pair with a wild floral pattern and a matching Nike shirt. I'm careful to leave everything as it was. I then go through a nearby set of drawers until I locate my bra and panties. Pretty, matching undergarments are one of my few loves. I choose a silky pair of purple boy shorts and a pushup bra and close the drawer. After a quick shower in Lee's luxurious bathroom, I dress and head toward the kitchen. I have no idea how long it's been, but I know how he is about punctuality.

He's sitting at the bar with a glass of juice in front of him and Rufus at his feet when I walk in. He glances up and smiles, and my heart does a funny somersault. *He's so freaking beautiful.* I've just taken a seat across from him when the cell phone near his elbow rings. He picks it up and glances at the caller ID before answering it with a curt, "Yes." He stays on the line for what seems like forever with only the occasional acknowledgment of whatever the person is saying. He doesn't add anything to the conversation—which seems bizarre. When I look up from my bagel and find his gaze fixed on me intently, I shift uneasily in my seat. I offer him a smile, but he doesn't acknowledge it in any way. I understand how seriously Lee takes everything in life, especially business matters, but this feels different. *Why isn't he speaking?* Surely, whoever is on the other end of the line has said something by now that would require Lee to say more than, "Yes" or "I see." But he hasn't, and even though I have no reason to be nervous, I am. I can't help it. I know instinctively that something is wrong. It's there in

the waves of energy radiating off him. I feel the desire
to grab Rufus and make a run for it—but I'm frozen in
place. I don't want to stay, but I can't leave. Then it hits
me with the force of a speeding train. *He knows.* I know
he's known something about Hunter Wrenn and me, but
clearly it can't have been as much as I thought. But now?
I've never been so certain of anything before in my life.
My nerves are at a breaking point by the time he ends the
call and tosses the phone down carelessly onto the bar. It
clatters loudly, and I can't control my flinch.

I gape at him in confusion when he picks up his half-
eaten bagel and takes a bite as if nothing out of the ordinary
happened. I almost believe I imagined the whole thing if
not for the weird current that still fills the air around us.
"Is everything all right?" I ask hesitantly, unable to stand
the silence any longer.

He doesn't answer the question, but says instead,
"Finish your breakfast." His face is impassive, and his
body language says clearly that any further conversation
isn't welcome. I take a few more bites of the blueberry
bagel, but it's like sawdust in my mouth. I finally lay my
napkin down, and as if he has been waiting for the signal,
he gets to his feet and clears the table. I don't offer to help
because I'm not sure my legs will work at this point. I'm
literally a prisoner to the barstool I'm sitting on. Even
upset, angry, or whatever the hell he is, he still carefully
cleans up all the remains of our food, right down to
wiping the crumbs away and loading the dishwasher. I
have never known a person in my life—and certainly not
a man—who is as much of a neat freak as he is. When
he's finished, he says stiffly, "Could you come into my
office please?" He may have phrased it as a question—but
we both know it isn't. *Gone is the man who couldn't keep his
hands off me.* I follow him out of the kitchen and down
the hallway to a door at the other end. He keys in a
code to release the door, then motions me inside. I didn't

notice the lock when he pointed his office out last night, but I'm not surprised. He's always been very security conscious, which made what my family wanted me to do virtually impossible—thank God. "Have a seat, Jade," he says softly, and I comply without hesitation.

Then it hits me with the force of a lightning bolt. *Jade. He knows my name.* A denial springs instantly to my lips, but I don't voice it. What is the point? It'll only make matters worse—if that's even possible. There has always been an air of danger around Lee, but I've never been afraid of him, and strangely, I'm not now either. I can't bring myself to believe he'd ever physically hurt me. But I know now that he doesn't have to, because he holds the power to destroy me with his words alone. "I wanted to tell you." I sigh. "I didn't know how to do that without you hating me."

He steeples his hands before him as he stares blankly at me. "Funny thing about betrayal; it does have a way of turning friends into enemies."

Leaning forward in my chair, I say huskily, "I didn't betray you, Lee. At least not in the way you think. I never gave my father any information he could use against you. And believe me, I had to withstand a lot of pressure from him and my sister."

He snorts as if he doesn't believe a word. "You betrayed me the moment you took a job at Falco with a false identity." He sits back in his chair, looking like the gangster he's reputed to be. "Now, let's start at the beginning. I know who you are, but I don't have the specifics as to why. Don't get me wrong. I'm aware of the past connection with your father and the company I took over. But this elaborate scam seems a bit extreme for simple retaliation. And don't even think of holding back on me. I want the fucking truth. You owe me that."

Without thinking, I raise my hand to the tender skin of my throat, and his eyes follow the motion. I see the first real sign of anger simmering there as he appears to come to a conclusion about how it happened. I look down to gather my composure before once again facing him. This is what I've worried about. This is why I left. I didn't want to see the anger directed at me. "You're right, this is about more than the company. Truthfully, I don't think my father would have been so bent on revenge if not for the fact that the company you stole from him resulted in my mother's death. Before you took Wrenn Wear, my father said she never drank more than a glass of wine with dinner. But afterward, she began drinking heavily. And the arguments—I remember they constantly yelled at each other. Sometimes, it seemed to continue all night. Until she went out one day—and never came back." My chest is tight as I add, "Her car left the road, and she hit a tree. The police said she never even pressed the brake pedal. She was killed instantly."

The mighty and powerful Lee Jacks did not expect that. He's clearly surprised—no, shocked. Even though his expression changes very little, I've learned to read him. And it's there in the way his hand clenches and in the slight tic of his cheek. "I don't see the connection," he says flatly. "It was but a small holding in the vast Wrenn empire. Of little consequence to anyone. I have no idea why Draco even wanted it," he adds almost as an afterthought.

"I don't know all the details. I was very young when it happened. But my mother was running the company you took over. According to my father, outside of her family, Wrenn Wear was the love of her life."

Lee pinches the bridge of his nose and closes his eyes for a moment before saying, "You must know what kind of man your father is. Well, he crossed the wrong people and got off remarkably light."

"You took the company for someone else?" I ask, already knowing the answer.

He inclines his head. "I did. He owed a debt to Draco Moretti, and he paid for it with Wrenn Wear."

"You tossed my mother and everyone else there out in the street," I say accusingly. This part of the picture hasn't made sense to me since I got to know Lee. He's ruthless in business, but always fair.

"The company was never officially mine, Liza . . . Jade." He catches himself after using my assumed name and spits the other one out in contempt. He pauses for a moment. "It was signed over to Moretti Holdings the second it was acquired. That was always the plan. Back in those days, I worked for Victor, who was best friends with Draco. I didn't question orders from either of them because they'd never once given me a reason to question their loyalty to me. Do you have any idea how rare that is in this fucked-up world?"

I don't think he meant to tell me as much as he has. Naturally, I've heard stories of Victor Falco through the years. Draco's name had also come up in passing, although there was very little information available on either man other than their supposed ties to organized crime. "I know my father's not a good person." I feel like I'm committing a betrayal of the worst kind, but what else is there to do? This has gone on for entirely too long. Eventually, someone would get hurt, and I don't plan to be a party to it. "I couldn't be around him for this many years and not be aware of that." Moisture gathers at the corners of my eyes as I add softly, "But there's one thing I can tell you that is absolutely true. He loved my mother. I might have been young when she died, but I clearly recall the way he worshiped her. He was different back then—even with my sister and me. Funny and loving— like other dads. Not this version that he turned into after her death."

"Honey, I'm sorry, I truly am," Lee says sincerely. I don't think he notices the endearment he's let slip because surely, he doesn't mean it—especially now. "But, regardless of what you think, I had nothing to do with whatever happened to her. And it was and still is standard protocol to make staff changes in companies you acquire. That would have especially been true of Wrenn Wear considering it was acquired through a hostile takeover. Draco wouldn't have felt comfortable leaving anyone in major positions there with loyalty to Wrenn. That would certainly include your mother."

"But why would he have wanted that company? I mean, you, yourself have admitted that you don't understand it."

He's getting irritated with my questions. His normally calm demeanor is fraying. His movements are abrupt and jerky. Very out of character for the man I know. "I don't fucking know," he snaps. "It never mattered to me back then. I was a kid off the streets, so taking a fucking company from someone was what I considered clean work. Sure, some rich bastard might not like it, but there was no physical force behind it. I took control by digging through company records until I found a weakness I could exploit. I won because I was smarter. I could think of scenarios that a team of lawyers couldn't come up with."

"And you loved that," I say as I begin to understand the side of the man he's always kept hidden from me.

"You're damn right I did," he says flatly. "I came from nothing—absolute filth, shame, and hopelessness. That was how Pete and I grew up. We were dirt on the shoes of people like your father. He wouldn't have given me a job washing his fucking car. So yeah, the fact I could think circles around Ivy League assholes and watch them look at me incredulously as I moved in for the kill was a fucking high unlike any I'd ever experienced before. I was their judge, jury, and executioner. But what I killed was their hope that they could possibly keep me from taking what I wanted from them at any time. I never made threats to families or them personally. I didn't have to. There was always a loophole somewhere in their company that I could climb through. I simply searched for it." I want to ask him to explain why he and Peter lived in such hopelessness, but I'm not sure I have that privilege anymore. *I want to know him. Dearly.*

"So you did this for Victor and Draco?" I ask, wanting to know more about the powerful men who had so influenced his life.

"In the beginning, yes. Eventually, I began to build my own empire. By the time Victor died, my holdings were almost as impressive as his. Then I combined them, and Falco was officially born."

I wasn't sure how to word this next question and finally settled on, "But it's run—differently now, right? I mean, than when Victor was in charge."

He doesn't pretend to misunderstand. "Yes, I've spent a lot of time and lost money making sure of that. I have a daughter and a grandchild who I want my part of Falco to go to eventually. I don't want them to encounter any difficulties when that happens. It's my desire for Falco to be a company they're proud of. I have earned and deserve the whispers and speculation that follow me—but they don't."

There is a pang in my heart at his words. It's so apparent that he's been to hell and back. His loyalty to a man who the rest of the world thought of a killer isn't surprising, but the fact that Victor was apparently just as loyal to Lee is downright astonishing. "Whoever said that there is no honor among thieves couldn't be more wrong." There's a code that goes beyond that of blood. These men weren't related, but they were family just the same. I have no doubt that Lee would have given his life for the one man who believed in him. "What happens now?" I ask haltingly. *Do I really want to know?*

Lee nods, appearing surprised by my words, before his

eyes drop to my neck and his lips tighten. "Did your father do that to you?"

It's on the tip of my tongue to lie, but I'm so tired of it all. Plus, he knows the answer; he always does. "Yes. I was summoned home last night. When I got there, he wanted to know what I'd learned since going back to work for you. When I told him there was nothing to find—that all men weren't like him—he lost it." I swallow hard as my fingers lift to rub the tender skin that is even more discolored today. "I thought . . . for a moment, I thought he would kill me. I've rarely seen him lose his temper like that. I mean, he's been a verbal bully for years, but not physical." I shudder, thinking of the look in his eyes as he held my throat. Took my ability to breathe away . . . "I've always been the outsider. My sister, Jacey, works with my father, and he doesn't make a secret out of the fact he prefers her to me." I drop my gaze in shame before saying, "A part of me was happy when he asked me to go to work for you. To help him get justice for our mother. It was the first time in so long that he acted as if I were worthy of being his daughter. It didn't take me long, though, to realize what a mistake I'd made. And I wanted out. I tried to walk away, but he wouldn't hear of it. Then some time ago, his interest in you became more crazed than it had ever been before. I don't know what changed, but instead of Jacey contacting me, he was as well, almost daily. He was impatient, insulting, and even threatening. I just—couldn't take it anymore. I cared about you, Lee, and there was no way I would be a part of anything happening to you."

"So you quit," he murmurs before rubbing his neck. He's stressed. "Goddammit to fucking hell, Liza! I mean, Jade, shit." He knocks a nearby book off his desk, and we both watch as it crashes into the wall and lands with a loud crash on the floor. It's so apparent that it's killing him to have it lying there ruining the otherwise tidiness of his office. Again, the tic in his cheek probably isn't noticeable to anyone other than me, but I see it. I get to my feet and retrieve it, returning it to where it was just seconds earlier, before taking my seat once again. He doesn't acknowledge the gesture in any way, but he visibly relaxes. I so want to know the rest of his story. The part that tells me why he can't handle disorder of any kind. It goes beyond being a neat freak. There's a driving force there and to know it would be to unlock an important piece of who he is. "I am so fucking angry with you that I honestly don't know how to handle it," he continues, as if the book thing has never happened. "You betrayed me in ways that no one has ever dared. I trusted you. I gave you access to files not many know exist. Falco is clean, so I'm not worried about that, but you've been lying since the very moment you walked into Falco. To me, it looks as though you were willing to do whatever was necessary to do your father's bidding, up to and pretending to have feelings for me."

"What? No!" I sit forward quickly, putting out a hand beseechingly. "I'd never do that. I fell in love with you, Lee." I know this isn't the time to hold back. "I could have witnessed you murder someone in cold blood, and I wouldn't have been able to tell my father. I told you I never gave him anything, even when he really turned up the heat." I point at my neck before adding, "This should show you that much. If I didn't care, I would have told him anything to avoid having this, but I didn't, and I never will."

He snaps his fingers, and I flinch. "So, just like that you can turn your back on your family? For me? You knew nothing about me. That's pretty convenient, don't you think?"

I straighten my spine, willing him to see that I'm dead serious. "I don't belong with them," I say clearly. "I've been a Wrenn in name only, and they'd be the first to tell you that if they were honest. You're the only one who's ever seen me. Maybe you didn't know my legal name, but I never pretended with you beyond that. You had the real me from the start. I found it impossible to be any other way. You always appreciated me—had confidence in my abilities when no one else did. They're my relatives, and there's nothing I can do about that, but my loyalty is to you. Surely deep down you know that."

He gets to his feet and walks to stand before a large picture window. His hands are in the pockets of his jeans, and he appears lost in thought. I know his mind is running through everything he's learned, and that I probably won't want to hear the conclusion he reaches, but what more can I do? Regardless of what happens now, a weight has been lifted from my shoulders. Everything is finally out in the open. I know in my heart I'll lose him. There's no way he can be romantically involved with someone he doesn't trust. Heck, he can't have that in his life, period. And for a man in his position, can I really blame him? It's not as if I've stolen company office supplies. No, I told a trail of lies for the sole purpose of ruining him. How could he possibly forgive that? "I'm at a loss here," he finally admits. I hear the confusion in his voice, and I ache to comfort him. He won't show any weakness, especially toward a woman he will want to destroy. "If you were anyone else . . . it would be so much fucking easier if you were. Part of me wants to destroy everything you hold dear—to burn it to the ground and watch as the ashes land at your feet. But a piece of me, that I don't even understand, feels compelled to save you. Yet the fucked-up thing is that I'm now your biggest threat. So how am I to battle myself?" I open my mouth, to say I have no clue, but he holds up his hand as if sensing it. "Please leave my office. Not my home. *For now.* I'll know if any exterior doors open, so don't think of going anywhere. I need time to process this."

I stay where I am for a moment as I consider pleading my case further, then decide against it. He's too divided right now, and anything I say at this point will only frustrate him. Lee is a loner, and I need to respect that or risk pushing him in a direction I don't want him to go. "I'm sorry," I say quietly, hoping he can hear the sincerity of it, before I stand to do as he's asked. I'm surprised that I'm not falling apart now that I'm away from him, but strangely enough, the sense of relief I felt earlier is still here. How long it will last, I can't say, but for now, I feel some hope.

Part of me wants to destroy everything you hold dear—to burn it to the ground and watch as the ashes land at your feet. What he doesn't realize is that he is the *everything I hold dear.*

———◆———

LEE

I HEAR THE DOOR CLOSE BEHIND her and allow my shoulders to sag. After all these years, I thought I was beyond being fooled to the degree that Liza—fuck, Jade—has fooled me. Of course, I knew something was off from the moment she was spotted going to Wrenn's house. I even guessed a family connection. But dammit, I hadn't seriously entertained the idea that she could be out to infiltrate Falco with the sole intention of discrediting me. And the horrific part of the whole thing is that I never suspected anything. Nothing about her had set off any alarm bells. And that was the scariest thing of all. I survived many harrowing years by instinctively sensing danger and deception. But fuck it all. Nothing. She never so much as caused a blip on my radar in either of those regards.

I pick up my cell phone with the intention of asking

Pete to come over, then think better of it. I'd rather not have to worry about Liza—fuck, Jade—overhearing our conversation. So instead, I send him a text and ask him to meet me at the sports bar a few blocks away. I then send an identical message to Lucian. Since he's the one who gave me the bad news earlier, I figure he may have some other information I can use.

Even though seeing her again right now is the last thing that I want, I can't leave without telling her I'm going. And reinforcing my order that she not go anywhere. I'm standing in the hallway trying to decide where to look first when I hear her voice nearby. It sounds as if she's in the bedroom—which irritates the hell out of me. I don't want to be reminded that mere hours earlier I was inside her beautiful body driving us both to an explosive release. *Goddamn you, little bird.* I school my face into its usual expressionless mask as I stand in the open doorway taking in the scene before me. She's lying in my bed propped up on a mountain of pillows with Rufus stretched out on her stomach. Even from here, I can hear her occasional bout of sniffles. Her face is wet, and her eyes are closed. It almost looks as if she's sleeping, but the steady stroke her hand over the cat's back says otherwise. Despite the anger I feel toward her, the urge to offer comfort is strong. Only, how can I? To do that will condone what she's done. So I harden my heart and clear my throat loudly. She jerks, which elicits a meow of complaint from her feline companion. In a gesture that's oddly childish, she wipes her eyes with the back of her hands before staring at my chest instead of meeting my gaze. Her avoidance is a relief, making it easier to remain aloof. "I need to go out for a while. If you need anything, dial one for the concierge, and he'll take care of it. There's also plenty of food in the kitchen, or if you'd prefer something else, then order takeout."

She turns away to stare at the wall before saying quietly,

"I know the drill, Lee. I'm not to leave. And you don't need to worry about that. I haven't the energy or desire to go on the run at this time. So you can rest easy." I stay where I am for a moment longer, but she says nothing else. She's dismissed me as surely as she uttered the words. Childishly, I feel the desire to have the last word but refrain. Haven't we said enough to each other for now? There's nothing I can add that will make her or me feel better about what's transpired today. That will take a fucking miracle, and the last time I checked, those were in short supply. So I take my leave instead. I stop at the front desk and inform them that I'm to be called if she leaves. Then I walk the short distance to the sports bar where I've met Luc at a few times. The crowd is sparse due to the early hour, which suits me perfectly. I glance around and see that both Luc and Pete are sitting at a table near the back, laughing like old friends. They've bonded easily since Lia came in to my life. "Oh fuck." I roll my eyes, before surveying my surroundings nervously. "Please tell me that insane bartender isn't here. I can't believe I didn't think of that. She's scary as fuck."

Luc laughs, while Pete appears lost. Surely, I've mentioned her before. "I haven't seen Misty yet." Luc smirks. "We can only hope it stays that way." He nods toward Pete before adding, "She'd probably be thrilled to see some new blood. After Aidan rebuffed her, she hasn't been the same."

Now Pete really looks intrigued before it seems to hit him and he smiles. "Ah, I remember Kara mentioning her. I believe they're friends now. She was at the cancer benefit we held. An interesting lady."

"She's crazy as a shit-house rat," I deadpan as I pull a chair out and settle my large frame into it. "I'd like to be able to talk without her mauling me the entire time. The stuff she comes up with is downright disturbing."

"True that, brother," Luc agrees as he takes a sip from

the beer in front of him. Even though we're meeting during business hours, a few beers are nothing to any of us. If it were later, it would be scotch or bourbon.

"So what's this about?" Pete asks curiously. "And why haven't you been in the office today? Obviously, it's not business related since you're wearing jeans."

This part is going to suck more than a little. I feel as if I'm betraying her trust by telling my brother, but considering all I know, how can I keep this from him now? There is simply no way to sugarcoat it, so I lay out the facts as I know them. "Liza's name is actually Jade Wrenn. She's the daughter of Hunter Wrenn. Twenty years ago, I took over Wrenn Wear for Draco, and apparently, Hunter has harbored a grudge since then. He concocted an identity for her and sent her to work for me to find anything he could use to ruin Falco. Well, me specifically. Only, apparently, she couldn't go through with it and finally quit when he began turning the pressure up."

Pete appears stunned as I pause, giving him time to process what I'm telling him. Finally, he asks, "How? Everyone at Falco is vetted thoroughly before they're hired. It shouldn't have been possible for her to get a job."

"I have an answer to that puzzle," Luc inserts grimly. "You hung up so abruptly earlier, Lee, that I didn't get to tell you everything." A sick feeling stirs in the pit of my stomach. "My guy found evidence that Sears was paid off to approve Liza's background check. There's also a good possibility that Jenkins is on the take as well. It's far too convenient that they were both completely incompetent with anything pertaining to her."

Pete curses under his breath as my rage hums through my veins. It's unfathomable to me that Falco has suffered this kind of breach. He not only opened the door for our enemies, but he also rolled out the fucking welcome mat. Sears was fired for fucking up information pertaining to Lia. At that time, I had no reason to question anything related to Liza. But Jenkins—other than pointing out that she'd been to visit Hunter Wrenn, has given me nothing of value. He's been stalling at every turn, so there's no doubt in my mind that he's been paid off. No one will ever hire him again, and he can only hope I leave it at that. I'd love to tear his fucking head off and spit down his throat, so firing and blacklisting his sorry ass will be far too lenient. I've been stumbling around in the dark for far too long and need the big picture. "Luc, can your guy dig up everything he can on Wrenn Wear? According to . . . Jade, her mother was running the company at the time of the takeover. She claims that after the management was replaced, her mother started drinking heavily and eventually died in a suicide car crash, thus spurring her father to seek revenge against me."

Pete puts a hand over his face, muttering, "Goddamn. This is like some kind of soap opera. I don't remember Wrenn Wear, but it sounds like an unusual company for Draco to want. Nothing like any of his other holdings that I'm aware of."

I've been thinking the same thing. "All I was told was that it was payback for a business deal gone bad. It seemed strange to me at the time, but you know that both Victor and Draco could be eccentric. I never questioned their choices: he wanted it—I took it, end of story. As I told Jade, it was never mine, and I haven't thought about it in years."

"And she claims that Wrenn suddenly started pressuring her more?" Luc asks as he flips through his iPad. "From the report, I don't see anything noteworthy from around the time she mentioned. Could be he just got impatient."

"I'm finished thinking anything concerning this mess is a coincidence," I say flatly. "We need to assume that any change in behavior is relative. Maybe have your guy concentrate more effort there. It could be nothing, but my gut tells me it isn't. Especially after him trying to strangle her last night."

"Wait—what?" Pete interrupts before I can continue. "Who strangled who?"

I told Luc about the latest developments earlier, but I've forgotten that Pete doesn't know as much about what is going on as Luc does. A fact I now feel like shit about. My brother was always my closest friend and ally. I regret now that I've let my need to shield my family keep me from sharing information that they should have known about from the beginning. If there's a threat against me, then it only stands to reason that Pete is also vulnerable. *Fuck, I've made a mess of this.* I sigh. "Apparently, Liza . . . Fuck it. Jade was summoned home to see her father last night, and when she made a remark he didn't like, he assaulted her."

"Are you fucking kidding me?" Pete snaps, clearly outraged. "We can't let that bastard get away with this. Things might be questionable where she's concerned, but I would have felt it in my gut if she were a danger to us. I don't know where all the pieces fit together, but I'm willing to bet that she's mostly guilty of being born a Wrenn. She would never hurt you. Hell, we all know she's been in love with you for a long time." *So perhaps she wasn't lying about that.*

"It's no secret." Luc nods in agreement. "I realize how it appears on paper, and you both know I'm always suspicious of the motives of others, but I have to agree with Pete on this one. I've never felt any negative vibe about Liza either. We need to know a lot more before we can draw conclusions, especially concerning her. Wrenn is up to no good, though." He flips through a few more screens before adding, "Hunter's wife, Jasmine Wrenn, died in 1998. As Jade indicated, it was a car accident. There's not much here on her, and if she's the starting point to this vendetta, then we need to thoroughly consider the years before and after her death. Why wait this long to come after you? That part makes no sense to me. I've heard of biding your time, but this seems excessive for a man who should hate you enough to go to all this trouble to destroy you. Hell, he could have hired someone years ago to get close to you. Why send his daughter?"

"It is bizarre," Pete muses. "Generally, people are more inclined to act when their grief or anger is fresh, hence so many workplace shootings within a few days after an employee is terminated. I'd say it's rare to let it fester for seventeen years, then go balls-to-the-wall for revenge."

Luc shakes his head in resignation. "After the shit that happened with Cassie, I didn't think anything else would ever surprise me, but this has. That's probably the part that unnerves me the most. The parallels between Wrenn and her. Not that the details are close to the same, but Max, Aidan, and I sat in this very bar and tried to make sense of it all. Then there was the whole mess with Lia's friend Rose and her family. I realize it's common that bad stuff happens to good people, but come the fuck on. I seem to be at the point where fucked-up shit constantly hits either me or those around me from behind, and we're left to run for cover while we attempt to find a rational explanation for some fucked-up stuff."

Pete raises his beer and taps it against the one in Luc's hand. "True that, my brother. If half of this happened to anyone else, I'd think they were lying through their teeth. We barely get back to normal before we're dealing with something new. Hell, I, for one, am tired of it." He gives me a meaningful look before adding, "And I'm ready to do whatever it takes to eliminate this threat from our door."

"Well, color me happy and drooling! I hardly ever get anything but angry rednecks who wanna drink beer in their truck and try to get their hands under my shirt. But it looks as if I've hit the stud-pot today." Our heads swivel as one, and I inwardly wince as the bleached blonde puts a hand on the back of my chair and chews her gum so loudly I wonder how her jaw isn't dislocated. Then I figure the muscles in her mouth are probably worked regularly and that brings up a whole other set of images I wish I could block out.

I give Luc credit for keeping his voice level and cordial as he says, "Hey Misty, how've you been?"

Her tits are fairly squashed against the back of my neck now as she leans closer. Not that I had any doubts going by the size, but they're fake and not great ones at that. They're so hard that with just a little force, she could probably knock me halfway across the table without every lifting a finger. "Oh, you know, sugar, just taking awesome to a whole new level as usual."

"I'll bet you are," Pete mumbles under his breath, while keeping a smile plastered across his face.

"It's a dirty job, but I'm sure you're more than up for it," Luc replies diplomatically. Of course, his double meaning is clear to me, but the giggle from Misty says that she hears only a compliment in the words.

"You know that's right, handsome," she purrs. She's so fucking close to me now that her breath stirs my hair. "So refresh my memory here. I know I've seen these two, but what're you boys' names again?"

Boys? She has no fucking clue who she's dealing with. I wish I'm the gangster Jade is accusing me of being. Hell, surely Tony Soprano wouldn't let this insult go. "This is my father-in-law, Lee, and his brother, Pete." Luc makes the introductions, saving me from saying something she'll likely never forget.

"That's right." She clicks her tongue before finally moving away from me, only to walk around the table until she has a view of all three of us. "How in the world can you be anyone's father? You're way too hot to have a kid that old. What were you, like ten when you created her?" I almost wish she'd stayed behind me. At least then I wouldn't be forced to make eye contact while attempting not to stare at the huge amount of cleavage she has on display. And then I make the mistake of reading the saying on her shirt. 'Nipples . . . they're not just for babies.' *Holy fucked-up shit.* Who comes up with something like that? And has anyone other than Misty bought one?

Apparently, she's waiting for me to answer her question. I fight the urge to roll my eyes. "Something like that." If I thought to shock or even disturb her, I'm sadly disappointed because if the look on her face is any indication, I've just moved up a few levels in her eyes. *Fucking perfect day.*

"I thought you were devoted to our boy Aidan," Luc says. Instead of being pissed that Misty has the hots for his future son-in-law, Pete appears amused. *Did I miss a memo somewhere?* It's like a private joke I'm not privy to, and I'm irritated. So much for a serious meeting. This has turned into a three-ring circus.

Misty rocks on her feet, and I wonder if gravity will have her face-planting on the table at any moment. "Oh no, I had to give that up. Kara's my girl now. We got each other's back." She thumbs her chest before adding, "Hoes before bros. Know what I'm saying? If he came in and begged for it, I'd show him the door, really quick like." She gets a faraway look in her eyes, then adds wistfully, "Damn, it would be tough, because I'd just love me some Aidan. But he's with Kara. Plus, since she was his first, they have that special kind of bond."

Luc and Pete choke almost simultaneously on their beer, while I wonder if I've heard her correctly. *Aidan's first what? Love?* Maybe she doesn't know about Cassie. That makes sense. But why are Luc and my brother laughing? I rub my forehead, as if willing away the headache that is once again pounding there. "There's no shame in remaining a virgin," Luc manages to say with a straight face. *Just when I didn't think this conversation can't get any weirder.*

"Sure, that's right," Misty muses. "Although, I've gotta admit, it's a tiny bit of a turn-off. Us women like to know that our man can wear the pants. You know, take charge and show us a good time. He's a handsome devil, so I would have been willing to give it a shot. But I prefer a little more experience under the hood. There's a big difference in being the driver for one night and having to sit in that seat all the time. You get my drift?"

"Loud and clear," my brother replies with a blank expression I truly admire. *And I thought I had a good poker face.*

"Anywho"—she smiles broadly— "I know these two are taken." She points at Luc and Pete. "But what about you, handsome? I don't recall Kara mentioning anything about you being married, and you're not wearing a ring."

Before I can come up with a reply, Luc quickly interjects, "He . . . um . . . bats for the other team." When I turn my head to stare at him incredulously, he shrugs. "Not all the time. Just some of it. He swings both ways." *What. The. Fuck?*

Misty looks as if she's just won a year's supply of tacky T-shirts. I can practically see her hormones surging, and I'm damn near ready to throw my beer bottle as a distraction and run for my life. I shoot my son-in-law a scathing look before telling Misty, "I'm currently involved with a woman. And I'm sorry to say that neither of us share."

Her huge tits jiggle alarmingly as she releases a breath before popping out her bottom lip in an elaborate pout. "I swear, why are none of you guys free? If you had an hour with me, you'd never be the same."

"I don't think any of us would disagree with that." Luc grins.

"Here, here," Pete chimes in, holding up his bottle to click against Luc's. "You're certainly one of a kind."

Misty preens, accepting the compliment at face value. "Toby should appreciate me more. Does he have any idea how lucky he is? I could go home with half the men in here every night, but do I? Nooo, I'm loyal to him." I'm hard-pressed not to point out that she'd just been trying to pick me up, but I don't want to draw attention to myself again. Hell, thanks to Luc, I'm already a challenge to her. She'll have bragging rights for years if she can turn a bi-man straight again. Little does she know, that the opposite would be more likely to happen were there any truth in the whole thing.

Thankfully, a table of guys who are apparently her regulars come in, and she smiles over at them flirtatiously. "We're fine here, Misty, if you need to take care of that." Luc nods in the direction of the new arrivals.

I must admire the way she seems to simultaneously pull her shirt down and her shorts up for maximum exposure before sashaying off with a roll of her hips that would do most anyone on a street corner proud. "What is wrong with that picture?" Pete chokes out.

"I'm thinking . . . a lot." I shake my head. I've gone from being irritated at the interruption to grudgingly amused. It is hard not to be. Misty is so overly confident on the one hand, and *almost* adorably clueless on the other. You have to be impressed at how she goes through life encased in her own little bubble. I'd wager a bet that she stays less stressed out than the rest of us. There's something to be said for picking and choosing your own reality. If you believe it's true, then fuck what the rest of the world says. Isn't that how a lot of life works? *Fuck, I'm getting philosophical in my old age.*

Seeming to echo my thoughts, Luc adds, "No doubt, but I kind of like her. She's fucking nuts on a good day, but she brings a certain something to everything around her. Kind of like fucked-up confetti."

"That's certainly one way to look at it." Pete laughs.

Luc glances at his watch, before getting to his feet.
"I've got a meeting in thirty minutes, so I need to cut this
short." He claps my brother on the back, adding, "Pete,
good to see you, man." Then he looks across the table at
me. "I'll be in touch when I know something." I nod as
he tosses some bills on the table.

When he's gone, Pete asks, "Have you considered
contacting Anthony?"

I don't need him to repeat the question, because even
though I probably know a dozen men by that name,
there's only one who could possibly be of use to us now.
Anthony Moretti, Draco's only acknowledged son. I've
heard rumors through the years that there are others
who claim to be his illegitimate offspring, but to my
knowledge, none have been tested to prove their heritage.
Whereas I inherited Victor's holdings, Draco left his
estate to Anthony. There's a ten-year age difference
between us, so I've been more like his big brother than
friend. I've bailed his ass out of trouble at the fancy
private school Draco insisted he attend and loaned him
money when his daddy cut his allowance off over some
shit he was involved in. Truthfully, I love the kid. He's
bright, funny, and charismatic. He inherited that air of
dangerous charm that always made his father so popular.
Victor and Draco have been dead for many years now,
and even though I've kept tabs on Anthony to ensure he's
okay, we haven't spoken in longer than I care to remember.
He used his money to open several nightclubs in North
and South Carolina as well as Georgia and Florida. He
took the Moretti fortune and built on it, instead of being
content to live the easy life. He's also gradually distanced
himself from his father and Victor's unsavory associations.
Although I knew he would always be a member of the
Moretti clan, I'm strangely proud of the man he's become.

I sigh as I realize my brother is still waiting for an answer. "I've thought of it, certainly," I concede. "He was barely twenty-one when Draco died, though, so it's doubtful he knows any more than we do about that time."

"He was young, yes," Pete says, "but to have broken the ties that he has, it would have been necessary to have an in-depth knowledge of Draco as well as his holdings. There may be something of benefit there."

He's right, of course. There's no one in a better position to help than Anthony. The fact that I've been hesitant to reach out to him is largely due to my guilt for not making more of an effort to remain in his life. We were once a family, but as I set out to turn Falco in a new direction, I left the old one and those associated with it behind. Anthony, unfortunately, was a part of that. It's not that I wouldn't have come to his aid should he have ever needed it, but that's never seemed to be the case. Quite the opposite, in fact. He was a born leader and is a decisive and successful businessman. "I'll get in touch with him." I nod in agreement. We talk for another few minutes before we leave. I've been fully prepared to throw Pete to the wolves or wolf and run, but luckily for him, Misty is nowhere to be seen. Poor bastard, he has no idea how close he came to being mauled. Regardless of what she said, I'm sure she'd bend all her moral rules in the blink of an eye.

I'm strangely hesitant to go home. With her there, it's no longer my sanctuary. Even though I rarely use public transportation, I hail an approaching taxi. It squeals to a stop with impressive accuracy. I grimace from the smell of old smoke and body odor as I settle in the back seat. It's amazing how easily these things offend me now when once I would have given them no thought. Have I become so used to the privileged life I now live? It's a sobering thought for a man who thought he'd always be more street thug than gentleman. I give the driver the address of Anthony's club from memory. I have no idea if he'll be there or not. But I do know that his personal quarters are on the top floor of the renovated industrial building that houses *Nyx*. I'll admit, I've been curious about the unusual name Anthony chose for his club, so I did some research and discovered it meant goddess of the night. The reference to darkness makes sense, considering how he was raised. As far as I know, he's never been in a serious relationship, so that part is a bit trickier. I don't believe it's random, though. Even when he was young, there was always a meaning behind everything he did. And from what I've gathered, he's become more intense with age.

The vehicle comes to a stop so abruptly, I'm forced to grip the back of the somewhat sticky seat. I try not to dwell on what has been there before me as I hand the driver the fare and a tip that has him thanking me profusely. I wave away his gratitude and step out onto the sidewalk. Even in the light of day, the concrete and glass façade of the club is impressive. I know from photographs that purple floodlights illuminate the exterior at night, making it appear almost iridescent.

I stride toward the double doors and am surprised when one opens easily under my touch. Somehow, I didn't expect that at three in the afternoon. Surely, a man like Anthony Moretti is more security conscious. Then a picture of Liza . . . fuck, Jade fills my head, and I realize that for all my attempts at safety, she'd waltzed straight through the front doors of Falco and fooled everyone there. *But what had she been after? Or more so, why after all this time had Wrenn targeted me? Did he really not know that Draco had purchased Wrenn Wear?*

I've barely taken two steps into the dim interior when my arm is gripped. I react instinctively, freeing myself within seconds, then pressing my unknown assailant against a nearby wall with my forearm against his throat.

He gasps and claws until I tighten my hold, effectively immobilizing him. "I'd appreciate it, Lee, if you'd release my manager before you kill him," drawls an amused voice from behind me. It's almost painful to bank the adrenaline pumping through my body. I force myself to relax, and the man before me wrenches away, coughing and cursing.

"Sorry about that, but in the future, you might want to know a bit more about who you're putting your hands on before you do it."

"Fuck you," the man wheezes out, from where he still leans against the wall.

"He's right, Jax." Anthony chuckles as I turn to face the man who is no longer a boy—and hasn't been for a long time. He's older, certainly, but that's not what I notice first. It's the hardness around his mouth that wasn't there before. Even smiling as he is now, he's alert and poised for any and all threats. It's a survival skill that cannot be taught—you're either born with it or you're not. Sure, a person can learn how to fight *and* win, but Anthony's eyes see things that aren't even there yet. His brain is scanning the area for things out of place. It's as instinctive to him as breathing. He *is* Draco Moretti's son and Victor Falco's godson. He's been taught by the best—but he's better. His skills are natural—I recognized that fact years ago. He never stood in the shadows of his powerful father. He is his own man. He extends a hand to me, all politeness and civility. "Lee, it's good to see you again, brother."

I hear the man behind me gasp in shock as I step forward and ignore his outstretched hand. Instead, I clap him on the shoulder, feeling oddly choked up as I say, "You as well, Tony. It's been too long."

"It has." He nods before telling his manager, "Jax, we'll be in my office." Anthony turns on a heel and heads toward a staircase in the far corner of the room. I follow behind him, paying little attention to my surroundings.

This is his home, and it only takes me a moment to know it's more than secure. He won't tolerate anything less. He removes a keycard from his pocket and opens a metal door before waving me inside. The interior is clean and expensively furnished, yet not flashy. He circles around behind a large, mahogany desk, and I take a seat in front of him. It hasn't escaped my attention that he opted to keep things formal, rather than use the more casual seating area in the corner that contains a well-worn sofa and matching armchairs. *Good for you. I would do the same.* He's clearly sending me a message that although we have a history, he doesn't consider us friends. Without preamble, he levels a direct stare at me and asks flatly, "Why now, Lee?"

I don't insult his intelligence by pretending to misunderstand. "I have some questions about a business deal that your father was involved in almost twenty years ago. I thought you might be able to shed some light on his reason behind it."

He quirks a brow, once again appearing amused. "You realize I was a teenager back then. Dad didn't make a habit of running anything by me, much less his rationale for the decisions he made."

"I realize that, Tony, but don't play the dumb-kid card, because I know better. Your father never tried to hide anything from you, and you certainly paid attention when it suited your purposes. I'm hoping this was one of those times."

"Touché." He shakes his head. "Be that as it may, it doesn't change the fact that it's been a long time. But you're free to ask."

"Do you recall a company called Wrenn Wear? I instigated a successful hostile takeover for it, then signed it over when it was complete. It was owned by—

"Hunter Wrenn."

"That's right," I say as I lean forward in my seat. There's

something here, I can feel it. This is no more random to him than it is to me. "What can you tell me about it?"

"Why do you want to know?" he asks instead, looking at me intently.

Honesty is the only way to go here. I'll just alienate him further with half-truths, which will get me nowhere. "I never understood his desire for the company. No, it was more of an obsession. I took it and walked away afterward, but it puzzled me. Everything about it was out of character for him. He claimed it was revenge for a business deal, but never said what. And to my knowledge, there hadn't been anything to warrant that kind of retaliation. In fact, I could find no evidence that there had ever been any dealings between them before."

"I can see you being curious about this back then, but why the sudden interest now? Both Wrenn Wear and my father have been gone for years. You're not one to get nostalgic and attempt to solve puzzles from your past just for the hell of it. So what's fueling this curiosity?"

"I recently discovered that my assistant is Jade Wrenn, Hunter's daughter. Apparently, he planted her at Falco two years ago to find what she could to destroy me."

The slight widening of his eyes is the only indication that I've surprised him. "How is that possible?" he asks flatly. "You probably have some of the best security in the country. Are you telling me that a woman managed to infiltrate your company for that long without you knowing it?"

I grimace, feeling strangely embarrassed by the amazement in his voice. "That's exactly what I'm fucking saying, Tony. And I really don't need another post-mortem. Believe me, it's already been done to death."

He gives me an assessing look before leaning back in his chair. He's the picture of relaxation—even though he's anything but. He's always been like a caged tiger, and I have no reason to think he's any different now. "Where is

Jade Wrenn now? I assume you've dealt with the breach accordingly."

What he's asking is if I've handled it in the way that Victor and Draco would. *Handled the breach. Not at all.* The question seems to have been asked more out of curiosity than a desire to see brutal justice served. It's only natural that he wonders if I've followed in my mentor's footsteps, although I must believe he's kept tabs on me through the years as I have him. We were too close once to completely sever the connection. Who gives a fuck if he thinks I'm weak? We're not likely to be engaged in any kind of turf war. I'm not Victor, and he's not his father. I get to my feet and cross the room to his impressively stocked bar. I don't bother to ask, but simply pour a hefty measure of what appears to be bourbon in a crystal glass, before tossing it back. The alcohol burns as it slides down my throat. It's smooth, though, in a way that only the expensive shit is. I refill my glass, before turning to give him a questioning look. He nods once, and I fix him one as well. I hand him the glass and return to my seat. "Jade is staying with me. I just found out about this today." I give him a brief overview of what I've learned from Luc as well as Jade.

He takes a sip of his drink before stating flatly, "You're in a fucking mess, aren't you? I never thought I'd see the day that the great and powerful Lee Jacks was felled by something as human as feelings."

"Fuck you," I snap. "What would you have me do, Tony, execute her? Maybe kill her whole fucking family in front of her before putting a bullet in her head?"

For the first time, there's real humor behind his laugh. The bastard literally shakes with the force of his amusement. "Damn, Lee, you watch too much television," he chokes out. "Sure, it's a fucked-up world and shit like that happens more often than anyone can even imagine, but that's never been what you're about." When I give him a sarcastic smirk, he adds, "I know you crossed the line a few times in the name of Victor and Draco. I also know you meted out justice when necessary. But you're not a cold-blooded killer. Both my father and Victor had plenty of people more than willing to handle that end of their business. You were the brains of the operation, and everyone knew it. People were terrified to fuck with you because you could bring them to their knees without ever laying a hand on them. You were the enforcer they feared the most. And that's why you had both the old man and Victor's respect. I heard them talk about you more than once. You were everything they weren't, so they not only respected you, they fucking revered you. The kid from the streets who would be king."

It's my turn to laugh now. "This isn't Camelot, Tony, and I'm not royalty. That's more your birthright than mine. I'm the son of a crack whore and who the fuck knows. I was a glorified thief and was lucky enough to be good at it. If I hadn't been, Victor would have still fed and sheltered me, because he knew I'd have his back in any way that I could. Honor and loyalty are the two hardest things to obtain in this life, and when they're given, they're priceless."

He tilts his head, reminding me so much of his father at that moment, that it's almost surreal. Tony had always resembled Draco, but as he's gotten older, it's become uncanny. It makes me curious about who his mother is. She'd been out of the picture before I'd come along, and no reference was ever made of her. It was as if she didn't exist. And in Draco's world, that wasn't unusual. "Say what you will. But modesty doesn't suit you, my friend. You and I both know that you wouldn't have been Victor's heir had you only been some charity project for him. You were his son in every way that mattered, and neither he nor my father was advocates of free rides. Hell, I think they were a little scared of the man you'd become. They knew that should you ever turn against them, you could topple their kingdom down around their feet."

I don't bother to deny his statement, because it's an unproven truth. I was privy to so many damning facets of Victor and Draco's personal and professional lives. Even without that insider knowledge, I could have dealt a heavy blow to their assets. But with it, I could have become the fucking grim reaper where they were concerned. But my loyalty had never been questioned, nor their faith in me shaken. Victor had told me once that he'd trusted me because he could see the integrity in my eyes the first time we met. I hadn't known what he'd meant then, but it's crystal clear now. A smart man knows how to read others. But it's not learned; it's a part of the DNA you're born with. And Victor had that. Which is why it's still hard for me to fathom how a junkie could have killed him. Dammit, were we all just one split second of oblivion away from meeting our maker? "Sometimes you have to take a chance in life and hope it doesn't fuck you over. I'm not happy with the position Jade has put me in. And if I believe for one moment that she's continuing to play me, I wouldn't be here now. The mystery of why wouldn't concern me as much as revenge."

"So you're in love with this woman." He's not asking a question; he's stating a fact. And even as I open my mouth to deny it, I know it's true. I've been in love with her for so long that there's no bombshell; it's more of a moment of clarity and acceptance. I wonder if I would have been capable of admitting it, even to myself a year ago. But when my daughter came into my life, it changed me. I'm vulnerable to those I love in a way I never was before. Opening my heart fully to Lia and Lara makes it harder to deny my feelings for Jade. I'm deeply shaken by the deception that she's been a central part of, but in my world, things are rarely black and white. And as fate would have it, I'm in love with the daughter of a man who wants to destroy me for reasons that I'm not fully privy to—yet.

"I am," I acknowledge. "That's why I need to find out what's going on. I don't believe Wrenn Wear is the reason he's after me, but it's certainly an important piece of the puzzle."

"I agree." He nods. "The only person I know who might possibly have that kind of information is my uncle. He wasn't involved in my father's business, but they talked."

"I met him a few times. You're right; he had nothing to do with any of Draco's companies. Hell, didn't he sell insurance?"

"He's a partner in the company now." Tony laughs. "He's nothing like my father, but they were brothers and stayed in touch through the years. Let me touch base with him and we'll go from there. Like you, I find that I'm more than a little curious about all of this now."

"Thanks, Tony," I say sincerely as I get to my feet. I've been gone from home far longer than intended, and I'm more than ready to see Jade now.

"Congratulations, by the way," he adds when I'm almost to the door. I turn, giving him a questioning look. "I heard about your daughter." He looks down at his desk, before saying softly, "And if you hadn't taken care of the problem, I would have seen it done. I owed you that much."

Lia's abusive stepfather. I'm moved by his words. Like me, Anthony may have distanced himself from that part of his life, but he still lives by a code. We were brothers once, and he would avenge such a wrong on my behalf if it came to that. I'd do the same for him. Where we come from, the family we make for ourselves is often stronger than the ones with a blood right. "I'm sorry it was necessary to cut ties, but it was in both of our best interests.   The attention that our continued association would've brought was the last thing either of us needed. But be assured that should the need have ever been necessary, I would have protected your door with my life. You were never forgotten, my brother."

"Nor were you."   He clears his throat before nodding once. "I'll be in touch."   And with that, my first meeting with Anthony Moretti in ten years is over.   I know instinctively that even though he's no longer involved in the family business, Draco would be proud.   There's strength and integrity there.   Tony is a force to be reckoned with in his own right, but he doesn't have to resort to violence to do it.   No, he rules with his head, and from the troubled look in his eyes when we were discussing love, I think that he too may have fallen victim to his heart.

CHAPTER NINE

JADE

THE BUZZING OF THE DOORBELL jars me from where I drifted off to sleep on the sofa. I stagger to my feet, once again disoriented at my unfamiliar surroundings, before I realize I'm still at Lee's home. When the bell sounds again, I smooth my clothing and attempt to tame my hair before looking through the peephole to see Lia in the hallway, holding Lara in her arms. I feel a wave of relief, like a prisoner being granted a temporary furlough. Lee is not likely to cause a scene in front of her daughter and granddaughter if he comes home while they're here. I turn the deadbolt and give her a bright smile. She blinks rapidly in surprise before recovering enough to say, "Liza . . . it's good to see you. Is, um, Dad here?"

I shake my head. "No, he had some . . . errands to run, I believe. I'm not sure when he'll be back." I reach out and take her arm, ushering her inside. "But I'd love some company, so please come in."

She looks a bit taken aback at the speed with which I get her into the living room. "If you're sure. Luc has a dinner meeting tonight, so I thought I'd come by and see Dad. Lara was a bit cranky, so I figured I could share the joy." She glances over her shoulder, before lowering her voice, "So does this mean what I think it does?"

My face flushes, and I know that I'm practically holding a sign that says, "I had sex with Lee Jacks." From the look in her eyes, she's come to the same conclusion. "It's um— well . . . really, complicated. That's an understatement," I add glumly. "It's more of a big, fat mess."

She lowers herself into an armchair before opening her purse and handing Lara a bag with crackers in it. Then she pulls out a sippy cup and sets it before her now beaming daughter. Sometimes a good snack can make all the difference. She waves me to a nearby seat as she curls legs up under her. "All right, spill it"—she nods to her daughter— "and don't waste time protesting. You never know when a teething toddler will explode, so time is of the essence." Even though Lia didn't grow up with Lee as her father, she shares his ability to talk frankly and not mince words. I've felt agitated all day, wondering when Lee would come home—and what mood he'll be in—so Lia's enthusiasm and kindness breaches my defenses. Lee may toss me out the minute he returns, but regardless, I've missed him so much today. I've felt . . . alone.

I'm horrified as the floodgates open, and I'm sobbing. She presses tissues in my hand and waits until I'm through the worst. "To start with," I gasp out, "my name is Jade Wrenn, not Liza Malone." I give her credit. She doesn't show a lot of surprise even though she clearly wasn't expecting that revelation. Hell, I've come this far, so why hold back? If Lee knows, there's no purpose in lying anymore. I take a shuddering breath, attempting to compose myself. "My father wanted revenge on Lee for something that happened a long time ago. So I was planted at Falco to find anything that he could use to take your father down."

And still, her expression is impassive. Her poker face is nothing short of impressive. Even Lee showed more emotion than she has. Then I remember all that she's been through in her life, and it hurts my heart knowing that her ability to hide her feelings is more than likely a coping mechanism that she learned long ago to survive. She confirms my suspicions when I pause. "So . . . I'm guessing you didn't really want to participate from the start. And then when you fell in love with Dad, you damn sure weren't on board. That's why you left so abruptly, wasn't it?"

She is so much like her father. Relief rushes through me at the understanding I hear so plainly in her voice. She's not judging me. She understands all too well that life can be anything but predictable and that we must adjust in any way we can. "Yes, it was." I take a deep breath, still trying to get myself together. "My father started pressuring me in the months prior to that. He was so angry and obsessed with Lee that it was scary. I felt like I was in a no-win situation. I had nowhere to go and no one to turn to, so I ran."

"And eventually, my father got his head out of his ass and came after you." She gives me a probing look before asking, "Why exactly is your father so hell-bent on ruining Dad? You said it was business. When did this occur?"

"It was almost twenty years ago." For the first time, I see her face register surprise. "I have no idea why he waited this long. According to him, Lee's acquisition of a company called Wrenn Wear is the reason for his hatred. My mother ran the company, and when Lee took it over, all management was terminated, including her. Afterward, she started drinking heavily and eventually slammed her car into a tree one night while intoxicated. My father blames Lee for her death."

Lia sits back heavily in her chair. "Wow," she murmurs. "I didn't see that coming. I can understand how he would be upset, but I still don't get this kind of delayed need for revenge. Have you attempted to confirm his account of what happened?"

"No." I shake my head. "I never had any reason to question his version of the truth until I got to know Lee. By then, I was in so far over my head that it was hard to think straight." Shrugging, I add, "But now that Lee knows everything, he won't rest until he gets all the facts."

"How did he find out?" she asks sympathetically.

"I'm not sure really. Apparently, someone finally stumbled upon the truth about me. I wanted to be the one to tell him—I would have. But I shouldn't have waited so long." Looking at my hands, I admit, "I knew I'd lose him, and I couldn't bear that. Not that I ever really had him, but at least he was in my life in some form, you know?"

"Trust me, I do." Lia laughs. "You worked with my father while Luc and I were getting it together, so I'm sure you were privy to some of our story. It wasn't exactly conventional in a lot of ways." Pursing her lips, she adds, "None of us have had a picture-perfect past, so maybe it stands to reason that we wouldn't do anything in the normal manner."

"I thought you'd hate me when you found out," I say honestly. "Frankly, I'm more than a little relieved you're still speaking to me."

Her eyes drop to my neck, and I raise my hand self-consciously to touch it. "If I thought for a moment that my father was responsible for that, I'd either help you kick his ass or drive the getaway car after you did it. But I know him better than that. He didn't raise a hand to my evil mother, so there is no chance he'd do that to the woman he loves. Which means I can only assume that someone in your family did this. I'm guessing your father?" I'm still stuck on Lia's words about her father loving me. Even if I had believed that last night, after what he now knows about me, I doubt he will want anything to do with me. He will quickly forget me, which I doubt Lia truly understands.

I give her an embarrassed smile before nodding. "I said the wrong thing to him. and he snapped." I swallow hard. "He's losing it, Lia. He's had moments through the years when he's been verbally abusive and insulting, but he's never hurt me physically. But as I looked into his eyes when he had his hands around my neck, I didn't know him. A wildness was there that scared the hell out of me. Even as he was hurting me, I don't think he was even seeing me. Does that make any sense?"

I see a shudder pass through her small frame before she smiles sadly. "More than you can imagine. To me, I think a person is only capable of violence when they completely remove themselves from the equation. Their physical being might be present, but their mind is somewhere else. Especially when it pertains to your own blood. A true father or mother should never be able to harm their child, nor stand by while another does."

I put my hand over hers where it sits rigidly upon her knee. "I'm sorry, I wasn't thinking. Please forget I said anything."

She surprises me by shaking her head with a laugh. "It's fine. I'm not a victim, and I haven't been for a while. I refuse to give those who hurt me that kind of power or satisfaction. I have a past, and some of it is bad, but I also have a future, and it's more than I could have ever imagined. I have everything that I dared to dream was possible. And my dad is part of that. I know he's a hard man on the outside, but when he loves someone, there's nothing he won't do for them. And he loves you, Liza . . . er, Jade." I hate that this is what my friends will endure. "Because of that, he'll forgive you, and he'll protect you." She puts her other hand on top of mine. "All that I ask is that you not give up on him. He's like Luc in so many ways. Stubborn, overprotective, and overbearing. Alpha right down to the core. Even though it can be exasperating at times, you'll never have to doubt his love for you when it's given."

"But that's the thing," I say glumly. "Your father has made no mention of love. I do believe he feels something for me, but I don't think it's love."

She gives me an amused look before saying, "You're still here, right? If he didn't completely lose it and kick you out, then he loves you. Come on, Jade, you know him as well as I do. Could you imagine him leaving the person who betrayed him in his home unless he was head over heels?"

"Keep your enemies close," I point out.

"Bullshit." She snorts. "He doesn't play games. He's direct in what he does, especially when it involves a threat to his family or Falco, and you're both." When I wince, she smiles sympathetically. "I'm sorry, but you would be both by most people's standards and especially to someone like my father. Yet you're in his home, and believe me when I say, this is very much his sanctuary. He only entertains family here. I'd be surprised if he's ever even brought a woman here before."

It's my turn to laugh when her cheeks turn red. I hold up my hand to stop her apology. "Trust me, I'm aware that your father has sex. Although he's always been very discreet about it around the office. That's not to say that there haven't been women who've dropped by. Plus, he's a favorite of the society page, and there have been plenty of sightings of him with pretty girls by his side at events over the years." *And that won't be me. Ever. Either beside him or as a* pretty *girl.*

Lia wiggles an eyebrow. "You've got a Google alert set up, haven't you?" She smirks when I look away guiltily. "Oh, don't worry about it," she scoffs. "I did the same with Luc. I think it's practically a given when you're in love. Especially if it's with someone high-profile." *God, I'm so thankful she gets me. I've felt so . . . stupid . . . watching him from afar.*

I don't think I've realized how lonely it's been over the past few years. Strangely, even though I have forged good friendships with Kara and Lia particularly, I always felt that because of my lies, I could never truly feel accepted. Yet here is Lia, someone who suffered so horribly at the hands of people she should have been able to trust, welcoming me despite my deception. She's seen through the name, the only thing that hasn't been true, and truly understood what I feel about her and her father. It feels so good to have a friend I can talk to. Living as Liza Malone has been isolating and lonely. Jacey may be my sister, but she's never taken the time to understand me. To embrace our differences and love me anyway. Yet Lia . . . *Don't cry, Jade. No more tears.* "I don't know how this could possibly work, Lia," I whisper miserably. "I do love him. But I fear that won't be enough. Under normal circumstances, a successful relationship with a man like Lee would be difficult. But how can it possibly work out, when almost no one wants to see us together?"

"That's not true," Lia protests. "Granted, there will always be some asshole who doesn't want you to be happy, but I think you'll find that our family will understand and won't hold what's happened against you." She shrugs her slim shoulders before adding, "As for your family, you know them better than I do. But from what you've told me, they're not likely to be happy should you end up with my father. I'm not sure that matters anymore, though. You must make a life for yourself, and either they'll get on board, or they won't. I think you're past the point of caring about what they want, though."

"You're absolutely right." *How did she get so wise?* "I've done things their way for far too long. If Lee will give me another chance, I'm not about to blow it for people who couldn't give a shit about me."

Lia holds out a fist. "Hell yeah, put it there." I giggle as we fist-bump. Then we both laugh when Lara rushes over and lays her tiny hand against ours as she grins proudly over the accomplishment. Lia picks up her daughter and kisses her cheek. "Now, let's discuss how we can turn this whole mess around. Between the two of us, I think we can solve the world's problems over a glass of wine and a little advice from Google."

The warm glow I feel is so foreign that I wonder what it means. And then it hits me. This is what it would feel like to be a part of a real family. I vow that no matter what, I won't give up on my dream of a life with Lee. I may have a father and a sister, but without Lee by my side, I'm deathly afraid I'll end up a bitter shell just as they are.

LEE

I PAUSE IN THE FOYER WHEN I arrive home a short time later. I hear laughter from what sounds like the kitchen. This is the last thing I expected. Jade was quiet and withdrawn when I left. But now, it sounds as if she's having a party. I take a hesitant step forward and freeze when something crunches beneath my shoe. I look down in confusion and see a trail of crumbs that extends as far as I can see. *What in the fuck?* My chest tightens and my shoulders twitch at the mess.

It needs to be gone. I need to sweep it up. Immediately.

There's no way I can concentrate until it's taken care of. With that in mind, I move toward the kitchen and what I find there shocks me even further. My daughter and Jade appear to be taking turns trying to toss something into each other's mouth from across the bar. Lia giggles as what I now see is popcorn bounces off Jade's cheek and lands on the floor to join the pile that is already there.

"You totally suck at this," Jade singsongs, then hiccups loudly. "I knew I shouldn't have had that last glass of wine."

"No kidding." Lia's speech slurs slightly as she opens her mouth and motions for Jade to toss a piece of popcorn her way. She catches it easily, and I feel a moment of pride before shaking my head. "I'm glad Luc came to pick up Lara. He's the best."

Jade nods enthusiastically, and I wonder snidely what my son-in-law has that causes her to give that dreamy sigh. "Well, he kind of had to after she got into Rufus's litter box. The poor thing had to wear one of Lee's shirts after we gave her a bath. It was sweet of him to insist that you stay here to enjoy the pizza we ordered. I swear you really hit the man—" She snaps her fingers clumsily a few times as if searching for the right word before she blurts out, "Jackpot! You won the man-candy lottery. You're rich in sexy hotness."

Lia reaches across the bar with her fist extended, and they bump them together. "Hells yeah, I did," she whisper shouts. "And you don't know the half of it. He's a god in the bedroom." *No fucking way.* I cringe when she opens her mouth. I need to put a stop to this conversation before she says something I'll be forced to kill Luc over. As it is, I'll never be able to un-hear what she's already said.

I clear my throat loudly, and they both swing around to look in my direction. Which is a mistake, because Jade teeters on her chair in an alarming fashion. I rush forward and barely manage to grab her before she face-plants on the floor. "Whoopsie." She laughs before wrapping her arms around my neck. "You're my hero," she adds as she gazes at me in a way that has my heart thumping firmly in my chest.

"You are," Lia states, and I can't help but smile at the daughter I love so fucking much it hurts. "I'd consider it a personal favor if you'd make her my—well, mother just sounds weird, but maybe friend of the father." Her nose scrunches up as if she's concentrating deeply before she shrugs. "There's father of the bride and stuff like that, so friend of the bride? If you married Liza—I mean Jade—then that's sorta what I'd be. Is that right?"

"I could be a mom," Jade offers. "After all, I'm older than you. And even though it wouldn't be physically possible to have a kid your age, I could still be called that, right?" She glances at me, as if awaiting confirmation, and I have no fucking idea what to say. Hell, I'm not even sure I know what they're talking about it's so jumbled.

"Er . . . sure, honey," I finally say when it becomes obvious they're both waiting for something from me. I'm trying desperately not to dwell on the disarray in the kitchen. It's not as if I can start cleaning with two drunk women who aren't safe to be left unattended. "Lia—sweetheart, I think you should sleep over tonight. I'll call Luc and let him know." The words have barely left my mouth when I hear the doorbell. *What the fuck else?* Jade still has a death grip on my neck, and now she wraps her legs around my waist, and I'm forced to either carry her with me or pry her loose. I glance at my daughter and say firmly, "Don't move." She gives me a comical salute, and my lips twitch in amusement before I retrace my steps with Jade plastered against me. I sigh in relief when I see Luc through the peephole. I throw open the door, and he blinks in surprise as I wave him inside. "Don't even ask," I warn. "And why in the hell did you leave these two alone here?"

He puts his hands up in surrender before chuckling under his breath. "I had to make an executive decision since you weren't here. I couldn't get Lia to leave, and my daughter had recently been covered in what I'm very much afraid was cat shit. I instructed your doorman not to let them leave the building, and then I hauled ass home to drop Lara off with the nanny. I wasn't gone for long. In my defense, they were both still upright when I left." Luc looks around and winces. "Man, this place is . . . Did the three of them do all this?"

I keep my eyes straight forward, refusing to take in all the carnage. If I do, I'll shut down, and that's the last thing any of us need right now.

It's just clutter. You can take care of it as soon as you've dealt with this. Compartmentalize. Pack it away for now.

I force myself to relax and shift Jade's weight. "Obviously, they did." I roll my eyes.

"You do know she's asleep?" he asks as he nods in Jade's direction. I feel something wet on my neck. *Yeah, I think she's out of it and drooling on me. Perfect.*

I shift her in my arms once again. Her body has become a lead weight, and I fear I'll either drop her or bang her head on something. "Give me a minute to get her settled, and I'll be right back." I've taken two steps when I hear a crash, followed by laughter.

"I've got it." Luc waves me away.

"She's in the kitchen," I throw over my shoulder as I stride toward the bedroom. Jade is snoring so loudly now that my ears hurt. *I'm in love with a woman who snores like a freight train, and whose father hates me. Karma is truly a bitch with a nasty sense of humor.* Although I do pause and consider the initial part of the sentence. *I'm in love with a woman.* It's not just that I love her. I'm *in* love. *Fuck.* I flip on the light in the bedroom and briefly consider changing her clothes. Her body is so lax that undressing her would be damned near impossible on my own. And there is no way in hell I'm asking Luc to give me a hand. So I snag the edge of the comforter and pull it back before depositing her gently onto the top of the sheet. Her blond hair half covers her beautiful face, and I sigh as I reach out to push it back. Her mouth falls open promptly and another loud snore fills the room, but she remains deeply in the throes of sleep. I smile despite myself. How can I not? I brush a tender kiss on her forehead before covering her and going to check on Luc's progress with Lia.

"Baby, we need to go." Luc is laughing as my daughter peppers his face with kisses. "You want to see Lara?"

"Mmhmm." She giggles. "Then you can tuck me in."

Fuck. At this rate, I'll be forced to burn the kitchen down. There's no way I can continue to eat where my daughter has talked to and about her husband in such a . . . *sexual* fashion. I clear my throat loudly. This feels like déjà vu. "Everything okay in here?"

Luc has the good manners to appear slightly embarrassed while Lia levels a sloppy smile my way. "There's my daddy," she says, then waves across the bar in my direction.

Luc wraps an arm around her shoulders and pulls her tightly against his side. "We're going to be on our way." He rolls his eyes as he coaxes my daughter across the room. "I'll let you know when we get home," he adds. I hear his amused voice responding to her nonstop chatter as they slowly disappear down the hallway. A door closes in the distance, and then there's nothing but blessed silence. *And then I look around me. Filth.* My shoulders tense.

No one can see it this way. I have to make it clean for us.

I get a broom from the nearby utility closet and begin methodically sweeping the floor. *Clutter. Mess. Disorder.* It's all I can see. My movements are quick and efficient. I've done this a million times before, and I don't waste time with indecision. The kitchen is returned to its normal pristine state. I then go from room to room, restoring order.

Get it clean, Lee. Don't make a fuss. Be calm and get it all clean.

I don't pause until I reach the bathroom where Rufus has his litter box. The cat is standing in the middle of the room meowing pitifully as he surveys the mess along with me. Then surprisingly, given the disarray around me, I find myself relaxing. Maybe it's the obvious disgust on the animal's face as he takes it all in. It's as if I've found a kindred spirit. *You're losing it. The cat is just pissed that someone played in his shit.* "I feel you, pal," I offer sympathetically. "I'm not real fond of people fucking with my things either." Then I feel like an asshole when I think of my daughter, granddaughter, and Jade. Would I rather they not visit? These are more than just *people.* Is a clean house worth never seeing the people who I love? Maybe Pete's right. It may be time to deal with this obsession that has haunted me for so many years. I don't want to be crippled by old voices anymore. I fear that at some point, I'll hurt the people who mean the most to me over some fucking crumbs. I lean down on my haunches in the middle of the litter-covered bathroom floor and rub the cat's bristling fur until he calms and begins purring. "We've got to learn to adapt, pal. It might not be possible to teach an old dog new tricks, but surely, you and I are capable of change." He meows plaintively as if to say, "*no fucking way,*" and I chuckle. "Yeah, it sucks, but one thing at a time, okay?"

It takes me another hour to go over the whole apartment, and by then, I'm exhausted. I strip my clothing off and take a quick shower before flipping on the bedside lamp. I freeze, so used to my bed being empty. The sight of a woman there is foreign to me. Sleepovers lead to expectations, and that's something I don't have the desire for—or at least I didn't.

She mumbles and turns onto her side, leaving me just enough room to slide in behind her. I pause to turn the light off, then pull her against me, cradling her head on my arm. *She's so warm and soft. God, she's feels so good in my arms.* A feeling of peace unlike anything I've ever known before comes over me, and I know that although the road ahead is long, I'll do everything I can to be the man she needs.   Because somehow, she's become the woman I can't fathom to live without. *Somehow, she's become mine.*

CHAPTER TEN

—◆—

JADE

I'M GOING TO BE SICK. I sit bolt upright in bed, which is a big mistake. The room spins at an alarming rate, causing my stomach to lurch. I make it out of the tangle of covers in the bed, then run into a wall. *What?* The momentum should have sent me sprawling, but something holds me upright.

"Whoa, honey, careful. You're going to hurt yourself."

This just gets stranger by the minute. "Lee?" I ask in confusion, before my stomach reminds me that I have no time to spare. I attempt to pull away, but he tightens his hold. "Sick," I gasp out, then clamp a hand over my mouth. Apparently, he gets the message, and I'm whisked into the bathroom and deposited in front of the toilet. "Leave," I mumble, but that's as far as I get before the heaving begins. He grabs my hair and curses under his breath, but his touch is gentle. And I know that instinctively he's upset for me and not at me. It seems like hours before the contents of my stomach are gone, and the nausea begins to subside. Still, I remain where I am for another moment, afraid to move too far from my porcelain helper. "I'm never drinking again," I shudder in revulsion.

"Said many, many people before you." Lee chuckles as he rubs a hand over my back. "Let's get you cleaned up and back in bed. Then I'll gather some breakfast from the kitchen."

"Ugh, no." I shake my head. "I'm pretty sure I'll finally lose those twenty pounds, because I'm off food as well."

"This too shall pass, little bird," he murmurs. He walks to the large shower and turns on the water while I'm brushing my teeth with a toothbrush he passed me. *It's so mortifying to have Lee see me at my worst. Mind you, I've sobbed on his shoulder, barfed in his toilet . . . Thinking it can't get much worse now.* Then he calmly begins to remove the boxer briefs that he's wearing.

"Um, what're you doing?" I ask in alarm. "If you think we're having sex now, you're crazy." When he throws his head back and begins laughing, I feel my face flush. "It's not THAT funny," I say, feeling embarrassed at my obviously incorrect assumption.

He points at the wrinkled clothing I apparently passed out in the night before. I grimace when I see what appears to be wine stains and God knows what else. "I thought you'd like to freshen up before you lie back down."

"Oh, okay. That's a good idea," I mumble sheepishly. "But why are you undressing? Do you want to go first?"

He gives me an indulgent smile, before stepping forward and saying, "Lift your arms." I do as he asks without thought, and he pulls my top over my head. I quickly cross my arms over my naked chest. At some point, I took my bra off, although I don't remember doing it. I'm still mulling that over when my pants are unbuttoned and the zipper is lowered.

"Whoa! I can do that myself," I stammer in protest as I attempt to bat his hands away. We may have had sex, but I was caught up in the heat of the moment. Now I'm standing in the bathroom under the unforgiving florescent lighting where there is no hope that he'll miss any of my imperfections. His body is all hard, chiseled peaks, and mine is soft and rounded. He looks as if he runs ten miles a day, and I look as if I have a serious M&M addiction. *Those fucking carbs.*

He rolls his eyes at my bout of shyness, but then the heat in his gaze is unmistakable. "I have a very good memory, little bird. I know the feel of every curve of that beautiful body." I'm so mesmerized by the desire in his voice that I'm hardly aware that he's picked up where he left off, sliding my jeans and panties down, then instructing me to step out of them. Then I'm horrified when it hits me. I'm completely and utterly nude. I don't know which area to cover first. *Dammit, when's the last time I did some maintenance on my lady bits?* He turns me gently toward the shower and swats my ass playfully. I yelp and throw him a dirty look over my shoulder. "Never hide your body, Jade. It's absolutely perfect to me. There is nothing about it I would change. A woman should look like a woman and not a toothpick."

"Oh, please." I snort. "I've seen pictures of the women who've accompanied you to various events." *And none of them had any extra junk in the trunk.* "They all looked like my sister, Jacey, who spends more time moving some lettuce around on her plate than eating it. Please don't lie to me, Lee, when I know differently." I hate my insecurities, and especially having to voice them in front of Lee. I just can't imagine how someone like him can like what he sees when he looks at me.

He takes my arm and spins me around so quickly that I'm disoriented for a moment. He's angry; it's there in the muscle throbbing in his cheek. "Let's get something straight," he says through clenched teeth. "I never say shit I don't mean, and you know that. If I wasn't attracted to you, then you wouldn't fucking be here. Not that I should have to explain, but I chose those women for one reason: there was absolutely zero chance of any feelings developing. *They* wanted to attend A-list events, and I needed a date. To me, it was a simple business transaction." His tone softens slightly when he adds, "Did I fuck some of them? Yes." When I swallow hard and drop my head, he reaches out to cup my cheek, forcing me to meet his eyes. "I'm sorry it hurts you to hear that, but it was a different time for both of us. No one before you meant anything to me. I couldn't even tell you their names or anything about them because I never cared to ask. I've been alive for forty-five years, Jade, but I never really lived until I loved you. I did my best to keep you at arm's length, but I won't deny it anymore. As fucked up as things are right now, how I feel about you is one thing that's not in question."

I can only gape at him in shock. *He loves me? Lee actually loves me?* Whatever I expected, it wasn't that. *You'll never have to doubt his love for you when it's given.* Lia was right? He loves me?

By all rights, he should hate me, but it seems to have changed something between us. We've removed the filters and laid ourselves bare before each other, literally and figuratively. Yesterday, I was certain he'd come home and kick me out. Or at least say he needed time to think. But here he is, saying everything I've longed to hear but feared I never would. And instead of telling him how I feel, I'm staring at him like a mute. "I love you, too," I manage to blurt out. As far as romantic declarations go, his was way better. But when he pulls me close and lowers his lips to mine, I figure he likes my awkward way of speaking just fine. And that's the way we remain until the bathroom is so filled with steam from the shower that I can barely see anything around me. As Lee's hands drop and cup my bare ass, I murmur, "I think I'm onboard with that whole sex thing now, if you're game."

His cock is hard and heavy against my stomach, and I'm beyond ready to have him inside me again. "Are you sure you're up to it?" he asks hoarsely.

"You certainly are." I grin as I wiggle against him provocatively. The words have barely left my mouth when he picks me up and deposits me in the corner of the shower. He adjusts the water and then puts his feet between mine and nudges them apart. "Bend forward," he instructs as I feel his cock nudging against me from behind. I'm breathless with anticipation. I've had so little sex that most any position other than missionary feels amazing. His dick slides through the slickness at my entrance a second before he pushes inside. "Oh God," I moan, feeling as if I'm going to come at any moment. He feels huge, and I'm so tight that I'm almost afraid to move. He places a hand on my hip to guide me into an easy rhythm as he goes a little deeper with every move. It feels so incredible that I'm desperate for a release, yet equally never want it to end. "Lee." I groan his name as his fingers touch my clit and begin rubbing. Within seconds, I fall apart, coming so hard that my vision blurs. I try to push away when he continues to touch me, but he doesn't allow it. Instead, to my astonishment, I peak a second time.

His movements intensify. I look over my shoulder and am completely mesmerized. *Oh God . . .* His handsome face as he gives in to his own release. He's so beautiful to me in that moment of unguarded passion. He slides out of my body and pulls me close, resting his chin on the top of my head. "Shit." He sounds incredulous. "I forgot to use a condom."

"It's fine." I sigh, because I feel so absolutely incredible. "I'm on the pill. You don't have to worry about any little Lees running around here in nine months."

"That's good to know," he says quietly. "But I wasn't concerned about that."

I turn properly until I can look into his eyes. I lay a hand on his chest and stroke it soothingly. "Is there something you need to tell me?" *Oh my God, surely, he doesn't have some kind of STD. What was I thinking?*

He appears so lost. "It's just that I'm careful about that. I mean, obviously I wasn't once since I have Lia, but I was a boy then. As a man, I've never lost control in that way. Never, Jade. But with you, all I can think about is being inside you."

Relaxing now, I attempt to offer comfort because I can see he needs it. "But it's different with us, right? You said so yourself. That's what love does to you."

"Apparently," he murmurs, sounding shaken. We're still standing out of the direct line of the water, and I shiver as my body begins to cool. "Shit. Sorry, amore," he says as he pulls me into the hot spray. He makes quick work of washing us both. Lee is a natural caretaker; I wonder if he knows that. I've seen him do it with both Lia and Lara, and he was incredible with me when I was sick. I know instinctively that if we can work through all that stands between us, he'll always be my rock. *Plus, considering what a cleaning fanatic he is, I'm not likely to ever worry about housework.* I grin at that thought, but then it occurs to me to ask him about it. So after we've both dried off and Lee has pulled one of his T-shirts over my head and donned a pair of boxer briefs, I say, "I'm sorry if we made a mess of the apartment. I don't remember a lot of the evening, but I'm sure we weren't at our best."

"It's no big deal. I've already taken care of it."

I sit on an armchair at the end of the bed, while he walks into the closet to dress. "You couldn't rest with the disarray, could you? I've . . . noticed that it really bothers you for anything to be out of place. And I don't think this is a recent issue."

There is nothing but silence. I think for a moment he hasn't heard me, but the serious look on his face when he steps into the bedroom says differently. He's wearing suit pants and a dress shirt but has yet to put on his jacket and tie. He takes a seat on the ottoman at my feet and slides closer until my legs are between his spread knees. He places his hands on my thighs before releasing a deep breath. "No, this is nothing new for me. This is the last thing I want to discuss, but you have a right to know what you're getting into. Hell, you'll need to understand why I am like this because I'm not sure I'll be able to change." I place my hands over his, showing my support without words. He intertwines our fingers. "I want to be different, to leave it all behind, but it's been a part of me for so very long that I don't know if I can."

"What is it?" I ask quietly. I don't mention that Lia has told me a little of his past. He wouldn't be happy knowing we'd discussed him in that way.

His answering grin is forced, and I can tell it's solely for my benefit. "I know you've heard bits and pieces about how I grew up. From the moment I was old enough to understand what it was, I knew my mother was an addict. And she slept with anyone who would toss a few dollars her way to feed that addiction. Pete and I never knew our father. For that matter, I have no idea if we were even sired by the same person. I doubt our mother did either. The only thing she cared about was the small amount of welfare money that the state gave her to care for us. But the bitch of it was that she stayed in trouble with social services after we got older because she'd disappear for days, and we wouldn't go to school. Then they started paying visits to our apartment, and that didn't go well at all. I guess they frown on kids living in filth."

"So you took over the cleaning," I guess as the pieces begin to fall into place. "How old were you?"

"Around eight." He takes a deep breath, and I wonder if he's ever shared this with anyone before. "It wasn't a big deal in the scope of things. I'd been taking care of Pete for years by that point. Doesn't do much good to get free baby formula if you're never around to feed the kid.

And our mother certainly didn't let little details like that keep her at home."

"Oh Lee," I whisper. "You were so young to carry that load. Was there no other family or anyone to help you?"

He looks at some point over my shoulder, obviously lost in thought. "According to our mother, she was an only child of a single mother who'd passed away years before. She said we had no family, and the evidence seemed to support that fact. No one other than our social worker ever seemed to give a fuck about our welfare. And being as we never knew when she'd drop in, I had to make sure that our pathetic home was at least clean at all times. Our mother told us in great detail what happened to kids who were put in the system, and it sounded far worse than how we were living. Plus, I couldn't risk being separated from my brother. He was all I had in the world."

I take in what he's told me and grieve for the incredible man in front of me. "You mentioned before that your mother passed away. How long ago was that?"

"She overdosed when I was ten—just a few days shy of my eleventh birthday. So Pete and I went into the system. We drifted through a dozen foster homes until I turned sixteen."

"What happened then?" I ask, almost dreading the answer. The neutral tone of his voice doesn't fool me for a second. There's so much more there than what he's saying. I already know he's mentally scarred by those years, and that's inevitably from how his mother treated him. I can only imagine the damage inflicted from other people who passed through his life. And I also know without a doubt that he'll only tell me as much as he wants to. I'll never truly know the full story behind the man. *But he's showing me he loves me at this moment. Sharing so honestly is his way of showing love.*

He pulls a hand from beneath mine and runs it through his hair restlessly. "Most of the foster homes we stayed in were the same. People just doing it to collect a paycheck. Those were the best kind. Because we knew how to do what was expected of us. We'd perfected the art of being invisible years before, and that's a good talent to have in those situations. Believe it or not, the ones who acted like they really gave a fuck were the worst. I'm not sure what they expected, but no matter what, we were never good enough for them. And they mostly didn't handle disappointment well. They either thought they could beat you to deal with it or they gave you back and you went elsewhere. But the last one was the worst. The husband was a mean fucker, and the wife was nothing more than a pedophile. So when she started showing a lot of interest in my brother, I knew it was time to go. I knew we'd be better off on our own than staying there. At least we'd have a fighting chance that way." He reaches his hand out and cups my cheek tenderly. His eyes are almost luminous when he admits, "But it was tough, Jade. You have no idea. We were hungry and cold all the time. Just living from one day to the next on whatever scraps we could find. We were little more than stray dogs. I . . . honestly don't know how much longer we would have made it. I tried to stay positive for Pete, but neither of us were oblivious to the reality of what we were facing."

"Then you met Victor," I prompt, when he goes quiet. This must be so hard for him. Yet in the midst of revealing the horror of his childhood, he caresses me. I wonder if he's even aware that his thumb is rhythmically stroking the side of my face.

"That night was the worst." He sighs. "We hadn't had anything to eat in a couple of days, and we were desperate. There was this big restaurant on one of the side streets that was always busy. It was a meat and potatoes type of establishment, and normally they had the best scraps in town. But they'd been closed the day before, and I was too fucking hungry to wait until they took the trash out, so when one of the employees left the back door open, I snuck in and began rummaging through the food scrap bin in the corner of the kitchen. I was hidden from view by a partial wall—or so I thought. Normally, my instincts were top-notch, but I was sloppy due to hunger. Before I even knew what was happening, someone had an arm around the back of my neck with just enough pressure to immobilize me. I have no idea why, but my usual fight deserted me, and I just stood there, ready to accept my punishment. I figured he'd call the cops, and I'd be hauled away. I planned to tell the police about Pete, so he wouldn't starve to death on his own. But nothing went how I thought it would. Instead, he released me then moved to stand in front of me. And there he was. This giant of a man, who should have scared the hell out of me, but he didn't. He shook his head before pointing at a table at the other end of the room and telling me to sit while he got me something to eat."

I smile as he drops his hand and leans back in his chair, looking more relaxed and less guarded. This is a part of his story he's comfortable with. The affection he feels when he thinks of Victor is clearly written on his handsome face. "He sounds like a very kind man," I remark, then give him a questioning look when he laughs dryly.

"At times he could be." Lee chuckles. "But make no mistake about it, Jade. There were many sides to Victor and most of them were scary. I believe he would have fed me that night and probably given me a few bucks no matter what. He wasn't heartless. He knew fear and hunger and was empathetic because of it. Yet I connected with a part of him that few ever did because he saw himself in me. He knew that, should I be given the chance, I'd do whatever necessary to rise above the filth that surrounded me. It didn't take him long to discover there was a part of me—humanity—that he wasn't so enamored with. I believed it was kill or be killed, and that if you were wronged, then you returned that two-fold. But I wasn't one to harm without a good reason, so that took several job possibilities out of the equation. There was something more valuable to him, though. I could read people, and over time, I proved I had a real knack for business and sniffing out the weaknesses of his rivals. That gave Victor a high unlike any he'd ever known before. I started out being a glorified errand boy while he schooled me in his holdings and that of his best friend, Draco Moretti. Within a few years, I was his right-hand, and to those who knew Victor and Draco, that basically made me mafia royalty."

"So what they say about Victor is true then?" I ask hesitantly, not sure I even want him to answer the question. Some things are better left unsaid, and this may be one of them.

He seems to be of a like mind because he doesn't deny it. "Much was speculated but never proven. Neither Victor nor Draco ever spent time in jail for organized crime. Men of power and wealth such as they had are connected far beyond anything that most can imagine. Hell, some of the most influential people in this state run in the same circles that they did—your father being one of them."

His words don't surprise me. I've known my father wasn't a typical businessman since I was old enough to notice his odd friends. Plus, like Victor, there have been just as many whispers about the type of man he is. I had no proof of any of it, and truthfully, I didn't want to know. Jacey had hinted at it a few times, but I had no idea whether she was a trusted member of my father's inner circle or not. For her sake, I hope she isn't. I raise a brow before turning up my nose. "If you're waiting for me to protest, then don't bother. I've never been privy to that side of his life, but it's hardly a shock."

He smiles wryly. "No, I don't suppose it is." He looks at me so intently that I find myself shifting in my seat uncomfortably. "Jade," he begins softly. "I've done a lot of things in my life that you won't approve of. Just because I wasn't a hired gun for Victor doesn't mean I didn't cross a lot of lines for him."

I reach out and place my finger across his lips. "Don't," I whisper. "I never want to know anything that could be used against you. There is nothing in your past that I need to know because it makes no difference to us. I love you unconditionally. Past, present, and future. You did what needed to be done. You thought each instance out and knew that however you handled it was the only way. I left you all those months ago because I love you for who you are, Lee. Nothing else matters to me. You are someone I admire and respect. Please forgive me for deceiving you." I'm not sure how he will handle my declaration. He almost looks . . . surprised.

Apart from Peter, and now Lia, how many people have told Lee that they love him? *That makes me sad.* But then I consider how many people have ever told me they loved me . . . and I realize that it's only Lee. *And for that I'm heartbroken.*

"Oh cuero mio, come here," he murmurs as he pulls me onto his lap and holds me close. The feel of his heart beating against my ear brings me the most incredible peace. I finally grasp what true love is. It's believing in each other and seeing past the flaws. *It's accepting the truth about each other.*

"What is it you call me?" I smile at the almost embarrassed look on his face. But then he strokes my cheek again and explains.

"Cuero mio means my heart. I didn't know until you that I'd ever love someone like I love you. Victor used it when talking about Jess, a lost love that he never quite got over. So it is instinctual somehow."

"And the other one? Amore mio?"

"My love. Another favorite of Victor's."

Said so simply, it brings tears to my eyes. "I never thought I'd have this love in my life, either, Lee."

He kisses me because words are no longer needed.

Physically, we are a new couple. Emotionally . . . I wonder if this connection we have is because we emotionally connected quite some time ago. We've survived a tough hurdle, and in his arms now, I can't fathom anything ever coming between us.

Yet I'll look back in the days to come and realize that we'll have to climb through hell to ever reach heaven together.

CHAPTER ELEVEN

———◆———

LEE

A NTHONY IS LEANING AGAINST THE wall of his club smoking a cigarette when Luc and I arrive. When he called to say he had some information for me, we were having lunch a few blocks from the office. So, instead of coming alone, I asked him to join me. After all, he knows as much about the situation as I do, and I want him to remain in the loop. "That your guy?" he asks as he parks his Land Rover at the curb.

"Yeah, that's him." I nod as I open the door and approach the younger man. "That shit'll kill you," I remark dryly, pointing at the smoke that he exhales before he stomps the remainder of the cigarette into a nearby canister.

"No shit." He grins before extending a hand to Luc. "You're Lucian Quinn. I'm Tony Moretti." After the introductions are complete, Tony opens the door and waves us into the dim interior. Instead of going upstairs to his office, he leads us to a table near the rear of the large room. "No one's around yet, so we'll talk here. Can I get either of you a drink?" We both decline and take a seat. "I talked to my uncle. My father apparently wasn't so much interested in Wrenn Wear as he was Jasmine Wrenn. According to him, they were lovers for quite a while, and Draco was crazy about her. He used the term 'obsessed.' I guess things were getting intense until Hunter found out about it. Draco wanted her to leave Hunter and be with him. But she claimed that he'd never let her take the children, and she couldn't leave them behind, so she ended it. My uncle said that Draco came around to see him and was drunk and out of his mind over it. He wanted to go to the Wrenn's and steal Jasmine away. And he didn't care if he had to go through Hunter to do it. But somehow, my uncle convinced him that if anything happened to her children, Jasmine would never forgive him. He told him that if he really loved her, then he needed to respect and understand her decision. A woman should always put her children before her man."

Luc sits forward looking thoughtful. "So he bought Wrenn Wear to be near Jasmine?"

Tony laughs softly, before shooting me a look. "Not quite. Draco may have been in love with her, but I know how he thought. It wouldn't have taken very long for jealousy and resentment to set in. He wasn't a man who was used to hearing the word no or being second best to anyone."

"He wanted Wrenn Wear because she loved it." I nod in understanding. That makes sense. I always knew there was more there than what I was told. Now the pieces are sliding neatly into place. "Then he basically kicked her out on the street and didn't give a damn whether the company survived or not."

Tony shrugs. "Revenge for her having the audacity to pick her family over him."

"Your father sounds like a real sweet guy," Luc quips.

I answer for Tony automatically, feeling that I know parts of Draco better than his son does. "Things were very black and white with him. Regardless of his feelings, he wasn't the type you'd want to disappoint. Her leaving him would have been the highest form of insult. There's no way he'd let that stand. So he went after something he knew was important to her."

"She's lucky that's all he did," Tony says quietly. "For him, it was an act of mercy. But in the end, he took more than he'd bargained for. My uncle said that he was a fucking mess when he found out that she'd died. Said he kept saying that Hunter had killed her. If he and Victor hadn't died, I'm not sure that Hunter would still be around today. Regardless of the truth, if he believed that Hunter was responsible, he'd have avenged her."

"Without question," I agree. Sitting forward, I add, "So now we know more about the connection, but this still doesn't make everything add up. Hunter knew years ago about the part I played in the takeover of Wrenn Wear. Why wait this long to come after me?"

"Delayed gratification?" Luc tosses out. "Although that seems highly unlikely. You've had no other interactions with him or any of his holdings since then, have you?"

I shake my head. "No, I've gone over it in my head more than once, and until the moment Jade came to work for me, there'd been nothing since Wrenn Wear. Hell, he doesn't have anything that I'm remotely interested in. Plus, he's dirty money, and I've tried damn hard to steer clear of that."

"There's still a key piece of the pie missing here," Luc states. "We need everyone we have on Hunter. I don't believe for a minute that he woke up one day two years ago and decided you needed to pay. Something set this in motion, and I, for one, want to know what."

"That makes two of us," Tony chimes in. "One of my men is digging into it. Fuck, I'd be curious even if this didn't involve my father. But seeing as it does, I want to know what in the fuck is going on."

"It's time for me to rattle a few cages," I add. "I'm going to pay Wrenn a visit. He's been sneaking around behind my back for years. I think even he'd expect me to confront him about it."

"You'll be giving away the fact that you know about Jade," Luc points out.

"I'm aware of that. But there is very little to be gained from keeping him in the dark to that fact. Plus, it forces Jade to continue playing a dangerous game with him. No, I think it's better to shift his attention fully to me and hope it pisses him off so badly that he gets sloppy and fucks up."

"You need to watch your back, brother," Tony interjects. "Wrenn is dangerous because he's unpredictable. If you push him into a corner, he may declare all-out war on you."

From anyone else, those words would sound overly dramatic, but with a father like Draco Moretti, Tony understands mobsters better than most people ever will. He spent too many years with a father who never bothered to shield him from the violence that was so much a part of his daily life. "I'll make sure I'm covered."

"We'll make sure everyone is," Luc adds firmly. "Your family is my family, literally and figuratively."

Fuck, my daughter did marry someone just like me. I bite back my grin at that thought. I'll never admit it to Quinn, but I like that he's fully capable of unleashing hell if the circumstances require it, and he'll go to apocalyptic proportions for Lia and Lara. I get to my feet, and the other two men follow suit. We say our farewells with a promise to keep each other updated. When Luc drops me in the front of Falco, I don't bother going inside. Instead, I walk to the parking garage where my car is waiting. I asked Denny to have it ready and it is. As I climb behind the wheel and drive toward Hunter Wrenn's office, I feel no fear even though I know that very shortly I'll be setting things into motion that are twenty years in the making. Love may have started this war, but I'll end it—any way necessary.

JADE

"WHAT?" I SHRIEK. MY VOICE echoes loudly off the walls of Lee's office as I sit down heavily in one of the chairs in front of his desk. "Are you sure?"

"I think I know who Lee Jacks is," Jacey says dryly. "But what I don't know is why he's here. Does the man have a death wish? Father has been in an uglier than usual mood lately, so this isn't a great time for a friendly, unannounced drop-in."

"I have no idea why he's there," I whisper as my heart hammers in my chest. "Couldn't you listen at the door?" I suggest. "Then call the police if you hear any loud noises." *Like a gunshot.*

"He came to the lair of the beast, so he brought this on himself," Jacey adds dramatically. "I couldn't believe it when I saw him in the lobby. I trailed him upstairs half expecting him to be thrown out, but instead, he made it in. I'm sure dear old dad's curiosity got the better of him, and he couldn't resist knowing what had brought his enemy to the door."

"He's going to tell Daddy that he knows about me and see where that leads. There's no other explanation for it."

"Jade . . ." my sister hisses, sounding appalled. *Oh shit. I said that out loud?* "You didn't tell Lee everything, did you? Surely, you realize that this could pour gasoline on an already blazing fire."

"He found out on his own," I say defensively. I don't bother to add that I would have told him anyway. It serves no purpose now other than to drive more distance between us. "He also saw the bruises on my neck from Father and was beyond pissed. It wasn't hard for him to come to the right conclusion. So I told him what little I knew and that was it. Truthfully, he handled it far better than I could have hoped." Lowering my voice, I add, "He told me he loves me."

There is dead silence for so long that I think she's disconnected the call before I hear a sigh, followed by a snort. "You are so delusional, Jade. You always have been. Lee Jacks is no different than our father. You serve a purpose to him now, which is why you're still around. But when this game between him and Dad runs its course, you'll be out on your ass before you can even process what's happening. Lee isn't going to take you away from your life and turn you into a fairy princess. Plus, let's get real. I'm sure you've seen the type of women who he spends time with, and they're nothing like you. You lick at his heels and stare up at him in adoration with those big eyes. So maybe he scratches you behind the ears a few times, but that's it. If he settles down with one woman, it will be a tall, thin trophy wife who knows how to play her part in his world."

My eyes narrow with anger as her words hit me like bricks. Piercing through my bubble of happiness with one small dose of reality. Damn her. She knows my weaknesses, and she's pushing at them all right now. *Why did I just give her more ammunition?* I manage to keep my voice level as I ask, "So I assume you're the type of woman who Lee will end up with? Isn't that who you're describing? Maybe you don't want to see me with him because you want him for yourself."

She laughs cheerfully as if I've said something truly hysterical. Finally, she gets enough control. "Rest assured, Jade, I'm not after Lee. And yes, while I might be the perfect woman for him, *he* is not what I want in my life. I've spent too many years as father's right-hand to want to marry a duplicate of him. At some point, I'd like some peace, even if it's only for a few hours in the evening. And that's not likely to happen with Lee Jacks by my side."

It irritates me that she talks as if he would be hers if *she* were interested. Her overinflated ego doesn't seem to consider for one moment, that maybe Lee wouldn't have her even if she begged. And regardless of all the uncertainty, that's one thing I know in my heart is true. She's everything he'd avoid in a romantic partner, but I don't bother to argue. Instead, I say, "Let me know if you find out anything on your end. Otherwise, I'll wait for Lee to return and see what he has to say."

"I have better things to do with my time than listen at keyholes, so you're on your own. Just check out the news tonight. If they kill each other, it'll probably make the evening edition."

"You're so not funny," I snap before ending the call. I drop my head onto the back of my chair as I whisper to the empty room, "What are you doing, Lee?"

I'm at a stopping point, so I quickly close the office and lock away a few important files before collecting my purse and removing the keycard Lee left for me. Within a few moments, I'm at the door of his penthouse, and strangely enough, it already feels like home. *But for how much longer?* What if my father attempts to discredit me by filling Lee's head with a bunch of lies? Will he believe them? It's certainly something my father would do. He'll be so angry that Lee knows about my deception that he's likely to do or say anything without thinking it through first. And that will be dangerous to us all. The urge to rush to Lee's side and protect him is so strong, but I know in my heart that my appearance there would make everything worse. My father has no respect for me, so it may discredit Lee in his eyes even more. No, I need to remain here for now and hope that somehow Lee gets whatever made him go there today. He's working some type of plan. He can take care of himself, and he won't be this brazen without a goal in mind.

Rufus strolls through the foyer as if he owns the place. He stops a few feet away and scans the area before meowing plaintively. I swear the damn cat is disappointed that it's me and not Lee. After only a few days, his allegiance has switched firmly to the man of the house. Their standoff that night was a real bonding experience. I shake my head before reaching down to scratch him behind the ears. "You can't complain, boy. We're both just lucky that he let you stay inside instead of putting you out on the balcony as he wanted to. I wouldn't push my luck, though, if I were you."

I go through the motions of feeding Rufus and making a sandwich for myself, but I'm a nervous wreck. There's no way I can relax until I hear from Lee, so I give up on doing anything other than pacing. By the time he gets home, I'll have either collapsed from fatigue or there will be a hole in his expensive marble floors. I halt in my tracks as one horrible thought occurs to me. What if Lee decides I'm not worth the hell I'm putting him through? Will there really be life after him? Realistically I know there must be, but in my heart, I'm not certain I'll survive it, and I pray I never have to find out.

CHAPTER TWELVE

———◆———

LEE

MY FIRST THOUGHT WHEN I see Hunter Wrenn for the first time in almost twenty years is that time has not been kind to him. If I look closely, I can see a vague resemblance to Jade, but it's faint. The thing I do notice immediately is the sense of evil that emanates from him. I've rubbed elbows with some soulless men in my time. Ones with zero empathy or conscience, and that's what I see in Wrenn. Victor and Draco did a lot of shit I didn't agree with or condone, but they didn't become soulless. Certainly, there were times when they could conveniently set being humane aside, but they suffered regrets over certain things in their lives. I doubt Wrenn can say the same. He remains behind his massive desk, not bothering with the formality of a handshake. No doubt, he thinks he's in the power position. "Jacks, this is a surprise." His voice is laced with amusement, but his eyes are coldly calculating. He's thrown by my visit.

I don't bother waiting for him to extend an invitation. Instead, I walk forward and take a seat in front of him. His mouth tightens at my audacity, but I could give a good fuck. I'm not here to ask for his daughter's hand in marriage. Hell, if I have my way, he'll never set eyes on her again. Any man who can use his child in the way he has doesn't deserve that privilege. He had no idea what I'd do when I found out about Jade, but with my reputation, he had to have thought that the worst-case scenario was possible—even probable. And I'm confident that it didn't give him one moment's pause. He remains standing—again another attempt at control. He's wasting his time. Nothing about this man intimidates me although the very fact he is breathing offends the fuck out of me. I make a deliberate show of straightening my cuff links before brushing an imaginary piece of lint from my slacks. A quick glance his way shows a muscle twitching in his cheek. He's angry. But he's also nervous, which proves he's not a complete idiot. Finally, I relax back in my seat as if I haven't a care in the world. "I thought after all these years that we should finally meet face to face. After all, you did think enough of me to send your daughter Jade to Falco." I force a smile to my lips. "I owe you my thanks for that. She's an amazing woman. She must have taken after her mother."

He may have had a sneaking suspicion that I know who Jade is, but he really needs to work on his poker face. "What the fuck is this all about?" Ah, the gloves are off and all pretenses of civility are gone. "You barge in here uninvited, spouting some nonsense. You may have nothing better to do, but I can assure you that I have. Now, if that's all—"

"Sit down and shut the fuck up," I bark in a voice that brooks no arguments. He stiffens but surprisingly takes a seat. *Pussy.* He's used to being the bully and doesn't know how to deal with an authority figure, so he looks like a sullen child now. But isn't that the way of all spineless cowards? I get to my feet and begin pacing his office. Fear literally comes from him in waves, and I wonder fleetingly if he's even aware of it. He's broken faster than I estimated, but I'm not a fool. Evil men are even more dangerous when they're backed into a corner.

He's not stupid enough to try anything here, but as soon as I'm gone, he'll be calling in reinforcements. He'll be too fucking scared not to. "Let me bring you up to speed here, Wrenn, so we can have a reasonable discussion afterward. You planted your daughter at Falco to acquire incriminating information that you could use against me. You also paid off several people in my employ to cover her identity. All this under the guise of revenge for my part in the acquisition of Wrenn Wear almost twenty years ago."

"You killed my wife," he blurts out, but it sounds scripted.

There's no real emotion there. Certainly, that many years might dull the pain a bit, but the only thing I can detect is anger, and I feel in my gut that even that isn't directed at me. But I have a pretty good idea who it is aimed at. "That's bullshit, and you know it. I think your real problem here is that you're still pissed over your wife daring to prefer Draco Moretti to you. That must have been quite a blow to your pride." Momentarily, I see the intense fury he's trying to contain. His fists are clenched, and his nostrils flare as he fights for control. *And we have a winner, folks.* He wants to lash out, yet he also doesn't want to give me the satisfaction.

"You don't know what you're talking about, Jacks," he spits out. "Moretti taking control of Wrenn Wear was the only association she had with him. And if you knew anything at all, you'd know that was the true love of her life. Not some thug who took things that didn't belong to him."

I shrug indifferently "Whatever lets you sleep at night. The word is, Jasmine and Draco were an item for quite a while. Not just a brief fling because she wanted to leave you. Take the kids. But you used them as your trump card, and she panicked and fell back in line. But I guess living with you was too much for her, hence the drinking. Draco taking Wrenn Wear, living without her lover . . . One drink too many and *boom*, she wrapped her car around a tree." I pause, stop my pacing, and look him straight in the eye. "Or did she?"

His face goes ashen at my insinuation. Truthfully, the last part had been thrown in for no other reason than to piss him off, but his reaction gives me pause. "Whatever you're insinuating, you're wrong. You know nothing," he all but shouts. Color floods his face once again as his temper soars. "My family is none of your fucking business!"

I stride to his desk and lean across it until he's only inches away. He moves back to get more distance between us. "You made it my business when you sent your daughter to Falco to spy on me," I snarl. I struggle for composure, as the urge to pull him from his chair is nearly impossible to resist. But that's not why I'm here. He'd love nothing better than for me to lay hands on him because he'll have me arrested for assault before I make it out of the damn building. So I carefully pull away and regroup. When I speak again, my voice is level—almost pleasant. No doubt, it's making his skin crawl. "You know, Wrenn, you're right about one thing. I don't know nearly enough about your family—but it's an oversight I intend to correct immediately." I stride toward the door and open it before turning around to lob my last grenade. "After all, Jade is mine now, so it only seems right that there be no secrets between us. I've always found that dirty laundry has the power to stink up a room at the most inopportune times, haven't you?" I don't wait for a reply. Instead, I leave him there with the look of a man who has been caught with his dick in his hand. Some days, I get off on being an asshole, and this is one of them. But for now, it's time to go home to Jade. The bait has been cast, and if I were a betting man, I'd say that Hunter picks immediately. *Game on, you smug bastard.*

JADE

MY CELL PHONE RINGS, AND I glance at the caller ID. I ponder ignoring it, but she'll just keep calling until I give in. So with a sigh, I click answer. "Yes," I say shortly. She never calls for a sisterly chat, so she wants something from me. I've often wondered who she talks to about things. I can't think of anyone she's ever been close to. Apparently, Wrenn women don't cultivate close relationships with other females. But I do have Lia, Rose, and Kara.

"I need you to come pick me up," she says without preamble. "My fucking car won't start."

"Call the auto club," I suggest. It's what I do rather than contacting her. Heck, hitchhiking is preferable.

She releases an irritated breath before saying slowly and deliberately. "I did, Jade. But they're backed up for like two hours. Everyone in this godforsaken city has an emergency tonight. I don't want to sit in a dark, deserted parking garage alone." Before I can answer, she adds quietly, "As if you'd really give a damn if anything happened to me. Just forget I even asked."

I roll my eyes in exasperation, but considering she's not there to see it, the gesture seems pointless. We both know I'll do what she wants because there's no way I could live with it on the outside chance that some poor bastard attacks her. "Where are you?" I ask, already getting to my feet.

Now that she's gotten her way, all trace of softness is gone, and she says impatiently, "At Wrenn, naturally. Could you get a move on, I have plans tonight." She disconnects the call without bothering to say *goodbye* or heaven forbid, *thank you*. I could carry her on my back across a freaking river and not receive any gratitude.

I grab my purse and rush out, making it to my car in record time. I consider calling Lee to see if he's left my father's office but decide against it. Surely, if Dad is still there, Jacey doesn't need me to rescue her. I'll wait until I get back to his place to find out what happened during his impromptu meeting.

Jacey is standing next to her car when I pull into the garage. It is rather deserted and creepy. I've never noticed the lack of after-hours security here. My father really should do better for his employees, but I doubt he gives a damn. I park next to her and lower my window when she doesn't make a move to get in the passenger seat. "I thought you were in such a rush."

"Could you give me a hand?" she huffs out. "I have a couple of boxes to carry, plus my briefcase." *Shit, what else, princess?* I leave the engine idling and the door open, hoping that one trip will do it. She has her trunk open, and I'm leaning over, looking at nothing but empty space, when pain explodes in my skull. My vision blurs as I struggle to remain on my feet. "I'm sorry, Jade. I don't want to do this, but it's either you or me. I really have no choice." *What?* Her words make no sense. I am attempting to steady myself and turn around, when there is another blow. This time, I can't hold on. My legs begin to buckle beneath me as the world goes black.

CHAPTER THIRTEEN

———◆———

LEE

I'VE BEEN HOME FOR ALMOST an hour, and there's still no word from Jade. I stopped by Falco on the way in to check my messages and to see if she was still there, but security said that she'd been gone for a while. I assumed she'd be here, so when she wasn't, I checked the parking garage. Her car is gone. I wasn't overly concerned at that point, thinking she may have run home for some clothes. I used the time to talk with Luc about my meeting with Wrenn and about hiring additional security for our families.

When all that has been taken care of, there still is so sign of her, and she isn't answering her phone, so I begin to get nervous. Warning bells are sounding in my gut, and that always spells trouble. I have my phone in hand, ready to call Luc again, when it rings. I look and breathe a sigh of relief when I see Jade's name—well, actually *Liza's* on the caller ID. "Hey, where are you?" I ask, feeling instantly better.

"Lee." Her voice is low and shaky, barely audible. *Fuck.*

"What's wrong? Where are you?" I fire off the questions, as I begin pacing. "Are you okay?"

Her line is silent for a long moment before she says,

"I–I don't know. I think Jacey hit me. It's so dark, and I can't sit up." Her voice is rising, and I hear the panic, bordering on hysteria. I want to lose my shit right along with her, but that will accomplish nothing. I need to calm her down and find out what's going on.

"Jade," I say soothingly, yet firmly. "Sweetheart, take a deep breath. You must focus so I can help you. Now start at the beginning and tell me what happened."

I hear her do as I've instructed. "Jacey called me to ask me to come get her because her car wouldn't start. I'm not sure, but someone hit me in the back of my head. Then she said something about being sorry and that's the last thing I recall. I woke up in the dark and tried to get up. But I can only move a little on either side."

I'm already racing through the lobby of my building before she finishes talking. My car is still parked at the curb, and I fumble for my keys before unlocking it and jumping inside. But I haven't a fucking clue which direction to head in. I consider going to Luc's briefly, but I don't want to panic Lia, so instead, I go to the man with resources I need. "Okay. Let's work this out. Can you find the flashlight button on your phone? Then you can flip it on and look around." I notice there is a roaring noise in the background, but I can't identify the sound. I hear her fingers touching the keys, then she shrieks.

"Oh my God! Lee, I'm in the trunk of Jacey's car. Or at least I think it's still hers. I remember now that she had some boxes she needed me to help her with, and that's when someone hit me. She must have pushed me inside."
What. The. Fuck? Her sister?

I'm furious. Her fucking sister will never walk if something happens to Jade. Keeping it together is almost impossible right now. "Listen to my voice, baby," I murmur soothingly. "You're going to be okay. I'll find you, I promise. Just stay on the line with me. If you hear the car stop, hide the phone. I'm going to have it traced." I pull to a stop in front of Tony's club and leap from my car, not bothering to shut the door. As luck has it, Tony is standing a few feet away smoking a cigarette with the guy I recognize from my first visit here. He gives me a questioning look. "I need your help." He doesn't ask questions. He nods once, then tosses his cigarette onto the sidewalk before turning to the entrance of his building and walking inside. I follow him as I tell Jade, "Hang tight, sweetheart. I need to tell my friend what's happened. Remember what you're supposed to do if necessary."

"I got it. Just find me—please." Her voice is still high and tight with fear, but she's holding her own. I'm so fucking proud of her. Most people would be freaking the fuck out right now, but she's hanging tough. *That's my woman.*

"I will, baby. I'm working on it now. I-I love you," I add. *I've never told anyone that before. Apart from Jade.* My voice sounds rusty as I utter the words. Yet as if they were always waiting for her, they're so right on my tongue. Tony is standing in the center of the club with his hands on his hips as I mute my side of the conversation. I don't want to cause Jade more panic as we discuss the situation. "Jade's been taken. She thinks she's in the trunk of her sister's car. She has her cell phone, so I need to trace the call before it's discovered. I haven't a fucking clue where she's being taken. I doubt she'll be at the Wrenn family home."

"What is Jade's phone number?" He tosses me a napkin and a pen from the nearby bar, and I quickly jot it down before handing it back. He has his own phone out now, quickly punching buttons before lifting it to his ear. "Marco, get here now. Trace this number," he says sharply. He relays the digits and ends the call. No other information is given, nor apparently are any questions asked. And I recognize the name of the man who he's just spoken to. Marco Moretti is no one's errand boy. He's a heavy hitter within the organization. Tony studies me for a moment before saying quietly, "This won't end well for the Wrenns. Jade has immunity because she belongs to you, but the other two are fair game. And you can bet your ass Marco will know the connection between Draco and Hunter."

I nod. "I could give two fucks what happens to them. They punched their ticket when they dared to take Jade. They should hope Marco is who they face because this is personal."

"Understood." I fill him in on my visit to Wrenn's office, pausing to check on Jade every few minutes. I've just finished relaying the last of it when a tall hulk of a man dressed in a black suit walks in. *Marco.* He and Tony were close growing up, and it's obvious by the way that they embrace that the connection is still there. "Thanks for coming so quickly, brother." Tony claps his shoulder.

Marco then turns toward me and extends a hand. "Lee, it's been a long time."

"It has indeed," I say warmly, seeing traces of the boy I knew in the man before me. "I appreciate it," I add, and he inclines his head.

"You're family," he says. And that explains it all. I hear my name and realize Jade is calling me. I moved the phone away from my ear when talking to Marco and hadn't realized it. I hastily raise it again asking, "What's wrong, baby? I'm right here."

"I think the car has stopped," she whispers. There is no longer any background noise, which unsettles me, too. While they were moving, she was relatively safe.

"All right, honey. Leave the call connected on mute, but put the phone back in your pocket."

"I'm scared," she says. "What if I never see you again?"

Her words, as well as the shakiness of her voice, nearly breaks my heart. I strive for confidence that I'm far from feeling. "I'll find you, piccolo uccello. Just hang on a little longer. Do what they say and try to buy us a little time."

"Okay," she says uncertainly. "I love you, Lee."

"Me too, baby," I murmur, then swallow hard as she does as instructed and puts the phone away. "We need to trace that call now. They've stopped. If we can at least find the general area, we'll have a starting point. Based on how long she's been moving, they should still be in the state."

Tony looks at Marco who is already typing on his phone. "My guy is talking to his contact. We have an approximate grid around the Pisgah Forest, but we'll be wasting our time without narrowing it down. There are so many subdivisions and wooded areas there that finding a needle in a haystack would be fucking easier."

Apparently having the same thought, Tony and I head toward the door. "We'll at least be mobile when we get some more information," he says. He pulls a set of keys from his pocket and clicks to unlock a black Land Rover a few feet away at the curb. "I'll drive so you can monitor Jade." He tosses me his own phone. "Call Lucian. Fill him in. Let's make certain everyone is on guard until we know what the fuck we're dealing with."

"I've tightened security and so has he. But too fucking late. I'll let both he and Pete know." I quickly fill both Luc and Pete in and am grateful how calm they are under pressure. They both agree to add another layer of protection to our family and ask to be contacted as soon as I have further information. Even though they want to help, I tell them they can do that by taking care of the people we love.

I hand Tony his phone back, then say softly, "Marco needs to know that the person who orchestrated this is mine."

Tony doesn't respond for a moment, then he glances my

way before turning back to the road. "Family is a funny thing, Lee. Jade may hate her father, but if you're the one who kills him, she might not be able to get past it. Something like that—even when warranted—has a way of changing the way a person looks at you."

I run a hand through my hair in frustration. "Don't you think I know that? But what kind of fucking man would I be if I let this stand?"

"I know you did shit when necessary for my dad and Victor. But at your core, you value human life. I also know that you believe in an eye for an eye," he adds. I know without him putting it into words that he's talking about the bastard who hurt Lia. I've never told anyone what happened the day I did what needed to be done to ensure the safety of my only child, nor will I. That's yet another secret I'll take to the grave. And I'll never lose a moment's sleep over it.

"Tony, you and I might not be involved in the daily operations of the Moretti's, but we're still men who think differently than most. Sometimes, the long-term potential of a threat must be weighed against the collateral damage that terminating it will bring."

He nods in agreement. "You may lose Jade to make that happen."

It's nothing I haven't already thought myself. And even though it guts me to think of a life without her, I can't let any further harm come to her. I'll gladly sacrifice my own happiness if it means she's out there in the world living a life without fear. "If it comes to that, then yes." I put my phone to my ear again, and there is nothing. Complete and utter silence. I pull it away and begin cursing when I see that the call has dropped out. *Fucking hell.* "We've been disconnected," I say tensely. "I bet they found the damn phone." The one link I have with her is gone. *What if I'm too late?*

"Maybe her battery died," Tony offers, sounding calm

and unruffled. I almost want to hit him for that, but rationally, I know he's trying to keep me from losing it. The sound of his phone ringing is like a gunshot in the car. I jerk involuntarily, before releasing a steading breath. "Marco," he says by way of greeting before going silent. Finally, he ends the call and once again hands the phone to me. "He's texting me an address. When you have it, enter it in the GPS."

"Did he have any other information?" I ask as I scan his phone for the incoming message.

"They tracked the signal to an area about five miles from here. It's a more remote section with only two houses in the two-mile radius near the cell tower. He's also sending the names those homes are deeded to. If we're lucky, she's at one of them and not the surrounding area. It'll make finding her a hell of a lot easier than looking through the dense forest at night."

His phone chimes, and I click to read the message. "Nicholas Hider is at 1122 Green Pine Way, and April Chester is at 1125 Green Pine Way." Something niggles in the back of my mind as I enter the first address. *Fuck, what am I missing?*

Tony does a U-turn and goes in the opposite direction as the route guidance begins. "Do either of those ring a bell?" he asks as he slows to take a sharp curve ahead.

"I'm almost certain I've heard of April Chester before. Or fuck, maybe it's the street name. All I know is that— wait a minute." I quickly punch in Luc's number, and when he answers, I don't bother with a greeting. "April Chester?"

He's quiet for a long moment before hissing, "Holy fuck. Tell me that bitch isn't behind this."

"Who is she?" I demand, then it's there. I barely hear him as I turn to Tony and say, "Go to the second address. 1125 Green Pine." He shoots me a questioning looks. "April Chester is Monique Chandler."

"What in the hell is going on?" Luc demands, sounding about as shell-shocked as I feel.

"We traced Jade's phone, and there are two houses in the area. One of them is in April Chester's name. Isn't she in prison for years to come?" I ask, knowing that Luc would have kept tabs on the deranged woman who had been instrumental in putting his family through hell.

"You're damn right she is," he grits out. "I'll call you back."

I hit the dashboard in disgust. Tony shakes his head in commiseration. "This is some fucked-up shit. I remember Monique Chandler from all that went down with your daughter." He pauses a moment before adding, "She's still in prison, Lee, because I'd have known otherwise." I glance his way. "Like I said, you're a Moretti, and that extends to your daughter and granddaughter." He laughs, but it's devoid of humor. "That bitch should have been taken out. We should have all known better than to let her live. Thinking of her suffering in that maximum-security prison gave me calm. We both know there are no coincidences where people like that are concerned."

"No, they're not," I agree flatly. "What I don't see if how this fits together. It's like trying to push a circle puzzle piece into a square slot."

"This shit does get weirder and weirder." Tony sighs. "I need to update Marco so the men aren't wasting their time looking at other areas." He quickly places a call and brings the other man up to speed. "I assume you're packing? If not, there's a 9mm in the glove box."

I open my jacket, showing him my shoulder holster also with a 9mm in it. "Got it covered. You?"

"Always. Would you leave a nightclub in the morning hours without protection?" The GPS announces our destination, and Tony turns down a small driveway, surrounded by trees. A few feet ahead are two black Escalade SUVs. Marco steps out of the back of one, when

Tony pulls in behind it. He rolls down the window, asking the other man, "Seen anyone?"

Marco shakes his head. "No. Mike did recon, and there's a house about half a mile further up. It's deserted other than that. There's a Mercedes and a BMW in the driveway. But no one outside. I told him to hold the perimeter and let me know if anything changes."

"Good," Tony says. He turns to me adding, "I think we should go in on foot from here. No sense alerting them to our presence until necessary. The element of surprise is always a good thing to have."

I'm already opening my door, having come to the same conclusion. By the time we've reached the first SUV, six other men are waiting. I recognize a few of them from years back. He turns to me and asks, "How do you want this to go down? We go in guns blazing and hope they're not prepared or try to slide in a back window and avoid detection for as long as we can?" Marco has the confidence a man can only acquire when he's faced his own death numerous times. He has no fear, only a healthy respect in his abilities to defeat anything thrown his way.

"Let's go low." My decision isn't based on trepidation for my own safety. Considering the anger I feel toward the people who abducted Jade, I want to choose the direct approach in this instance. But, my reason is centered solely on Jade. If she is caught in the crossfire of a shootout, I'll never forgive myself.

Tony nods. "Especially as we don't know exactly who we're dealing with. Or where they're keeping Jade."

Marco nods. "Mike says there's a door to what appears to be a basement in the back. I think that's our best point of entry. I'll leave a man there and in front to nab anyone attempting to come or go. Eight of us should be more than enough to handle anything from them."

I motion for Marco to fall back as we start moving out.

When I reach his side, I say quietly, "I want to take care of the person responsible for this."

He shoots a questioning look at Tony, who nods once in affirmation. Marco shrugs before saying, "Your woman, your revenge." Then he adds, "But if it becomes a matter of one of our lives—yours included—safety will supersede that."

"Of course," I reply without question. He's right. The Morettis are not a group led by their emotions. The survival of the family is of paramount importance to them. Especially after several senseless deaths high up in their organization. Draco's murder was a classic example of what can happen when you let your guard down. Had there been due diligence in his protection detail that day, both he and Victor might still be alive.

As we all prowl through the rapidly darkening forest, I feel a foreboding that makes my blood run cold. For as simple as our plan is, I know that what we face will be anything but. I have no idea exactly how it will happen, but tonight there will be a loss of life. It had been there in Tony's expression as well before we began walking toward the house. That's the fucked-up thing about intuition. You may be certain that disaster is just around the corner, but without the specifics surrounding it, there's no way to predict the outcome. After the smoke clears, Jade better be still alive. Because she is probably the only truly innocent one among us. If I go down, I'll be taking the fucker with me who put Jade in this position. There's no way I'll die and leave her behind to face any more hell. This fucking ends tonight.

JADE

MY SISTER PACES THE FLOOR while our father and one of his goons talk quietly in another room. "We need to get out of here, Jacey," I implore her yet again. "Surely, you can see that someone is going to get hurt."

She snorts before rolling her eyes in my direction. "Tell me something I don't know. This was a big mistake from the beginning, but you know Daddy dearest. Your boyfriend is the one who created this whole mess. If he hadn't rattled the old man's cage, none of this would be happening. But no, he had to drop by and make threats." She looks almost pleased as she adds, "I've never seen our father so freaked out before. Whatever Lee said must have been good."

My head still throbs, and the feeling has long been gone from my hands that are bound in front of me. "You hit me," I accuse. "I'm your sister, and you kidnapped me. What in the hell is wrong with you, Jacey? You could go to prison for this. And do you think Father would cross the road to bail you out? No, he'll make you the bad guy, while he swears he knew nothing about it."

"First off, I didn't lay a hand on you." She rolls her eyes. "That was Daddy's henchman. I mean really, do you think I could have lifted you on my own and put you in the trunk of my car?" She snorts at the absurdity. "As for him turning on me, I'm smart enough to have a little insurance." She holds up her phone before lowering her voice. "You've got to love these handy recording apps. I never attend a meeting anymore without turning mine on."

She acts as if she expects praise for her ingenuity, but I simply look at her in disgust. "What made you such a bitter person?"

She ignores my question, then surprises me by tossing her phone in my lap. "That's my favorite one, check it out." *Is she insane? Wait, what?* I squint down, trying to make out the writing on the screen. Then my eyes widen in shock.

I SAVED YOUR LIFE TONIGHT. DAD WANTED TO HAVE HIS GOONS HANDLE EVERYTHING, BUT I VOLUNTEERED TO DRIVE YOU HERE AFTER LENNY HELPED YOU INTO THE BACK OF MY CAR. YOU NEED TO PLAY ALONG WITH WHATEVER I SAY UNTIL I CAN FIGURE A WAY OUT OF THIS. KEEP THE NASTINESS GOING. IT'LL SEEM REAL SINCE THAT'S THE WAY YOU USUALLY TALK TO ME. OH, I KNEW YOU HAD YOUR PHONE IN YOUR POCKET, BUT I TOLD LENNY I'D THROWN IT AWAY. I HAD TO TAKE IT BEFORE ANYONE FOUND IT, THOUGH. HOPE YOU MADE GOOD USE OF IT BEFORE THEN.

I read the words again, barely daring to believe them. Is she on my side? *Careful, don't trust her.* My head is screaming for me to exercise caution, but when I look into her eyes, there's something I haven't seen in a long time—hell, maybe ever. There's sorrow and possibly even love. *I must have taken a harder hit to the head than I thought.* With no other options, I clear my throat and decide to go along with it for now. "Where are we, and what in the fuck is going on?"

Giving me a smile of approval, she reaches out to take her phone and squeezes my hand before pulling away. Then she assumes her usual role of a condescending bitch. "I have no idea and couldn't care less. I'm sorry it isn't up to your recent standards. I imagine Lee has a pretty sweet place." She puts her hands on her hips and shakes her head mockingly. "But he really should learn to keep his mouth shut. You have him to thank for this. Well, *if* you ever see him again, which is doubtful."

Our verbal sparring continues for several more minutes. I'm at the point where I no longer know what's real and what's pretend. Then I see something out of the corner of my eye that has me jerking to attention. *Lee?* I have only a split second to wonder if I'm hallucinating before all hell breaks loose. Jacey squeals in alarm and grabs my bound hands, pulling me up and across the room. We crouch down in the corner behind a chair, and she unties my hands as the sounds of shouting fills the air. I hear what I think is someone fighting and then there is silence. Jacey and I look at each other in dread, wondering if we're about to be saved or if all hope is lost. *Dear God, let him be all right.*

CHAPTER FOURTEEN

———◆———

LEE

MARCO INSISTS ON TAKING THE lead as he quickly picks the basement lock and we file into the dark space. I can make out what looks to be some old furniture, but otherwise, the space appears unfinished. One of Marco's guys brings out a small flashlight and does a quick search of the area, making sure there's no one here before we move toward the staircase in the center of the room. "This feels off," Tony murmurs behind me, and I incline my head in agreement. The unease of earlier is becoming progressively stronger.

Marco doesn't seem to share our sentiments as he approaches the first step confidently. We reach a door at the top of the landing, and he turns. "Follow my lead and everyone stay low." I see the glint of his gun in the shadowy light. My own feels cool and unusually heavy in my grip, but also comforting. I'm an expert marksman— something else I can thank Victor for. He believed in being prepared for all eventualities in life. Marco opens the door silently, and one by one, we step into a wide hallway. He motions toward the right, indicting where we'll check first. We make our way steadily through three large bedrooms and a bathroom before we reach what looks like the foyer. Then almost as if we've stepped on a hornet's nest, shapes begin pouring from every direction. Warnings are shouted and blows are exchanged, but strangely, no one attempts to fire their gun. In fact, Marco and his crew appear to have holstered theirs in favor of hand-to-hand combat. *Fuck it. I need to blow off some steam.* Tony and I follow suit, and even though we're massively outnumbered, we still manage to inflict considerable damage on Wrenn's crew before a shot is fired, freezing everyone in his place.

"Welcome to the party, gentlemen," purrs an amused voice that I heard only hours earlier. "I must say, it took you long enough." Hunter Wrenn strolls into view, looking absolutely thrilled at our arrival. He pauses before me. "Good of you to bring some friends along, Jacks. How about we make ourselves comfortable?" He barely spares a glance at Tony and the rest of the Moretti men as he motions for his guys to escort us into a nearby room. At first, there seems to be no one else here, but then I see movement, and my heart surges as I recognize Jade. *Thank God, she's alive.* The other woman I assume is Jacey. I've seen her a few times in passing over the years but never for more than a moment. She's thinner than Jade—tiny and waif-like. They share the same blond hair and bone structure—but there's a hard weariness about Jacey that says she's seen far too much in her life. At present, she and Jade are holding hands and staring at us with varying degrees of surprise and anxiety. I see Jacey dart a glance in her father's direction before straightening and dropping Jade's hand. Jacey was instrumental in Jade's kidnapping, so I feel absolutely nothing but revulsion toward her.

Not giving a damn what Hunter thinks, I wipe what is no doubt a trickle of blood from my lip from the melee in the foyer and ask Jade gently, "Are you all right, piccolo uccello?""

Her eyes are huge as she nods. "I'm good. Are . . . you?" Her voice breaks before she finishes her question, and I know that I'm probably banged up. Although I've had worse.

Hunter clicks his tongue. "So touching. Obviously, my daughter took after her mother in more ways than one." He spreads out his hands before him. "You give them every advantage, yet they still prefer slumming." He points at Jacey. "This one has potential. She's almost as ruthless as I am. But she's a woman, so I'm afraid she's already reached the top of her potential. There are things in life that only men are capable of." Jacey's jerks as if struck physically, but she keeps her mouth shut. Waves of resentment emanate from her, yet Hunter appears to be the only one utterly oblivious to it.

The gun in my holster is burning a fucking hole through me as I long to grab it and put an end to this arrogant motherfucker. But first, I want some answers. *Patience, then he's all yours.* I put my hands in my pockets and rock back on my heels as if considering his words. "Your parenting skills are illuminating. However, I'm curious as to how you've come to be in April Chester's house. Or is it Monique Chandler? Frankly, it's hard to keep up with who she is these days." From the fisting of his hands, he didn't expect me to get that connection. He's grappling for a plausible explanation, while trying to figure out exactly how much I know. His mouth moves, but no words are uttered. *Fool.*

I survey the room as I'm awaiting his response and almost smile when I see Marco appearing so relaxed that he almost looks bored. Looks can be deceiving, though. I know without a doubt that he's aware of everything, right down to the smallest detail. Beside me, Tony doesn't seem concerned about our predicament either. *Fuck, maybe I'm losing my edge.* Although I'm in no way panicking, my mind is racing as I try to formulate an escape route for Jade. I don't give a fuck about myself, but I need to know she'll be safe should anything happen to me. I know without asking that Tony will ensure that. Hunter forces out a laugh as he crosses the room to a bar and pours a large measure of amber liquid in a glass. He tosses it back in one swallow and grimaces. Then he repeats the process once more before facing me. "That's an interesting story," he begins. "You see, I saw the news coverage when that crazy girl almost killed your daughter. I didn't think much of it other than disappointment, of course, that she didn't succeed." There's no malice in his tone, just a simple statement of fact. Regardless, I want to tear him apart with my fucking hands. Tony touches my arm in warning, sensing the rage simmering inside me.

"How disappointing for you," I snap out, hating this fucker more than I ever thought possible.

"Indeed," he agrees, and I half expect him to thank me for my understanding. That would be an epic mistake on his part. "So, anyway, where was I? Oh, yes, I felt a certain kinship with the lovely Monique, as she prefers to be called. I sent her a letter explaining that I had been unfortunate enough to fall victim to you. We began corresponding on a regular basis, and I've also paid her quite a few visits. That part was tougher, though, as you never know who's watching." He shakes his head. "Monique feels considerable hatred toward your daughter and son-in-law. So being the gentleman I am, I offered my assistance."

I'm still processing his revelations when Tony says coldly, "This bullshit was never about revenge, was it? It's been two decades . . . You never cared about your wife's death. You got the sudden desire to go after Lee when you met Monique."

Both Jade and her sister gasp as they stare at their father in confusion. The final pieces are almost clicking neatly into place. This wasn't vengeance for Jasmine's death.

It was for Monique. Hunter's eyes are locked on Tony's now, and I see the exact moment he puts it together. "The bastard son," he hisses. "What an unexpected bonus. Never believed I'd have Anthony Moretti at my mercy." He rubs his hands together in glee. He points at two large men a few feet away. "Cuff this one. I don't want him getting away." Just when I think this can't possibly get any weirder, Wrenn's men, except for two, turn in a move so smooth it almost appears scripted. Their guns are suddenly pointed at Wrenn, who stares at them in confusion. "Wh-what are you fools doing? I'll have your fucking heads for this. Do as I say!"

Marco steps forward with a lazy grin on his face. "These are Moretti men, asshole. We had people infiltrate your organization months ago. Long before we knew all this shit. You've been helping yourself to things that don't belong to you. Guns, contracts, job sites." He pauses for a moment to let it sink in. "You're done, Wrenn."

Wrenn's gaze swings wildly around the room before landing on Tony once again. "Hell yes, I stole from you and your family. And you know what, you little punk? I'd do it again. Your father dared to take what wasn't his, so I'm simply returning the favor. If not for the fact that there's always goons shadowing your every move, I'd have gone after you first instead of Jacks. Everyone was always so fucking impressed with his brilliance. Made me look like a laughing stock when he yanked Wrenn Wear out from under me." He shakes his head as if he hadn't meant to reveal that much, before once again focusing on Tony. "Be grateful it's just money and not your fucking wife," he sneers.

Tony smirks at the older man, which seems to infuriate him. If he thought the son of Draco Moretti would bow down to him, he's sadly mistaken. "Don't blame me because you couldn't satisfy your woman." *Nice.* Not many guys can ignore that bait, and Wrenn will be no exception.

But what happens next is something I never expected. Again, time appears to almost stand still as Wrenn's face turns molten red. He moves to the center of the room directly in front of Tony as he speaks in a near shout. "You think you're so fucking smart, boy. Well, you don't know shit." He gives Tony a smile that is pure evil before dropping his bombshell. "Wanna know what happens to people who cross me, Moretti? They die—whenever and wherever I want it to happen. And as you can see, I have plenty of patience when need be. Although I must admit, I'd grown tired of the pace of this piece of payback. I even had Jenkins toss some crumbs at Jacks to speed the process along. He certainly didn't seem to be putting it together on his own. Possibly because he was too busy playing the besotted fool with my daughter." Tony has the audacity to yawn, which damn near has me smiling, despite the sting I feel at the reminder of Jenkins' deception. That is, until I meet Jade's tearful gaze and see the fear lurking there. I attempt to offer her comfort without words, and hope that some of my confidence eases her.

Tony makes a show of checking his watch. "If you don't mind, Wrenn, I need to wrap this up. I've got a business to run, and frankly, I'm bored with you."

Wrenn nearly convulses he's so filled with fury. "I killed the fucking Moretti king *and* his whore. Still bored, you fucking piece of shit?" The room has gone deathly quiet. Tony's fully focused on Wrenn now, and a muscle clenches in his jaw. This is the moment I knew was coming. The specifics aren't there, but I recognize it just the same. Tony will kill Hunter Wrenn to avenge his father, and I must let him. Moretti men surround us. They'll expect the son to exact retribution. It's the way of the family. I take a few steps back, signifying without words that I understand what must be done. Wrenn's two men have been disarmed and are no longer a threat. Jade stands next to her sister, looking as if she understands far more than I imagine. She too realizes what will transpire. And although a silent tear trickles down her cheek, she makes no sound. She's so fucking strong that I'm in awe of her. If I wasn't already in love with her, I would be for this moment alone. This beautiful woman who stares down death without flinching or hiding away. Jacey appears to be in some kind of trance. Her eyes are huge on her stricken face as she stares at her father. I know Jade is hurting, but I believe that her father's confession has hit Jacey the hardest. Possibly because she has more of a relationship with her father than Jade does.

"Exactly how did you kill my father?" Tony asks, injecting just the right amount of skepticism in his voice. Wrenn wants the younger man to be impressed, and he's more likely to continue talking if he thinks Tony doesn't believe him.

Wrenn chuckles, appearing absurdly proud of himself. "I gave that junky who killed him some premium coke for a fucking month. He was good and addicted. So I let him run dry for a few days, then told him that if he killed Draco, he'd be set for life. Wasn't too hard," Wrenn brags. "Your father was a man of routine. So he simply followed him around for a while and waited until he had the kill shot." Shrugging, he adds, "I'm not going to lie, taking out Victor Falco was an unexpected bonus. I might have even let the bum live for a while, but that was never an issue. I knew all along he'd be taken care of by the Morettis, and he was. Hell, it was almost too easy. And to think I assumed he'd be the difficult one, and Jasmine would be simple. I had that shit backward." He rolls his eyes in exasperation. "Do you have any idea how many people I had to pay off to ensure the reports stated she died in that car accident? The fucking coroner was a greedy bastard. I couldn't exactly hide the bullet hole in her forehead, but if she'd simply disappeared, I wouldn't have inherited all her holdings. It's a damn shame that my old man was so infatuated with my wife that he left her more in his will than he did his own son." Releasing a long-suffering sigh, he adds, "But it all worked out in the end." He looks away from Tony and focuses on me. "And Monique? I imagine by now she's one less drain on the prison system. Certainly couldn't leave that crazy bitch to run around spreading rumors, now could I?"

It's so quiet. Everyone appears to be waiting with bated breath for something to happen. Then it does. There's a loud boom that literally shakes the windows. "Oh my God, Jacey," Jade croaks out drawing all eyes in their direction. Jacey stands there with her thin frame shaking, yet the gun in her hand remains remarkably steady as stares at her father. He's gasping and flailing about. I hear a gurgling sound. She's punctured one of his lungs.

"Fuck," Tony hisses. Somehow Wrenn remains on his feet as he swings around to stare at his daughter in disbelief. Seemingly without blinking, Jacey pulls the trigger once more, and her father falls forward, twitching a few times before there is nothing more.

Jacey calmly places the gun in the chair next to her and smooths down her hair. She walks forward and stands over her father before shocking the room even more by spitting on him. "That's for my mother, you fucking evil bastard. I won't let you hurt us anymore." And with that, her eyes roll back in her head, and she pitches straight into Tony's arms.

A loaded silence descends for several moments as we all attempt to process what happened. Marco steps forward and lowers his large frame to check Wrenn for a pulse. He shakes his head when he gets up before looking over to where Tony is holding Jacey in his arms. "That was the hottest fucking thing I've ever seen in my life. I'll marry that girl tomorrow if she says the word." Even though he says nothing in reply, I don't miss the way that Tony's arms tighten protectively around Jacey as he cradles her gently against him.

Jade launches herself across the space and barrels into my chest. I breathe easy for the first time in hours. She's back where she belongs. She lets me hold her for a moment, before she pulls back and studies her sister in concern. "What's going to happen to her, Lee? Will she go to prison? It was self-defense, right?"

Jade was raised by an evil man, but she's still immune to the ways of a family like the Morettis. There's no way to shield her from it, because she's seen too much tonight. Tony, who has been staring at Jacey's face as if in a trance, appears to hear the questions and nods to Marco. "Take care of this. Whatever you think is best. But nothing touches her," he adds as he stares once more at Jade's sister.

"My fucking pleasure," Marco answers easily. He huddles around his men, speaking with low undertones. Tony strides from the room, not bothering to look back, and I put an arm around Jade and follow him. She doesn't need to see any more. As it is, Jacey may never recover from what she's done. But regardless, they'll need each other in the days ahead.

At some point, Tony's Land Rover was brought around near the door. He stops next to the Mercedes and glances inside before tossing me his keys. "I'll drive her car. No use leaving it here for the guys to get home. I'll touch base with you tomorrow."

I open the passenger door of Jacey's car so he can deposit her inside. She's awake now, but makes no protests at being cared for by a stranger. She simply stares straight ahead, saying nothing while he fastens her seat belt. "Um, where are you taking my sister?" Jade glances from Tony back to Jacey. The worry is evident in her eyes as well as helplessness. She's never had a close relationship with her sibling, and I don't think she knows how to comfort the other woman.

"She'll be safe," he replies. "Lee knows where to find me." Without anything further, Tony walks around and gets in the driver's seat. The car roars to life, and we watch until his taillights disappear in the distance.

I help Jade into Tony's SUV, then follow suit. I hold her hand on the way home, hoping it'll give her a small measure of comfort after all she's been through. We don't speak until we're settled on my sofa. She's sitting sideways across my lap with her head against my chest as I gently stroke her back and drop kisses onto the top of her head. I gave her Advil as soon as we arrived, hoping to alleviate the headache she's complained of. I tried to convince her to see a doctor, considering she lost consciousness after the blow earlier, but she refused. In the end, I made her promise to tell me if she had any other symptoms that might indicate a concussion. When my phone rings, I bite back a curse, just wanting some quiet time with my woman. But it's Luc. "Hey, did Pete call you?" I contacted my brother on the way home to let him know we were okay. I was vague, not wanting to go into details over the phone. Tomorrow is soon enough for that. I also asked him to update Lucian as well.

"Yeah, he did. I assume we'll get together soon." When I agree, he pauses. "I received a call from Woodbridge Correctional. Monique was killed today in an altercation with another prisoner."

I sigh, shaking my head. "I see," I say simply. "Maybe there is some justice in the world after all."

"My sentiments exactly," he says. "Anyway, just thought you should know. Do you or Jade need anything tonight? Happy to help out in any way that I can."

I smile at his thoughtfulness. "Thanks, Luc, but we're good. Just take care of my daughter and granddaughter."

"Always," he says adamantly. I end the call and lay my head against the cushions, feeling the stress begin to drain out of me.

I must have dozed off at some point because movement beside me has me jerking awake. I look around groggily to see a grinning Jade staring at me with Rufus sitting in her lap. He stretches his paws up, and they land on my chest as he surveys me. Then very deliberately, he leans closer and licks my cheek. "Holy fuck," I groan in disgust. "Please tell me that was the first time he tongued me while I was passed out."

Her giggle has me shuddering. "It's so cute, honey. I swear he adores you. He jumped in my lap and rubbed his head all over you."

I roll my eyes at her amusement but can't bring myself to be angry. I'm too happy to see her smiling, and the sound of her laughter is everything I didn't know I needed. "So you're basically saying I'm covered in cat hair and spit? Need I remind you what he does with those paws?"

She shrugs before saying impishly, "Better add shit to that list as well. He does lick himself a lot, but I'm not sure how clean you would consider him. He probably misses a few spots."

"Thanks for bringing that to my attention, baby," I grumble as the fur ball snuggles next to me. The sound of his purrs literally fills the room. "Fuck," I sigh, but it's more in resignation than irritation. If living with Rufus is the price for having Jade in my arms, then I'll gladly pay it. Not that I'll tell her that, but I'll take every family member of the feline for another day with this gorgeous woman smiling at me. "Do you have any idea how much I love you?" Maybe not the smoothest delivery, but the question is certainly from my heart.

Her eyes go soft and heavy, and there's a hint of moisture there as she whispers back, "If it's half as much as I feel for you, then I'm the luckiest woman in the world. Because I fell madly in love with you the moment I first saw you at Falco."

"I'm sorry it took me so long to tell you how I feel. I'm the best version of me with you, but I've still done a lot of things that would make you look at me differently if you knew."

She puts a finger to my lips, silencing me when I want to continue. "You saw my family today. I wasn't raised in a traditional household." She rests her forehead against my chest before adding shakily, "For God's sake, my sister killed my father, Lee. She shot him twice. And the bad thing is that I understood. A part of me even wants to applaud her for having the strength to do it. Because he killed our mother and let us spend our lives believing she died because she was driving intoxicated. *But he killed her.* Do you realize that half of my family killed another family member? Who does that?" She sounds bewildered as she shakes her head. "So stop thinking you're corrupting me because I'm not exactly Mary Poppins."

I nod solemnly before dropping a kiss onto her frowning lips. "I see your point, sweetheart. But regardless of those things, you're still all that's good and pure to me. And maybe in a way, those parts of you make us a perfect match. Your halo is beautiful but a tad crooked, and baby, that's one of the many things I adore about you."

She turns in my arms until she's straddling me and our lips meet in a kiss that reaffirms our words. It promises today, tomorrow, and forever regardless of what comes our way. Our life may have shades of normalcy at times, but it'll always be anything but. Quite simply, we're two people who grew up in a world shaded in gray, and although there will be moments in the light, there will also be many in the darkness. *She is my home. My sanctuary.* If we have each other, we'll hold on tightly until the storm passes and the sun breaks through the clouds once again.

EPILOGUE

———◆———

JADE

"I SWEAR I'D LOVE NOTHING BETTER than to cut your dick off," I snap at my husband who is trying hard not to smile. The poor man has been through hell with me these past three months, and it's not getting any easier for either of us. After my father's death, the Morettis *magically* made him disappear, and his holdings were divided between Jacey and me. She's taken over running the company, and I've been content to put my part in a bank account and try to forget that the money was probably as dirty as my father. Lee proposed to me the very next day after Dad's death. I said yes immediately but didn't want or need a traditional wedding. He arranged a pastor to perform the ceremony at our home with only Pete and his family and Luc, Lia, and Lara in attendance. I invited Jacey, but she declined, saying she simply couldn't handle it, but she wished us well. I completely understood, and we were married two days later. Then less than a month later, I found out I was pregnant. So much for those birth control pills. Thus, bringing us to our familiar morning routine of me being bent over the toilet puking my guts out while Lee stands behind me, holding my hair and rubbing my back. Oh, and the loving way I toss out threats to his manhood between bouts of heaving. After he'd gotten over the initial shock of having me spew such violent rants, I think he quite enjoyed them. He's even recorded a few and played them back for me later so I can hear what I sound like. He only made that mistake twice before I tossed his phone across the room and shattered it on the marble flooring. Yes, I think I've really got this pregnancy glow down.

"Is there anything left in you?" he asks with a note of concern in his voice. For as much as I amuse him with my profanity, he always hovers like a mother hen. I'm not sure who this pregnancy has been harder on: him or me. I'll wake up sometimes at night to find him staring at me. Once, I'm almost certain he was checking to make sure I was breathing. The man is seriously overprotective, and I love it. I've never felt so cared for, pampered, or cherished as I do now. It's as if once we said, "I do," what remained of his walls simply crumbled. He opened his heart to me, and I never doubt that I am his world just as he is mine.

He tenderly washes my face, and I brush my teeth before he helps me back into the bed for what is one of my favorite parts of the day. When the puking subsides and we cherish those last few moments before we rise. We argued about it, but I'm still working at Falco part time. Kara has kindly agreed to check on Denise, my job-share partner, after the baby is born and we decide on when and if I'll be returning to work. Denise, a fifty-year-old detail-oriented ninja, has been an awesome second assistant to Lee. *And* he likes her, which is certainly a bonus. Possibly because she doesn't put up with his shit and keeps him in line. That's my theory anyway. "I'm sorry for being mean to your pecker again." I giggle as he pinches my butt playfully.

"Might I remind you how fond you are of that particular part of my body, Mrs. Jacks? I feel certain you'd be very sad if it were no longer there for you to use as often as you like. Which we both know is frequently. I fucking love these crazy hormones you have now," he declares reverently.

"I can see that," I whisper throatily as I push my hand inside his boxer briefs and encircle his hard length. This is also part of our daily routine. I go from being sick to horny in the blink of an eye. Lee had been stunned the first few times, but he's come to REALLY look forward to morning time as well. I begin sliding his underwear down, intent on taking him in my mouth, but he has other plans.

In a move that has me blinking rapidly, I'm hovering over his cock as he controls my downward descent with his hands on my hips. I moan loudly as he begins to fill me. I've become more comfortable with my body since being with Lee. Just seeing the adoration in Lee's eyes every time he looks at me has resolved my inhibitions. And with that, I've turned into some kind of wanton, sexual being who demands satisfaction from her man— and Lee always knows how to bring that and more. My body is finely tuned to his every touch as if it recognizes its master and performs only for him. "So good," I pant as he sucks a sensitive nipple into his mouth while pinching the other one.

"Fuck, you're so damn beautiful," he groans, raising his hips from the bed as he brings me down to meet them. "Love you, cuero mio. Always." He never fails to say those words several times when our bodies are joined, which usually sends me spiraling toward my climax. And today is no exception. I tighten around him as he continues to murmur praise and words of love into my ear. All too soon, I'm screaming his name as we come together. Each time I think it can't possibly get any better, it does. I'm gasoline, and he's the match. Put us together and we burn brighter and hotter. Our fire will never be extinguished, just as our love will never fade. Two pieces of a puzzle that should have never fit together, yet somehow ended up being a perfect match.

LEE

I SIT AT A LARGE TABLE in Leo's restaurant surrounded by our family and friends. My wife is seated next to me with our son, Victor, asleep on her shoulder. His hair is dark against his pale skin, a fact that I've teased her about countless times. Just like his namesake, little Victor is his own man. Simply because his parents both have blond hair doesn't mean he wants to. His features, though, are the perfect mix of us. He has my eyes and Jade's mouth. She swears he has my temperament when he's pitching a fit. I then remind her that I'm more of a silent brooder than a verbal drama queen. But considering these tantrums earn him a trip to his mother's breast, she may have a small point there.

I've also seen a psychologist who helped me understand that I don't have OCD. After reading more about it with Jade, I am so relieved. It is a crippling disorder where an anxious thought can lead to recurring, obsessive behavior. Knowing that has freed me somewhat. The psychologist taught me strategies to use when I struggle with clutter or mess, so I no longer feel so choked or distressed. But at forty-six, my learned behaviors are hard to change, so I'm a work in progress. It's still not easy, but I can walk away from clutter and not completely lose my mind until it's cleaned up. When Victor was born, the constant disarray, coupled with the lack of sleep, had driven me a little crazy. But Jade had been there for me, always understanding and supportive. And together, we took it one step at a time. There were victories and setbacks, but I've come to accept that the world will not end if there is a mess, and that nothing is so important that it can't be put aside to spend time with my wife and son. I know I'll never be fully cured of the phobia that has been so deeply ingrained in me since childhood, but I can and will be better—always for them.

Tony laughs at something Luc says, but his eyes rarely stray from my sister-in-law, Jacey. True to his word, he made the disappearance of Hunter Wrenn a non-issue. The Morettis are the most powerful family in the city, so I doubt it was difficult. Wrenn wasn't a well-liked man. I'm sure most considered whatever happened to him poetic justice. Jacey has downsized their assets considerably, selling off parts of the company that were operating in questionable areas. She is brilliant in business, but she is beyond fucked up personally. Even now, as she carries on a conversation with my daughter and Kara as if she's completely normal, her eyes are haunted. A lot of people don't notice that, but for those of us with our own demons, she may as well be holding a flashing sign. I have no idea what has happened with her and Tony, nor do I ask regardless of how much my wife prompts me. They're adults, and it's their business.

Lia glances my way and flashes me an affectionate grin as she raises her wineglass in my direction. I smile in return, loving the amazing woman she has become. She's a phenomenal wife, mother, and a hell of a businesswoman. She's taken the company I bought her and turned it into a profitable entity. She adamantly protested, but I signed it over entirely to her a few months ago. I wasn't there when she needed me the most, but if I have anything to say about it, I'll never miss another important moment in her and her family's lives. Luc, who is chatting with Pete, absently drops a kiss on the side of her head, always needing a connection when his wife is near. He's proven himself again and again.

The table erupts into laughter when my granddaughter, Lara, climbs up into Aidan's lap and puts her spaghetti-covered hands on his white shirt. Kara makes a halfhearted attempt to dab at the mess with a napkin, but the damage is done. I see Pete and Charlotte shoot each other a look, and I know what they're thinking. Their daughter has finally set a wedding date, and they're already looking ahead to some grandkids of their own to spoil. Lord knows their son, Kyle, isn't in a hurry to settle down. My nephew hasn't put down his cell phone since he arrived. Even now, his fingers fly over the keyboard as he texts God knows who. His generation has no fucking manners.

My wife's hand lands on my leg, and I automatically cover it with my own. We've been married for over a year, and I never thought it possible to know the kind of peace I do now. We're sleep deprived because our son has his days and nights mixed up, and even when we can nap, we often choose to enjoy each other instead. Luckily, with the arrival of Victor, Jade's morning sickness stopped, but our love of that quality time didn't. She's always been a beautiful, desirable woman to me, and the fact that she was completely unaware of it just made her more attractive. But now—there is a confident glow about her that a woman gets when she's loved and desired. She's stopped the insanity of trying to lose weight because she finally believes me when I say that she's perfect just as she is. Her curves and softness drive me wild. Smacking that round ass of hers is one of my favorite things. Hell, I can't keep my hands off it. As always, her proximity has a stimulating effect on my cock, and the devilish grin she flashes me says she damn well knows it. I move her hand over slightly, letting her feel what she's doing to me. "You have something to take care of," I murmur near her ear.

She curls her fingers around my length, rubbing the tip

teasingly. *So much for leaving anytime soon.* I laugh wryly, knowing once again she's turned the tables on me. *Little minx.* At this point if I stand, everyone is going to be aware of my predicament. "I'll be more than happy to do it when we get home," she purrs before licking her lips. *Fuck.* "Oh, and by the way"—I raise a brow, waiting for her to finish her sentence— "I'm not wearing any panties." *Double fuck!*

"You'll pay for that." I shake my head as I attempt to get my body under control. Luckily, she's distracted from her evil intentions by something her sister is saying. I glance around the group gathered, and it hits me with the force of a punch to the gut—a good one. I have a family. Not the dysfunctional kind I grew up with, but people who love and support each other through good times and bad. None of us are perfect, but we're there for each other.

My daughter distracts me from my moment of introspection as she gets to her feet excitedly, waving her phone in the air. "Rose and Max got married in Hawaii! They finally did it."

Applause fills the air before Aidan sighs and tosses some money to Luc. "Guess I lost the bet," he grumbles. "I was sure they secretly hitched ages ago."

Luc winks at Lia before saying, "Never bet against a man whose wife is the best friend of the party involved. You know girls tell each other everything. At least those two do, which is downright disturbing."

Everyone laughs as the interrupted conversations resume. I take my sleeping son from Jade and cradle him in my arms. I was given a second chance to be a father from the beginning, and I don't want to miss a single moment of it. I've been spit-up on, pissed on, and damn near shit on, but it's all a part of this crazy, beautiful life that I have with this amazing woman by my side. I have no idea what the future holds, but whatever it is, we'll face it together.

THE END

ACKNOWLEDGMENTS

A special thanks to Brittany Babb.

A thank you to Kim Killion with Hot Damn Designs for the wonderful cover. And to my editors: Marion Archer and Jenny Sims with Editing4Indies. Love you ladies!

And to my blogger friends, Catherine Crook with A Reader Lives a Thousand Lives, Jennifer Harried with Book Bitches Blog, Christine with Books and Beyond, Jenn with SMI Book Club, Chloe with Smart Mouth Smut, Shelly with Sexy Bibliophiles, Amanda and Heather with Crazy Cajun Book Addicts, Stacia with Three Girls & A Book Obsession, Lisa Salvary and Confessions of a Book Lovin Junkie.

COMING SPRING 2018

ANTHONY

CHAPTER ONE

I LEAN MY HIP AGAINST THE second-floor balcony and glare at the dark-haired woman below. "What in the fuck is she doing?" I snap to my club manager, Jax Hudson.

Jax shrugs his shoulders indifferently. "Don't know for sure, boss. Seems like a weird place to hold a job interview, but that's what it looks like. She's got people filling out paperwork, and hell, there's even a pen stuck in her hair. She's hot, though, so maybe I should go apply for whatever this position is. I've always had a thing for the nerdy accountant look. Shit, look, she's wearing glasses with those granny neck straps." He licks his lips in a way that makes me want to punch his face. "That's smoking."

Rolling my eyes, I shake my head in resignation. If I've learned nothing else in my time as owner of one of the hottest clubs in town, it's that people are basically nuts. I'm not surprised anymore, but seeing the woman below in a pale silk blouse collecting papers from the group of men who surround her table is a first. Even from a distance, something about her is vaguely familiar. Her slim build and the curve of her neck stir something in my conscience, but I can't place what it is. Even my body is reacting to her, which is downright insane. I'm surrounded by scantily dressed women every night—most of whom throw themselves at me regularly. So why in the fuck would I look twice at some uptight broad who's obviously picked a bad place to conduct whatever business she has. "Go down and see what's going on. Her little enterprise is blocking the entrance to the bar."

Jax straightens away from the banister saying, "You got it, boss," before leaving to do my bidding.

I remain where I am out of curiosity as he reaches the bottom floor and approaches the table in question. He weaves his through the group of men and leans down to speak in the woman's ear. She nods a few times, then looks up. Her eyes search the area before locking on mine, and I hiss in shock. *Holy fucking shit.*

Jacey. The hair is different, but I know the face. It's haunted my dreams for months.